I0733496

Cedar Creek Crossing

A Southern Tale

By

Robert L. Wilkins

All Rights Reserved.

No part of this publication may be reproduced in any form or by any means, including scanning, photocopying, or otherwise without prior written permission of the copyright holder.

Copyright © 2024 Robert Wilkins

ISBN-13: 978-1-944662-88-2

Cover Design by Diana Henderson

Dedication

This is for my wife, Debra, without whose patience, support, encouragement, and ability to get my butt into action, this book would not be possible.

Acknowledgements

I would like to thank Bernie Ashman whose belief in this manuscript and continued encouragement were instrumental in bringing this book to fruition. I would also like to thank my editor, Diana Henderson, who took my unruly words and wrestled them into what you are about to read. Finally, I extend my gratitude to Realization Press and to Drew Becker whose expert and inspired work we now hold in our hands.

Table of Contents

Chapter One

In a Southern family, disaster is always lurking in the shadows. I guess it's probably the same for the Yankees, but I can't say for sure, never having had the opportunity to visit the home of a certified Yankee family when the "shit hits the fan." The most pleasant of Southern gatherings can erupt into an inferno or chill to an icy silence with just a word, a glance, or the turn of a head by that most dreadful of creatures, the Southern lady.

The deadliest of the species is the matriarch, no matter which branch of the family tree upon which you perch. Hardly ever is permanent damage done, but to the unfortunate observer born north of Richmond, the jungles of Vietnam might seem like a haven in comparison.

My Mama was a perfect example of the Southern woman phenomenon. She was a fluffy woman with hardly the strength to open a car door or carry a bag of groceries into the house, but, if left alone for the day, she might move every stick of furniture in the house and then rotate the tires on her car. Her strength and health seemed to be at their worst when surrounded by her husband and sons and a particularly distasteful project lay ahead. There appeared to be a sliding scale of acceptance as Mama and Daddy grew older. Mama accepted the fact that her methods got results, and Daddy accepted that he had no choice but to comply.

My Daddy was like a God to me. He was a big man with a barrel chest and an ample stomach for it to rest upon. I remember him always smelling like the cigars he smoked, an aroma as wonderful to me as it was "simply horrible" to Mama, which probably accounts for my love of cigars. Daddy possessed the patience of Job, the understanding of Billy Graham, Gandhi's wisdom, and Lewis Grizzard's sense of humor, all of which he needed every day of his life with Mama. Although never one for outward expressions of love, Daddy saw the family as the center of his universe. A touch on the head or a slap on the shoulder was about the most we could expect, but to us that was the equivalent of having knighthood bestowed upon us.

My Mama and Daddy loved each other dearly, although I never heard one admit it to the other. I don't believe that either of them would have let another person come between them except Uncle Rodney.

My Uncle Rot-ney, as Mama called him, was a character delivered straight to us from an adventure novel. He always seemed larger than life to me. He was loud and boisterous; we always heard him before we saw him. Uncle Rodney's arrival created electricity in the house that sent my brother Jason and me to join Daddy so we could all greet him at once. The sound of Uncle Rodney's entrance made Mama dry her hands on the kitchen towel and lean against the sink for support. Uncle Rodney must have had the nose and instinct of a hungry hound because he always showed up just as Mama was fixing a meal.

To describe Uncle Rodney, I must choose a certain period of time because he looked different every time I saw him. Depending upon his phase, he could be fat or thin, have long hair or no hair at all, be dressed in a pair of secondhand clothes from Goodwill or a tailored suit from Hong Kong. We never knew just who would blow in behind the Rebel yell he always sounded from the end of the driveway. Rodney stood a little over six feet tall and was muscular. Even when he carried weight, he obviously was no stranger to physical work. His face was sharply lined and generally clean-shaven with eyes as blue as the deepest water, but his right eye tended to drift a bit since an unfortunate meeting with a wine bottle in a bar in Thailand.

"Musta been a hunnerd dollar bottle of juice. It made me see stars so quick," he would always say when we asked him about it. Then he would laugh and roll his eyes in one direction and his head in the other while bowing his knees in and out and staggering about the room. All we knew was he had been something called a Green Beret, had fought in a war, and was gone a lot. Mama said that was what made Rot-ney so crazy and why he didn't think or act like normal folks. Jason and I just thought he was funny and exciting, and his visits always made Daddy happy. Those were the only days that Daddy would ever leave the house without either Mama or us with him.

Mama was never openly hostile to Uncle Rodney; she just tolerated him as she would endure cleaning up the messy diaper of someone else's child. Mama liked an orderly life, and Uncle Rodney always set the world on its ear. I think it frightened her to see the change that came over Daddy when he was in Uncle Rodney's company. They wouldn't do anything bad. They would just laugh and go off together to the Moose Lodge to drink a few beers and pass the time with the other men who happened to have a few minutes respite from the routine of work, meals, sleep, church, and more work.

As I said, Mama had her own idea of how life should be lived. Based largely on a strong Southern Baptist upbringing and several movies that she had seen many times, Mama felt she knew just how to act in any situation. She always did what she thought was "the right thing." That's how Mrs. Amanda Cotton came to be at our house that night in August when Uncle Rodney showed up just at suppertime.

Chapter Two

Mrs. Amanda Cotton was not a native of North Carolina. She was born Amanda Louise Stewart in Kingsport, Tennessee, where she grew to a lofty five feet, ten inches by the time she was twelve years old. Her classmates caught up with her in varying degrees by her high school graduation, but her size kept the list of early teenage suitors to a minimum. Not having the distraction of pimply-faced, hormone-driven young bulls, she turned her energies to athletics, in which she excelled. Her size, dedication, and well-honed physical skills earned her a position with the volleyball team at Vanderbilt University, where she majored in English. After an unusually arduous contest with Southern Methodist University, she met Craig Cotton, a divinity student at nearby Atlantic Christian College in Nashville.

Teammate Sharon had set the ball perfectly and Amanda spiked it so viciously that the girls from S.M.U. had no hope of returning it. Thus, her team won the game. The victory was sweet, and Amanda savored it with a long hot shower that left her renewed and in love with the world. After dressing, she walked through the field house one more time and exited by the main door instead of the tunnel used by the rest of the team.

Craig had drawn the assignment of handing out brochures advertising the upcoming revival to be held at A.C.C. He had worked the Vanderbilt campus the entire day and happened by the field house as the game was ending. He was packing to move along when he heard the door open.

Amanda saw the young man and smiled. He walked toward her and offered a brochure. Their eyes met, and then she looked at the paper that proclaimed that "The Day of Decision Is at Hand." When their hands touched during the exchange, a current of electricity ran between them. They both knew this was a momentous event in their lives.

Though tenuous because of inexperience and rigid Christian edicts, their romance blossomed over the next two years, and upon graduation they were married in a fine Southern style. After his ordination, Craig received the traditional assignments as youth minister and associate minister at churches of varying sizes throughout Tennessee and western North Carolina. Amanda worked as a substitute teacher in each community where they lived, not taking a full teaching position because of their frequent moves. Of course, starting a family was out of the question on Craig's salary as associate minister.

When the offer of an interview for a church in Cedar Creek, North Carolina, came, they were both overcome by joy at the possibility of being able to settle down. The process was long and unnerving, but in the end their prayers were answered. They moved to Cedar Creek in November and spent Christmas in the parsonage built beside and slightly back from Union Baptist Church of Cedar Creek.

Craig was determined to be the minister of and for the people of Cedar Creek. He saw the inaccessibility of the clergy as a major contributor to the lack of church growth. To accomplish his goal, he arose each morning at 6:00 a.m. and headed for town, where he walked and spoke with people as they went about their daily routines.

By 9:30 a.m., he was seated in Sybil's Diner, enjoying a bowl of Raisin Bran with skim milk and coffee. Often, he would work on the outline of Sunday's sermon as the diner transitioned from breakfast to lunch.

Sybil's Diner was made up of four rows of booths, and each day the reverend would take his seat at booth 3-B facing the window so he could watch his flock as they moved about the town. If anyone needed the preacher, they knew just where to find him.

Mary Alice Darnell came to work at Sybil's in May. Mary Alice was a petite ex-cheerleader whose presence did more to decorate Sybil's than to further its reputation for service and good food. That Mary Alice had an aversion to clothing in general and panties in particular coupled with the most provocative way she sat in booth 1-A to wrap silverware in three-cornered napkins ultimately led to the reverend's moral downfall.

By the end of June, everyone knew of the preacher's tryst, including Troy Jacobs, a 265-pound ex-linebacker turned outlaw biker who called Mary Alice his girl. Craig persuaded her to leave town quietly with him under the cover of darkness.

Amanda Cotton withdrew from the community and began making plans for her return to Kingsport while the deacons formed a search committee to find another preacher. The townspeople gossiped constantly, as they tended to do. Mama watched events unfold in Cedar Creek for about two weeks, then decided to take matters in hand. She had seen this very situation discussed by Oprah and four matronly abandonees, and she knew that the last thing Amanda needed was to be alone. Mama made one of her pineapple cakes that could coax even the most reluctant fox out of the den and set out to single-handedly save Mrs. Cotton. She took the cake to Amanda and invited her to have dinner with us on Thursday night, refusing to take no for an answer.

The silence-to-conversation ratio was overwhelming on that first Thursday night, but Mama was determined. She visited Amanda almost daily; before long they had beaten a path between our house and the parsonage. Mrs. Amanda Cotton became a regular at our Thursday night table. It was in the fourth setting that Uncle Rodney appeared.

Chapter Three

Cooking was akin to religion in Mama's kitchen. She began her ritual at about 4:30 with peeling potatoes. She approached each vegetable with reverence: cleaned, sliced, anointed with spices, and prepared not only to nurture the body but to pay homage to the meat that was the centerpiece of the table. No altar was more beautiful than her table prepared to receive guests. The aroma of Mama's kitchen drifting on a lazy summer breeze held as much promise to me then as the hint of perfume worn by a Southern belle does today.

Jason was in the yard playing some imaginary game of adventure, and I was reading a Louis L'Amour Western when Mama yelled for us to get ready for dinner. I had forgotten that it was Thursday and Mrs. Amanda was coming for supper. I really didn't mind her much, except she caused us to take an extra bath and wear shoes. I think Daddy felt the same way because we were all pretty much one-bath-a-day men, but we all knew better than to protest for fear of incurring Mama's wrath. Anyway, we all went to work on ourselves, and by 6:00 p.m. there wasn't a cleaner group of folks in the country. All spit and polished, we were sitting in the living room waiting for the guest of honor when it happened. The sound, shrill and loud, sent the chickens scattering and the dogs running, tail-tucked, under the front porch. We glanced back and forth among the three of us to figure out what to do next while a groan of great despair emerged from the kitchen.

"Sam, tell me it ain't true," said Mama, appearing ashen and weak in the doorway. "Rot-ney can't stay. He'll destroy all I've set out to do with his crazy stories and wild ways."

"No, he won't, Edna," said Daddy walking over to Mama and helping her back to the kitchen. "I'll talk to Rodney and tell him to mind his manners. He'll understand and behave just fine."

Jason and I looked at each other and giggled quietly, knowing something grand lay ahead.

The driveway bore Uncle Rodney's signature whirlwind of dust as he raced up in a 1948 Willy's Jeep. Entering the yard, he cut two doughnuts and was out of the Jeep before it came to a halt. The cloud of dust was catching up as he jumped onto the front porch.

"We gotta pave that driveway," he yelled, wildly waving his arms and faking a few coughs.

Jason and I ran to meet him, knowing that he'd brought us presents from whatever far-off place he'd been, but Daddy brushed past us and took Uncle Rodney out to the shop to tell him about Mrs. Cotton and save us both from Mama. Uncle Rodney knew something important was up, but glanced back at us boys and gave us a wink, as if we were all conspirators in some subversive plot to undo mankind.

Jason looked at me as we walked back into the house, and, as the next man of the house, I knew it was my job to go check on Mama and reassure her that Daddy had the situation well in hand. The clanking of pots and pans warned me that I had my work cut out for me. Now I knew how the Christians must have felt as they stood in the coliseum and listened to the lion's roar across the way. Mama dried dishes in a frantic fashion, tossing them into cabinets without regard. The advertisement in the catalog had said they could withstand heat up to five hundred degrees, and I figured they were getting the test.

"Mama, Daddy's talking to Uncle Rodney now, so don't worry about supper. Everything's gonna be just fine. Supper smells really good, and I know Mrs. Cotton will enjoy it. She really likes your cooking too," I said, trying my fifteen-year-old best to convince both of us.

Brushing the hair back from her eyes and wiping her hands on the towel, she saw right through me.

"You'd be better off talking to old Duchess hiding under the porch; at least she would wag her tail and let you know she was listening. The only way your daddy could control Rot-ney is if he would lock him up in the shop with a six-pack and a bucket of chicken. If I'd known he was coming, I woulda bought a chicken. It's too late now. We can only hope for the best."

Mama was a brave woman and reminded me of Scarlett standing on the porch of Tara as the Yankee's rode through the gate.

As Mama dressed for supper, I went back to the living room with Jason. Neither of us had much to say as we played out different scenarios of the evening in our heads. Time passed until the headlights of Mrs. Amanda Cotton's car turning into the driveway broke our revelry.

Mrs. Cotton had no more than stepped on the porch when Mama came out of her room looking as fresh as a spring morning. The transformation was complete, although I knew the package was bound by the frailest ribbons.

Mrs. Amanda wore a simple print dress that was loose at the waist and fell well below her knees. She had put her hair back in a French braid and tied it with a bow the same color as the flowers in her dress. Her shoes were flat, and she wore no jewelry other than a simple watch with a leather band. Her face was pretty in a wholesome way, looking more clean than made-up. She fought a constant battle to keep her round glasses on the bridge of her nose, always pushing them up with her middle finger. The first time I saw her do it, I wondered why she was shooting me the bird on the sly.

After realizing the truth, I would play a mental game, imagining the prim Mrs. Cotton shooting the bird to whomever had spoken before the adjustment was made. I even let Jason in on it, and together we had hours of fun saying things like, "Boy, did she get pissed when Daddy said it might rain tomorrow," or "she even gave Mama the finger for sneezing. Probably woulda cussed the whole lot of us out if she had farted." The sordid minds of young boys left to wander.

Mrs. Amanda spoke to us as she came through the door, then followed Mama into the kitchen, where I'm sure she heard several disclaimers concerning Uncle Rodney's presence and probably a warning as to the possibility of this dinner not being as serene as the others.

After ten minutes alone with Mrs. Amanda, Mama sent me to fetch Daddy and Uncle Rodney. When we got back in the house, Mama introduced them, and Uncle Rodney bowed slightly (a trait he had picked up in Southeast Asia) and said how happy he was to meet her. He took her hand ever so lightly and led her to the table. Mama was not impressed.

Uncle Rodney had not come prepared for a dress-up dinner, so he was wearing old worn-out jeans with holes in the legs and back pockets. He had on his favorite boots, which had once been brown but now took on the colors of the earth. They were scuffed, and the toe was worn through. He had on a faded chambray shirt and a brown leather vest. His hair was shoulder length and pulled back into a salt and pepper ponytail. He was in a forty-year-old-hippie-cowboy stage. The contrast between him and the rest of us in our Sunday clothes was severe enough to draw Mrs. Amanda's eyes to Uncle Rodney and Mama's eyes to Daddy, who looked like he was having trouble swallowing.

Uncle Rodney may not have come dressed, but he sure came hungry. He ate with total abandon and twined his fork around his fingers every few minutes, a trick that always made Jason and me happy. Mrs. Amanda didn't seem to mind, and Mama tried not to notice. When Mama served the pineapple cake and got coffee for the adults, a full Uncle Rodney told us of his latest adventure. He had been building a bridge in the Florida Keys for the last six months and was home for two weeks "to let his tan fade." Mama sat on the edge of her chair the whole time, poised to save the delicate Mrs. Amanda if the story became too sordid or the language too coarse.

With the meal complete, Uncle Rodney issued the challenge for a men versus women game of Scrabble. Mrs. Amanda said she loved to play and looked forward to it after she helped Mama clean up the dishes. Seemingly harmless enough, Scrabble between Mama and Uncle Rodney had become as serious and deadly as pistols at twenty paces. The challenge, however, had been issued and accepted. As the women cleared the table, the men went out on the front porch for Jim Beam and cigars, evidence that the icy fingers of women's liberation had not yet encircled the throat of Cedar Creek.

It took an extremely long time to clear everything away, but Mama was preparing Mrs. Cotton for the upcoming battle while allowing Mr. Jim Beam more time to take the edge off the competition.

Mama was rightfully proud that she read over thirty books a year and had a command of English, although spoken with a slow drawl, which immediately endeared her to anyone above the Mason-Dixon Line. Scrabble was Mama's way of showing off to her friends. She loved to watch the look on their faces as she wove her tapestry of words across the board, all the time pushing her score far out of reach. Mama was a sure winner with or without the help of her partner except when she played Uncle Rodney. He was widely traveled and prided himself on being able to speak with people from every walk of life. He would always say, "I might be walking down the street with my lawyer, talking about real estate, and an old drunk in the alley might holler: 'Hey, Rodney, come on over for a drink, and I'd love 'em both." If Uncle Rodney ever heard a word he didn't know the meaning of, he would immediately look it up and then try to find a way to use it himself. Over the years, he looked up quite a few words and almost always retained them. The battle lines were drawn.

In most parts of the country, Scrabble was never considered a team sport, but in the South we found ways to pit one group against the other, especially men versus women. All they had to do to make it work was to take positions opposite each other on the board and add the scores together. Mama and Daddy were usually partners. Daddy was a simple man and just played because Mama loved it so much, and it gave her a chance to shine. He was happy to dwell in her shadow. The only other person who he would consider playing with was Uncle Rodney.

Mama would usually shy away from a game with Uncle Rodney because it always led to words (no pun intended). But tonight the thought of a male versus female match appealed to her, mainly because the other female player just happened to be an English major from Vanderbilt University. Uncle Rodney had no way of knowing the deck was stacked against him, so Mama planned to have some fun.

Mama called the game to order and smiled across at Mrs. Cotton with an air of confidence, but before long it became apparent that it was Uncle Rodney's night. As the game progressed, Mama shifted in her seat and became increasingly quiet. To those of us in the know, that could only mean trouble. Nature provides warning signs that precede every disaster. Time after time, Mama and Mrs. Cotton scored only to have Uncle Rodney squeeze out the win on the final turn. The straw that finally broke the camel's back came about an hour and a half into the game. Mama slumped down in her chair and set her jaw. The tension was about as tight as the e-string on an old fiddle. Uncle Rodney threw in all his tiles and took the last seven on the table. Mama's left eye twitched like an owl that had just spotted a field mouse. When it came around to Mrs. Amanda, the women had a ten-point lead and felt this was surely the final round. She only had to think for a moment before forming the word "plaque." The word's point value was seventeen, and she had covered a double word value space, giving them a lead of forty-four points with only Uncle Rodney left to play. Mama could sense victory. Without even a thought, Uncle Rodney threw all his new tiles down and using the Q formed the word "quixotic," which automatically gave him a bonus of fifty points, once again snatching victory. It was more than she could bear. You would have thought he was caught pulling an ace from his sleeve in old Dodge City.

Mama jumped straight up, sending her chair flying out behind her and yelled, "You know damned well that ain't no word, you cheatin' son-of-a," and then she caught herself. Around the table, six eyes tried their best not to look at Mama.

"Why, Edna, it most certainly is," said Uncle Rodney as if she had asked him if the food was good. "It means chivalrous or romantic like old Don Quixote or Sir Walter Raleigh."

As he explained the definition of his word, he rose with a flourish twirled his brown leather vest over his head and let it settle on the floor. He then bowed deeply to Mrs. Amanda Cotton and took her hand as she stepped across his vest. She played the perfect Queen Elizabeth to Sir Walter Raleigh. When she had completed the three steps necessary to traverse the vest, she curtsied and stood before Uncle Rodney. Mrs. Amanda sighed audibly, and instead of letting go of Uncle Rodney's hand placed her other hand on top of his and gazed into his eyes. Mama fainted.

Chapter Four

T he next two days were touch and go for Jason and me. As soon as our feet hit the floor in the morning, we would go outside for the day. The only time we crossed Mama's path was when she called us. She didn't lose control very often, but when she did, time was the only cure. She played out the scene a hundred times in her mind until she rationalized her every action and figured out how to proceed to minimize any damage to her image.

When the smell of freshly baked pies reached all the way down to the creek, we both took a deep breath and smiled, knowing that the end of the crisis was near. By the time she called us to eat, we were salivating and gulped down the chicken, cabbage, and green beans, knowing they were the prerequisite for dessert. Upon finishing the main course, we sat silently, thanking God for our having been born in the South and to Mama in particular.

"If ya'll are through, run on back outside. I've got to clean up and run a few errands."

"But, Mama, we smelled pie cookin' and cleaned our plates, snap beans and all," said Jason while I sat quietly, thankful for his youthful impatience.

"Them pies ain't for ya'll. I'm gonna take them to Mrs. Cotton and explain to her how your Uncle Rot-ney always plots to embarrass me in front of my friends. I should know better by now, but he always does it. Once she realizes what kind of person he is, she'll understand what happened. I owe it to her to explain."

It was then that I saw the Tupperware pie dishes sitting on the counter, the kind with the top that seals when you push your thumb in the middle and the plastic strap that runs along the top to lock in freshness and lock out the hungry hands of twelve- and fifteen-year-old boys.

Feeling much like the tomcat who tracked the canary to the door of the cage to find out that the bars work equally well from either side, Jason and I shuffled back outside while Mama readied for her mission.

* * *

As she drove along the road to town, Mama thought of what she would say to Amanda. Her remembrance of the ill-fated evening was vivid, especially the look on Amanda's face as Rot-ney carried out his foolishness.

"The poor darling probably didn't know what to think. I'll bet she was embarrassed to death by his antics. She'll probably never feel comfortable coming to my house again," Mama mumbled to herself as she turned off the highway onto the main street leading into Cedar Creek. "I'm right back where I started. She's frightened and probably feels as if I've betrayed her. I'll tell her not to mind Rodney—that he always shows up at the wrong time and does the wrong thing. I'll have to make her understand, and then maybe I can bring her back around."

She turned left onto Whitbow Avenue and saw the steeple of the Union Baptist Church as it rose above the elm trees just three blocks away. Approaching from Whitbow, Mama's view of the parsonage was obstructed by the church building, so she started to slow down for the turn into the driveway. She glanced at the rearview mirror as she applied the brake and then looked straight ahead as she turned the steering wheel to the left to safely navigate the drive. One more peek to the right, and then she turned her head toward her destination. When she looked at the parsonage, Uncle Rodney's 1948 Willys Jeep filled her vision. Mama meant to apply the brakes, but her motor functions were in shock. She missed the brake altogether and instead pinned the accelerator to the floor. Her arms were locked, so the car continued its arc, running through the driveway, jumping the small curb, and proceeding into the churchyard, while gravel, dirt, and grass rooster-tailed from the spinning tires. Ahead she saw the sign announcing the upcoming sermon: "The Narrow Path to Salvation." She unconsciously smiled as she twisted the wheel to the right, where the steps leading to the sanctuary came into full view. She found the brakes and tugged the wheel to the left again, eluding a crash. Mama's heart was pounding in her chest when the car finally came to a stop. Vanity immediately took over as she looked to see who had witnessed her little faux pas. Not seeing anyone, her only thought was to put distance between herself and the churchyard. Mama eased the car down the hill and into the street. The churchyard looked as if it had been the site of a monster truck rally. As she sped toward home, she imagined the scene from *Smokey and the Bandit, where every cop with a car was in hot pursuit of Burt Reynolds, and she just knew that by now they had an APB out on her.*

* * *

There was so much dust flying we thought Uncle Rodney was coming up the driveway. As we ran to the top of the hill, we saw it was Mama. She drove the car all the way around to the back of the house and slid to a stop. She threw the car door open and ran, crouching, toward the back door. She clutched a Tupperware pie holder in each hand, swinging them by the plastic straps. Mama's size was a testament to her meandering pace, so to see her bulk at a full gallop aroused imaginary scenes of hungry dogs nipping at our heels or a band of Gypsies coming to steal Jason. Forsaking all else, we made a beeline for the back porch. When Mama yelled "Boys!!," we lit the afterburners and almost beat her to the back door. She slammed the door so hard that the Venetian blinds rattled loudly and then swung from side to side. She quickly closed the blinds and ran into the living room to repeat the action. While she was in the living room, I examined the pie plates and could see the stains on the inside of the covers made when the pies were tossed about inside the holder. I knew in my heart that Mama had been attacked by thieves and had gallantly fought them off by wielding the pies like the hammer of Thor.

"Ya'll run upstairs and stay in your room. Don't answer the phone and don't come down till I call you."

"Mama, what's wrong? Who's chasin' you? What—"

"Just go upstairs and be quiet. Ain't nothing wrong. I've just got to think for a minute," she said, cutting me off.

We went upstairs to Jason's room and pretended to play Yahtzee while speculating on Mama's dilemma. We had to be in Jason's room to play a game because I was fifteen and way too cool to have games stored in my room. We took turns sneaking to the top of the stairs to try to see what was happening. Mama sat quietly downstairs without turning on either the lights or the television. The only time she would move was to slip to the front window and slightly lift one blade of the Venetian blinds to look out onto the driveway. I must confess to feeling a flood of relief when I heard Daddy's old truck pulling into the yard. Whoever had us surrounded could not and would not prevail against Daddy. He would single-handedly turn back the forces of evil and deliver his family to safety. Never had the rattles and knocks of that old Ford sounded so much like the trumpet of the Archangel Gabriel. We wanted to run to him and tell our version of the siege but knew better than to be seen without having been summoned by Mama.

The light came on in the kitchen, and we heard Mama's voice speaking in rapid but hushed tones. It took about an hour for her to complete the tale. I don't think Daddy spoke more than once or twice, but whatever he said must have settled Mama right down because it wasn't long before I saw the lights come on and caught the sounds of supper being fixed. I turned to sneak back into the room and bumped into Jason. We both screamed as if we had been attacked by a band of renegade Apaches.

"Boys, ya'll cut out that fuss up there and run on outside till supper's ready," yelled Daddy, further adding to the confusion of the day.

Daddy was dialing the telephone as we ran down the steps and out the back door. I would have given the rest of my summer vacation to listen to that phone conversation, but I knew that hesitating would invite disciplinary action.

We ran to the edge of the woods, stopping to reflect. Neither of us could explain the events of the day. I wish I had known the word bizarre back then.

Chapter Five

Saturdays start slow in Cedar Creek. Any vehicle moving before daylight is either delivering something to the local supermarket or has a bass boat hitched to it. Most folks in Cedar Creek work in one of the three textile mills within a thirty-mile radius of the city. After spending forty hours a week manufacturing designer sheets and pillowcases for the rich folks up north, they hesitate to leave the comfort of their beds on Saturday. Don't go conjuring up an image of the entire community sleeping till noon. Waking at eight a.m. is sleeping in to a person who is usually up by five. Daddy was a mechanic, a fixer, at Holson Mills, the smallest plant in the area. Daddy sacrificed about a dollar an hour to work for old man Holson instead of one of "the big boys." When Granddaddy Wilson died, Mr. Holson not only helped pay for the funeral but told all those gathered about how "Pappy" had helped him keep things going in the early days and had been an inspiration to all who knew him. Daddy grumbled about machines and breakdowns, but you couldn't drag a derogatory word about the company or the owner out of him.

I loved Saturdays because Daddy stayed with us all day. I could always hear him and Mama talking as I awoke. The smell of freshly brewed coffee and cigar smoke remains forever etched in my mind. I would dress quickly and bound down the stairs to see what the day held for us. Depending on the week, we would either begin by taking care of the yard work or going down to Mr. King's Barber Shop for a haircut. The rest of the day, we would follow Daddy around and dream of the day when we would be big enough to have a cigar of our own and go to work with him at Holson's. Daddy was not fond of either idea but would not discourage us, figuring that time would change our priorities.

This particular Saturday, the sound of the lawn mower woke me. I had been dreaming that Sue Ann Landsbury, the head cheerleader at Cedar Creek High and the hottest babe in town, had given up her pom-poms and renounced a scholarship to State in return for a chance to go to the prom with me. She had said that no sacrifice was too great to be my date, and I could not dispute her logic. My subconscious mind wrestled to hold onto the dream, but the roar of the Briggs & Stratton engine would not be denied.

I should have known better than to expect a normal Saturday after the events of the week. I pulled on my tennis shoes and jeans and ran downstairs, pausing only long enough to bang on Jason's door.

Standing on the porch with no shirt and my hair in total disarray, I must have been a sight because Daddy stopped the mower and shook his head.

"You and Jason get cleaned up and put some decent clothes on. We've got some company coming this morning, and we want to make your Mama proud of us."

I knew immediately that the company was somehow related to the events of yesterday. It had to be important for Daddy to handle the yard work with no help and for us to bathe so early. Usually, we just threw our caps on and would not shower until all the work was done, another benefit of the weekend. I walked back into the kitchen, where a big plate of country ham biscuits sat in the middle of the table. I was about to grab one to take with me upstairs when Mama stepped through the back door and stopped me.

"Leave those biscuits alone. We'll have them when Deacon Miller gets here. Ya'll clean up and put on some decent clothes."

Well, now I knew who the company was going to be, but that only presented me with more questions than answers. This was a strange turn of events. Daddy was a good man but never much for church activities or meeting regularly with members of the clergy or board of deacons. He accompanied Mama to morning services on most Sundays but appeared visibly relieved when the last hand had been shaken, and he was in the car with his tie pulled loose. Uncle Rodney told us once that he and Daddy couldn't see much sense in attending social gatherings where the fine traditions of cigar smoking and whiskey sipping were denied.

I figured it was Deacon Miller that Daddy had been talking to on the phone and had invited him to our house this morning.

I was pulling on my socks when I heard the car. I looked out the window and saw the jet-black Cadillac Eldorado easing up the driveway. The car was as wide as the path that led to the house and as long as a bus. Sitting behind the wheel, taking up as much space as a pencil mark on a poster board, was Mr. Royster Miller, the longest-standing member of the board of deacons at Union Baptist Church.

"Royster Miller: the man with two last names and no butt." That's what Uncle Rodney said each time the subject of Deacon Miller arose. He said that because there was no sign of any protuberance south of Deacon Miller's belt. Deacon Miller was a painfully thin man whose weight could not have been over one hundred and ten pounds. His height of six feet, two inches gave him the appearance of a walking skeleton with loose skin pulled over it. His eyes were dark and deep-set, defying you to name their color, and his ears were large with a tuft of hair growing from each. His Adam's apple bounced in and out of sight behind his shirt collar as he spoke. Daddy said the deacon had looked the same all his life, attested to by the fact that he had played Ichabod Crane in the town's presentation of *The Headless Horseman of Sleepy Hollow* each October since he was sixteen. He was known as a "no-nonsense person" who rarely smiled, never joked, and always insisted on being called Royster instead of Roy. He always wore a suit and kept on the coat regardless of the temperature. His necktie was always pulled tight with the material of his shirt collar gathered beneath it. Deacon Miller never had a job that anyone could remember. People said his mother left him very well off when she passed away, but nobody knew where she got her money either. The speculation ran the gamut from her family being rich industrialists from up north to her husband being into black-market goods and moonshine liquor during World War II, but nobody was sure. The deacon was a classic study in overcompensation. He surrounded himself with large objects. He lived alone in an old Victorian home in downtown Cedar Creek, which must have had twenty rooms, and drove his Eldorado around town as if it were a land yacht. His only companion was a Great Dane named Icky, which outweighed him by ninety pounds. The dog was stubborn and had a mind of its own, which many times led to trouble for the deacon, but that's another story. Anyway, the deacon was not without insight as to how things could get out of hand in a hurry.

We all went through our "howdy dos" and went inside to the kitchen. By 11:30, we had thanked the Lord for the chance of fellowship, all the blessings of this life, and especially that big plate of biscuits. By 11:35, we were chewing like there was no tomorrow. The conversation ran thin as we marveled at the deacon's ability to devour so much food. I think he quit when he finally realized we had been finished for several minutes.

"Mighty fine biscuits, Sister Wilson. The Lord truly blessed you with the ability to prepare his bounty," said the deacon as he wiped at his mouth with a napkin and washed it all down with a big gulp of Maxwell House.

As he drank the coffee, his Adam's apple bobbed up and down, and Jason giggled, earning him a stern look from Daddy. I contained myself because I had plans to stay for the duration so I could see how all the pieces of this puzzle fit together.

"Thank you, Deacon Miller. I'll wrap those last three up for you to take with you," replied Mama as she basked in the glow of his compliment.

"Boys, ya'll go outside now. We have some business to discuss with the deacon."

Daddy never left much room for debate when he spoke to us, so we got up to go outside while Mama put the remaining biscuits in a paper bag. My curiosity had been whet to such a razor's edge that it completely cut off my better judgment. Instead of minding my own business, I found myself crouched under the window where I could hear it all.

Daddy sat by the open window and began to unwrap a cigar. He offered the box of cigars to the deacon, knowing that he would not think of taking one. Mama and Deacon Miller talked while Daddy went through the ritual of clipping and lighting his cigar. Daddy took great pleasure in his cigars as I do today. It is a private satisfaction that, like love, you can't explain to anyone who has never fallen. The pungent odor reached me, and a grey cloud of smoke slowly drifted through the window as Daddy cleared his throat to speak.

"Thank you for coming out this morning. As I told you yesterday afternoon, my wife lost control of her car and did some damage to the churchyard, and we want to take care of the repairs. Have you had a chance to check into it for us?"

"Yes, Brother Wilson. I met Abe Caldwell this morning, and we looked at it together."

Daddy took an extra-long draw on his cigar and exhaled slowly. He never was fond of most church folks' habit of calling each other brother and sister. He always said that if a person's heart were filled with brotherly love, you wouldn't need to keep calling people's attention to the fact. He said that Christians like that were like duck decoys that look good floating on the water until a real duck lands among them. Then they become just painted chunks of wood.

As far as Daddy was concerned, a beer fart could not have fouled the living room any more than the mention of Abe Caldwell's name. They had grown up together and had bumped heads too many times to recount. If they ever came close to agreeing on anything, they would immediately change the subject to something they could fight about.

"Brother Caldwell said that he could put the grounds back into condition for around eight hundred dollars. Of course, I have entertained the thought of having a day of fellowship and asking for volunteers to work on the grounds and a few other projects that need attention."

"I think that would be a wonderful idea, Deacon Miller," Mama said, grabbing the chance to save the eight hundred dollars and keeping Daddy and Abe Caldwell from coming together.

From under the window, I could feel the tension in the room. We never talked much about money, but I never saw much lying around, and I knew that eight hundred dollars was a lot. I silently vowed to till and reseed the whole churchyard myself if given a chance. I was about to slip away, since what I was hearing was not as juicy as I had imagined it would be, when the deacon began to get to the point.

"I am very much in favor of a day of fellowship, but before I can schedule it, a matter must be taken care of. Sister Wilson, you could be a great help and comfort in this matter, and then we could move directly to the problem of the church grounds. The sooner we take care of it, the sooner we can put it all behind us. Will you help me with the problem?"

"Certainly, Deacon. I am always willing to do anything for the church," Mama said, thinking in terms of cooking, cleaning, sewing, or various other churchy activities. The fact that she had just been the victim of ecumenical blackmail had not yet entered her mind, but judging by his grunt, followed by an enormous grey cloud of smoke, the implications were not lost on Daddy. Mama thought of herself as the keeper of the vault and would stand steadfastly over the checkbook, determined not to let a single dollar escape without a gallant fight.

"Tell me how I can help you, and I'll begin immediately if necessary."

Daddy stood up and turned toward the window. The squeak of the rocker was all that saved me. I flattened myself under the window and had no choice but to stay.

What I heard next made me happy I had not made my escape. The deacon retold the story of how the preacher had left his wife and how the entire congregation had suffered right along with her. He said we had all been betrayed to a certain degree and that Sister Cotton had been fortunate indeed to have a friend such as Mama to help her in her time of need.

I imagined Mama purring like a kitten as the deacon laid the praise on thick. Daddy grunted once or twice and took long pulls on his cigar as he waited for the deacon to get to the point. Daddy had a knack for looking into the heart of the matter and was already thinking that the eight hundred dollars may be the cheapest way to handle the situation. Still, he said nothing, preferring to hear the entire story without putting the deacon on guard.

"Sister Wilson, as you know, we have been happy to accommodate Mrs. Cotton by letting her continue to live in the parsonage while we conducted the search for a replacement for Reverend Cotton. In the past few days, it has come to our attention that Mrs. Cotton has been seen about town with your brother-in-law Rodney. Although the church has not found a new preacher as of yet, we don't think it is proper for Mrs. Cotton to be courting while living at the parsonage, especially with Rodney Wilson, a man who is not known for furthering the reputation of any young lady he takes up with. Sister Wilson, I'd like you to talk with Mrs. Cotton and ask her to vacate the parsonage as soon as possible but by October first at the latest."

The deacon's cards were on the table, so he sat back and waited for Mama to speak. He probably did not realize what a mistake he had made. As I said, the deacon lived alone and did not have any family to speak of. In the South, nothing is more sacred than family. No matter how we may argue, fight among ourselves, or slander each other, we have no tolerance for anyone outside the family saying anything negative about one of us. The deacon had committed the unspeakable by talking about Uncle Rodney. Daddy exhaled a huge cloud of smoke and cleared his throat to speak, but Mama beat him to it.

"I'll be happy to speak with Mrs. Cotton about the decision that you and the other members of the board have made. I wouldn't think of letting anyone else do it, especially anyone as pompous and self-righteous as your group of do-gooders. As long as she was heartbroken and pitiful, you showed off your Christian charity for all to see, but as soon as she showed the first sign of being human, you're ready to cast her out."

Mama was getting wound up, and I knew that nothing anyone could say or do short of knocking her unconscious would save the deacon. I heard Daddy chuckle under his breath and knew that he had just settled in for the ride. He turned his back on the window, but there was no way I would miss this. It is rare for us to hear Mama at her best without one of us being the target. I wished Jason could be here for this, but I knew he would enjoy the retelling almost as much.

"But Sister Wilson, I only meant that…" the deacon tried to interject.

"And another thing, you pencil-neck geek, how dare you say anything about Rodney Wilson?! There is not a harder working or kinder man in this county. I don't know what his relationship is with Mrs. Cotton, but I can tell you that he is a fine gentleman, and if I were not related to him, I would be proud for any daughter of mine to be seen with him. Now, if there is nothing else, I'm sure you have other places to go."

With that she got up and walked over to where the deacon was sitting, reached down and snatched the bag of ham biscuits she had packaged for him and turned for the door. He and Daddy had no choice but to follow, and I had to hurry to get away from under the window before they came outside. I saw Jason at the corner of the yard and motioned for him to come running. We stood off to the side to watch as they came out on the front porch.

"I'm gonna do your dirty work, so you plan your day of fellowship, you conniving bast… That's the only way you'll get your yard fixed."

With that she tore the top off the bag and threw the ham biscuits to old Duchess as the deacon looked on. She then turned and walked back inside, leaving Daddy standing on the porch and the deacon climbing behind the wheel of his Cadillac.

Daddy took one last puff from his cigar and sent the butt flying into the yard. He turned and smiled at us as he headed for the door. That's when Mama came back outside.

"That no-good brother of yours can't be around for ten minutes without screwing up my life. You tell him to stay out of my life and mind his own damn affairs."

With that, she stormed back inside, leaving Daddy standing alone, scratching his head.

Chapter Six

"**B**oys! Boys! Ya'll get up and get dressed for church," Mama yelled from the bottom of the stairs.

I opened one eye and looked at the clock: 7:30 on Sunday morning. Jason and I had hoped Mama's run-in with the deacon might buy us a chance to sleep late on Sunday and miss church, but we should have known better. Daddy had said little the rest of the day on Saturday, but every once in a while he would stop what he was doing and laugh out loud, smiling with approval at how Mama handled the situation. I'm sure he wasn't hurt by what she said about Uncle Rodney and would never mention it to him. Daddy told us that long ago Granny Raspberry warned him not to put much stock in what Mama said when she was angry. When she got mad at him or us, he would wink and say, "Well, boys, Mama's words outran her thoughts again."

Having accepted that we would not be skipping church today, I got up and went through the steps necessary to gain access to the breakfast table. Mama laid a fine breakfast of scrambled eggs, milk gravy, sausage, grits, and buttermilk biscuits before us. This was a spread guaranteed to warm the heart, satisfy the appetite, and keep conversation to a minimum. Having a full understanding of boys and food, Mama would not let us put on our white shirts until after breakfast.

Daddy always dressed in his best suit and got ready for church before the rest of us so he could step outside and enjoy a cigar as he waited patiently for us, doing the better part of his worshipping while walking around the yard. He always said you could learn more about God working in a garden than by visiting every church ever built, but he understood people's need to gather. He said, "It's like taking a shower when you come in out of the rain; it ain't that you need any more water on you; you just feel better by doing it."

We saw several people already assembled in the churchyard as we drove into the parking lot. They were divided along the lines of gender and topic of conversation. The men examined and discussed the damage to the churchyard while the ladies speculated about why Uncle Rodney's Jeep was parked in the driveway of the parsonage. Our arrival quieted both groups.

Sunday worship consisted of Sunday School, where we learned the basics of Christianity, and Sunday service, where we were instructed to abide by those teachings in our daily lives. I liked Sunday School because we all got to talk about the lessons. In comparison, the sermon was often an extensive monologue that showed what a few years in seminary could do to a rational person's imagination. By far the most anticipated part of the morning was the 30-minute break between Sunday School and the sermon when smokers lit their cigarettes and gossips passed on juicy tales and braced themselves for the hellfire and damnation that was to come. During this break, Uncle Rodney and Mrs. Amanda Cotton decided to make their first appearance in Cedar Creek as a couple.

I stood under the maple tree beside the church talking to Billy Adams. The subject of our conversation was Laura Grinstead from our art class. Laura had a habit of sitting in a haphazard manner at her table opposite us so Billy and I could not help but look up her skirt. We were speculating as to whether she had a secret account at Frederick's of Hollywood or if her mother bought those multicolored bloomers for her. Jason stood beside me with his mouth open, wishing he were more mature and hoping one day to be blessed with his own "Laura Grinstead." Jason saw them first and tugged on my arm to get my attention.

I had to look twice to be sure it was Uncle Rodney. This was only one of a handful of times I'd seen him without first being alerted by a bloodcurdling yell. I never considered the possibility of Uncle Rodney entering a church in an upright position. An idol had fallen. They were coming across the yard of the parsonage, walking side by side, not touching each other, but it was obvious they were a couple. For the second time today, a member of our family had stopped all conversation in the churchyard.

Uncle Rodney was dressed in a blue pinstriped suit with a double-breasted coat. He wore a pink shirt with a navy and red tie. Instead of shoes, he had on snakeskin boots, and his hair, pulled back in a ponytail, made him a striking figure. Uncle Rodney was every mother's nightmare and every schoolgirl's dream.

Mrs. Amanda Cotton was wearing a deep blue dress trimmed in white that fell just below her knees. Her shoes and purse were a perfect complement to the trim of her dress. She wore a pair of white gloves that brought the whole outfit together. Her hair was pulled back and held in place by a white ribbon. I don't believe I had ever truly looked at Amanda Cotton until that moment. She was beautiful. From the looks on the faces of those around me, I think many people were seeing her for the first time.

Deacon Miller and Ms. Sarah Doolittle, the church secretary and first female deacon in Cedar Creek, were standing at the top of the steps discussing what role the Union Baptist Church should play in saving the souls of some remote tribe of Aborigines in the outback of Australia, a tribe that until now had done quite well without the help of anyone from North Carolina. Their conversation abruptly halted when Deacon Miller saw Amanda and Uncle Rodney enter the churchyard.

"Good Lord," muttered the deacon as he reached for the railing to steady himself.

It's a good thing he grabbed the rail because, at that instant, Mama appeared at the door of the church and brushed right past him as she made her way down the steps. I don't think she would have bowled him over on purpose, but I doubt she would have gone out of her way to avoid a collision.

"Hello, children," she said a little louder than necessary. "I saved ya'll a seat with us. Now, let's get inside so we can chat before the service begins. Come on, boys!"

I looked at Jason, Jason looked at me, Uncle Rodney and Amanda looked at each other, and everybody else looked at us, and Mama looked directly at Deacon Miller as she slipped between them and took each of them by the hand as if this were all part of a well thought-out plan.

Uncle Rodney had a keen sense of irony and recognized Mama's act for what it was. He would make her pay for the part she expected him to play. He took his hand out of Mama's and slipped his arm around her waist, drawing her close to him and planting a loud kiss on her cheek. Mama smiled and looked up at Uncle Rodney as if he were a son just back from a foreign war, but if her thoughts had been verbalized, we all would have been kicked out of the church.

The proceedings may have confused Mrs. Amanda, but she did not show it. She knew that every eye in the churchyard was on them but was determined not to let it bother her.

As they ascended the steps, Rodney reached for the door, faced Deacon Miller, and said, "Those gophers get more vicious every year, eh, Deacon? You should really try to get rid of them. Let me know if I can help. Good morning, Mrs. Doolittle."

We filed into the pew reserved for us and looked like the closest family in Cedar Creek sitting there: Daddy on the end, Mrs. Amanda next to him, Uncle Rodney next to Mama with his arm on the pew behind her shoulders, Jason next to her, and then me. Every once in a while, Uncle Rodney would pat Mama on the shoulder and hug her. I struggled to keep from laughing out loud.

The visiting preacher for the day was Reverend Elijah Dupree from over in Black Mountain. Preacher Dupree was "called to preach" when he was 13 and continued preaching for fifty-two years until he retired two years ago. Now, he spent most Sundays in the amen corner of Ebenezer Baptist Church in Black Mountain unless moved by the need of an orphan congregation like ours to once again preach the word. Reverend Dupree never crossed the threshold of a college or seminary, learning instead to preach by studying the Bible and practicing on any group that would sit still long enough to get him fired up. Daddy always said that if Jesus Christ were to come back to earth today, it would be six years before he could get a church of his own, providing that he could get into college with no money. Preachers like Reverend Dupree were a dying breed. Never having been to seminary, Reverend Dupree was not bothered by either the need to intellectualize his sermon or keep to a schedule. He came out of the chute preaching fire and brimstone and kept at a torrid pace until he whipped even the most cold-hearted sinner into submission without once looking at the clock.

By 1:15, every heart in the church was heavy, and every stomach was growling. After twelve verses of "Just As I Am" and several series of raised hands and closed eyes, the reverend ended the service with a prayer to which we said, "Amen," and truly meant it.

As we made our way to the door, the ritual of handshaking and "glad to see yous" was in full swing. Folks who won't even acknowledge your existence Monday through Saturday will grab and squeeze your hand on Sunday and act as if the day would not have been complete without spending those precious moments with you.

Reverend Dupree stood by the door, flanked by Deacon Miller and the other members of the board. Everyone told the reverend how much he or she had enjoyed his sermon. I personally did not see how anyone could enjoy being told how contemptible they were in the sight of God and how they were sure to burn in hell if they continued to live in such a manner. I certainly did not think that the prospect of eternal damnation was enjoyable. I would not even have enjoyed two and a half hours of hearing about the virtues of a trip to Disneyland while my stomach tried to chew away at my backbone, let alone promises of fire and never-ending agony.

Uncle Rodney made the most of the situation. He must have shaken a couple of dozen hands on the way to the door and called each person by name, asking about their family and their health. You would have thought he was the goodwill ambassador from the Baptist State Convention rather than a man who had not been in a church building since the last time a pretty lady cajoled him into attending.

As we got to the door, Uncle Rodney grabbed Reverend Dupree's hand, placed his other hand on the preacher's shoulder, and said, "Mighty inspiring words today, Reverend. Gives a man a lot to think about as he travels the roads of life."

"Well, thank you, Brother, uh…"

"Wilson, Rodney Wilson. My family and I would be mighty proud if you would come out to Sunday lunch with us before you make that ride back to Black Mountain. Wouldn't we, Edna?" he asked, patting Mama on the arm. "My sister-in-law here is the best cook in this county." With that, he leaned over and kissed Mama on the cheek again.

"Payback is hell," she thought but smiled broadly and nodded.

All the deacon's eyes opened wide and their heads snapped to the left to witness the preacher's response.

"Well, Brother Wilson, that's mighty nice of you to invite me to break bread with you and your family, but I really must be getting back home. I would be proud to stop by and enjoy a glass of tea with you on my way out of town. You certainly have a fine-looking family. God bless you all."

Royster Miller looked like he had been staked through the heart. On the other hand, Mama drew in a long and victorious breath. She squeezed Uncle Rodney's arm and proudly led her flock down the steps of the church, pausing only long enough to tell Deacon Miller to be sure to let her know when the grounds committee was going to have its day of fellowship so the Wilson family could do their part.

Everything was right in our little corner of the universe for a brief period.

Chapter Seven

Reverend Dupree came to the house just as he said he would. Preaching the old-fashioned way must raise a mighty thirst in a fellow because he drank almost a half-gallon of tea before leaving. As we watched the back of Reverend Dupree's Oldsmobile disappear down the drive, Mama asked Ms. Amanda to give her a hand in the kitchen so we could have our Sunday lunch. It was 2:30, and my body had made it about as far as it could on the love of God and the euphoria of the moment, so I was glad to hear any rumors of food being served.

When we finally gathered at the table, we were short on conversation and long on appetite. Mama always outdid herself on Sunday. Most of the time, there was plenty left over for snacking as the day went on, but now, even the gold binding that encircled the platters was in danger of being scraped off.

After the meal, while they were washing dishes, Amanda jumped right into the middle of the subject that Mama had been trying to figure out how to approach for two days.

"Edna, you have been a wonderful friend since Craig left. I don't know what I would have done without you. I was a little taken aback when you had Rodney over Thursday night, but he's such a wonderful gentleman. I'm beginning to think that you know more of what is good for me than I do myself."

Mama's head was spinning. Amanda thought she was playing Cupid. How could she tell her that Rot-ney was the last thing she would wish on any young woman?

"Well, that's mighty sweet of you to say, Amanda. I really don't deserve any credit for anything," said Mama, thinking of all the times that Rodney had invented innovative ways to anger and disappoint her and hoping that she had enough time to figure a way out of this mess. Mama could not help but feel flattered that Amanda thought she was wise enough to know when and how to devise a scheme to help her out of her unfortunate position.

"Did you see the looks on the faces of the people at church today?" asked Amanda, breaking Mama's revelry. "You would have thought Rodney and I had just landed in a flying saucer. I was almost ready to turn tail and run when you came to our rescue. Anyway, I no longer feel right living in the church house. I was thinking about moving back home, but that seems like giving up. I told Rodney that I was going to get a job and find a place to live right here in Cedar Creek. He said I could move into his place down by the river since he's going back to Florida the week after next anyway. If we have time, he's taking me down to see it this afternoon. It sounds wonderful when he talks about it."

Mama's heart was in her throat, and her head was pounding. It was all she could do to keep her composure. The thought of Amanda living in Rodney's cabin was as unimaginable to her as the idea anyone would choose to live in Minnesota or New York. Her panic was about to break the surface when it came to her that she would never want to live there once Amanda saw the place. The cabin was Rodney's toy and served as a roof over his head when he came off the road for a few weeks. He had been working on it for over five years, and Mama's image of the last time she had seen it would surely cause Amanda to reconsider that option.

Mama took it upon herself to find Amanda a place to live. She would start tomorrow. Once again, Mama had found a way to help Ms. Amanda, something with which she was becoming quite comfortable. Mama was proud of herself and began to hum "Onward, Christian Soldiers" as she made short order of the last few dishes and wiped down all the appliances in the kitchen.

Amanda took Mama's actions for approval and joined in on the chorus. When they both broke into song, it caused us men, who were headed out to the workshop, to pause and look toward the open kitchen window.

"I don't know what's behind all that fuss," said Daddy, "but when women get that happy, it usually means a man is in deep trouble."

It took me years to truly realize what a profound understanding of life my Daddy possessed.

Uncle Rodney had been awfully quiet since we got home. He had talked some with Reverend Dupree as they had sipped tea on the porch but mostly had let the reverend carry the conversation. That had not been much of a trick as most preachers can easily get wound up and run for quite a while with just a nod or an occasional "amen" from someone. I believe he was worried about what Mama was telling Ms. Amanda.

Daddy opened the door to his workshop and stepped inside. This was his domain. Placed all around the walls were his hand tools, all in immaculate condition. A table saw, band saw, drill press, and lathe were positioned on the floor to give him plenty of room to work and maneuver his projects. Throughout time men have sought solitude to contemplate the twists and turns of the human predicament. Jesus went to the desert for forty days, Moses took to the mountains, Gautama, the Buddha, sat under the Bodhi tree, and my Daddy went to his workshop. Jason and I spent many hours watching Daddy shape wood into useful and decorative objects. It was a rite of manhood in our family to learn how to operate the tools with skill and safety.

Daddy walked over to the cabinet above the workbench and pulled out his "emergency" bottle of Jim Beam and two glasses. We didn't wait to be asked to leave since liquor in the workshop was a sign of serious business.

Uncle Rodney listened while Daddy told him about Amanda and Craig Cotton and laughed as much as he thought prudent when Daddy told him about the churchyard. Mama's bargain with the deacon made him angry but gave him a full understanding of Mama's actions. He wished he had known all this earlier so he could have really given the deacon hell.

Daddy reached for the whiskey and poured two more fingers into each glass. "What's going on with you two, Rodney? I know this is none of my business, but that poor girl has been through a tough time and may be very vulnerable right now. I know you don't mean any harm, but another disappointment may just be too much. Edna doesn't have any faith in you when it comes to women, so I want to be able to ease her mind a bit."

"Sam, Edna don't have much faith in me when it comes to anything, but you can tell her not to worry. I wouldn't do anything to hurt Amanda. This one scares me. I'm going to take her out to the cabin this afternoon, and if she likes it, she can live there. No matter if she likes it or not, I'll get her moved out of the parsonage this week. When Deacon Miller finally hits hell, fire will splash a mile away."

Daddy laughed, and they spent the next fifteen minutes trying to top each other with quotes concerning the disparity between how most Christians perceived themselves and how God probably viewed them. They laughed and horsed around, making lots of noise, until Amanda called for Rodney. They climbed into his Jeep and said thanks for everything. I braced myself for the spray of dust and gravel that Uncle Rodney always left in his wake, but it never came. As they slowly drove down the path to the road, I was overcome by the fear that I was witnessing the end of an era. It was still two years until May Southerland would teach me the difference between foolishness and fun.

Chapter Eight

When you throw a pebble out into the middle of a pond, it doesn't just punch a hole in the water and sink to the bottom. When the rock hits the water, it creates waves that extend from that point outward until there's not a still place to be found.

The same is true when an event, good or bad, takes place in someone's life. When Craig Cotton ran off with Mary Alice Darnell, it didn't just affect him, Amanda, and Mary Alice. It touched the lives of Mama, Uncle Rodney, and the rest of our family, but that was just one circle on the pond.

One of the people most affected was Troy Jacobs. Troy could not understand why Mary Alice would choose a Bible-thumping wimp over him. Not that Troy missed her all that much. It was that she walked out on him, and everyone knew it.

Troy had been what you would call a "big man on campus." He was elected class president in the eighth grade and was re-elected each year until his graduation. He loved sports and excelled in football, basketball, and baseball, becoming the captain of each team in its respective season. Cedar Creek was not a hotbed of athletic talent, so when Troy was earmarked as a genuine contender, everyone took notice and wanted to get on his bandwagon. Parents of the other players may have gone to the games to cheer their own sons and to support the team, but they also went to see Troy play. The pride of the community was perched squarely on Troy's shoulders.

Sports and academics were not the only areas in which Troy excelled. He also shone with girls and cars. He really didn't care much for cars, but he realized early on that girls liked them. He developed his own theory of relativity: The hotter and faster the car you drove, the hotter and faster the girl you could get to ride with you.

After much consideration, Troy decided to bestow his talents upon the University of North Carolina at Chapel Hill. He had decided to dedicate himself to basketball, but soon after the beginning of his sophomore year, his focus changed to music, marijuana, and motorcycles. After losing his scholarship and eventually dropping out of school, Troy returned to Cedar Creek with only a thorough knowledge of motorcycle mechanics and an outlaw attitude to show for his time away.

Troy now moved in different circles from his former teammates and high school friends. He hung out in bars and clubs and only associated with other bikers. His athletic ability served him well when there was fighting to be done, so he soon became the recognized leader of the bike subculture in Cedar Creek. Now don't go having thoughts of Hell's Angels or of Marlon Brando in *The Wild Ones* because Cedar Creek would have never stood still for such. Troy's bunch were "wannabes," aspiring to outlaw biker fame. They were really just a group of local boys who rode motorcycles and acted tough among themselves but generally left everyone else alone.

A hill could be mistaken for a mountain if viewed without reference. So too Troy's gang took on the appearance of the real thing to the untrained eye. The untrained eye was exactly what Mary Alice Darnell possessed when she met Troy.

Mary Alice remembered Troy from high school. He had graduated three years ahead of her and was the sports hero by which all others were measured. When Mary Alice graduated, she moved to Asheville to live with her sister. After a year, she returned to Cedar Creek to find Troy a transformed person and completely available. Although she was attracted to the rough edge, she soon grew tired of playing second fiddle to a Harley Davidson. Craig was kind and respectful when he showed up at Sybil's and made her feel important. She was ready for a change.

Troy did not care about all the tangled paths that led to this point. He only knew he had been left for a "fancy Dan" preacher, and it pissed him off. He knew that Mary Alice would probably go back to Asheville, so he packed his bike and headed west to kick some ass.

Chapter Nine

Mary Alice's sister Victoria ("never call me Vickie") Pritchard had not anticipated her younger sister's visit, let alone her moving in with a man in tow. The proper Southern lady, as Victoria pictured herself, could never turn family away, but she could be sure the way they had to live would encourage them to leave soon enough. To ensure that Mary Alice and Craig conducted themselves properly, she assigned them separate bedrooms on either side of her own.

Victoria did not work as her only foray into the job market had left her injured. She had received a handsome settlement that, when coupled with her social security and the insurance money from the death of her husband, "Dear Lawrence," allowed her to live comfortably without having to go out and grovel with the masses. Victoria felt satisfied with her life and did not relish the thought of Mary Alice and Craig moving in. She had often wondered how the same parents who bore her could have spawned someone as noisy as Mary Alice. So Victoria contrived to see that Mary Alice and Craig would have absolutely no time alone, a situation that no two run-away lovers could tolerate for long.

Money was another factor that worked into the equation of the estranged couple's new life. Neither Craig nor Mary Alice had much in the way of cash when they left Cedar Creek. Both secretly wished they had planned better, but in a duel between the sensible and the sensual, the libido always triumphs.

The fact that they both would have to work did not escape them. Finding a job for Mary Alice was just a matter of locating a café or bar that needed an experienced waitress with a great body and effervescent personality. She knew that she would have no problem, so she could shop for just the right place.

The job market did not look quite so bright for Craig. There weren't any listings in the classified section for ex-Baptist ministers who had left their church and wife without notice and moved into the city with a panty-less waitress. After three days of self-evaluation, Craig realized he had absolutely no skills of value to secular society. The combination of the cold, hard truth about himself and the cold, hard tactics employed by Victoria threw Craig into a stupor. Self-pity and sexual deprivation are formidable forces against a man's ego. Mary Alice, although never appreciated for her mind before, came up with a solution.

She diagnosed the problem with speed that would make an emergency room doctor envious. She knew which problem must be addressed first. There can be no reasoning with a man possessed by his basic animal desire. She knew they must have some time alone and that there was no money for a motel room. First, she decided that her 1973 Volkswagen Super Beetle would serve as the magic carpet that would bear them off to a sexual Mecca.

The economical and dependable Volkswagen Beetle was the car of choice for an entire subculture of Americans. Its simple body style and Spartan appointments attracted the type of person who was more cerebral and less concerned with fashion. Thousands of counter-culturists used their hair length, mode of dress, and Beetle to make a statement about their lives. Mary Alice bought her Beetle because it was all she could afford. The only social statement she was trying to make was that she had made a purchase within her budget.

No one would describe the small, utilitarian interior of the Volkswagen as comfortable. To think of it as a vessel of amour would cause you to stretch the imagination and contort the body in ways that would confound Harry Houdini.

Mary Alice knew Craig would never think of making love in a 1973 Super Beetle, so her seduction would have to be convincing.

"Craig, darlin'," Mary Alice said, "will you ride with me down to the laundromat. I need to do some clothes and hate to be there alone."

"Could we wait till tomorrow? I'm not feeling very well right now and want to rest for a while. Anyway, won't Victoria let you use her washer and dryer?"

"I can't do what I want to do here, and if you come along, I'm sure you will feel better."

Something in her voice caught Craig's attention, and he finally turned to look at her. She was sitting sideways on the chair next to him, wearing a deep blue A-line skirt cut about three inches above the knee. When Craig looked her way, she shifted her position, giving him a covert peep at an overt promise.

I don't know how many of you hunt rabbits with beagle dogs, but those who do know that no matter how hard you hunt or how tired the dogs may seem, the briefest glimpse of a cottontail will have them up and running again. Craig bolted upright in the chair and ran his hands through his hair.

Mary Alice's memory served her well as she drove out of town. She had made this trip many times in her youth but never as an adult. Mary Alice slowed, turned the Volkswagen onto the path, and proceeded up the hill at a thirty-degree angle. She knew there was a clearing at the top, but she also knew that other roads led to that clearing. On a sultry August night, other cars and people would be there, so she pulled off the path and parked. She kissed Craig and crawled over into the back seat, a task that was made easier by the angle of the road.

As a Southern gentleman, I cannot in good taste give many details from that point except to tell you that the dance was progressing wonderfully until the ballerina's foot knocked the car out of gear at the most inopportune time. The sexual act can be likened to a jumbo jet at takeoff. With much force, the plane starts to taxi down the runway. As the plane picks up speed, the pilot still has time to cut the engines and return to safety if he feels there is any cause for concern. Just before the jet becomes airborne, there is a brief period when the speed is too great and the runway is too short to abort the takeoff safely. At that point, the plane will either fly or crash, and it is completely out of the hands of the flight crew. This is called "the point of no return." Craig and Mary Alice had reached the point of no return as the Super Beetle began to roll slowly down the hill.

They both felt the motion of the car and, at some subconscious level, knew they should try to do something about it, but neither of them was willing to stop what they were doing to set about this new task. The only saving grace in the situation was that the Volkswagen was very lightweight. The movements of their bodies shifted the weight of the car, turning the front wheels to the left, causing the Beetle to cross the path and come to rest in the middle of a honeysuckle patch instead of rolling straight down the path and across the main road. Neither Craig nor Mary Alice was sure whether the other's moans resulted from ecstasy or the sudden stop as the Volkswagen became entangled in the honeysuckles.

Slowly, they unknotted their bodies and looked at each other with a combination of love and wonder. They knew they were all right, but they weren't so sure of the car's condition. Craig forced the passenger-side door open and climbed out of the back seat. As he reached back inside, his feet became entangled in the vines, and he fell naked into the honeysuckle.

With Mary Alice behind the wheel and a slight push by Craig, the Volkswagen moved easily back onto the path. They got dressed, laughed, and joked, hugging and kissing like teenagers. It would be two days before they realized Craig had fallen into poison ivy and was covered from head to toe.

Chapter Ten

The ride back to Asheville had been just as productive as their backseat adventure. With the most immediate problem solved, Mary Alice set about talking to Craig about his prospects for gainful employment. She explained that he was in a wonderful position. The fact that he could no longer follow his previous path did not mean that he couldn't help people, which was the main point of the ministry. She suggested he might even be in a better position because knowing he was a preacher may put off people. After all, she reasoned, Jesus himself never had a church but did his work while moving among people. Nothing could take his training and compassion away from him. Having no practical experience should be viewed as a plus because now he could seek employment anywhere.

Craig virtually leaped out of bed the next morning, determined that he would find a job. He attributed the tingling sensation that he felt over his body to excitement derived from the understanding that Mary Alice had helped him achieve concerning his new position in life. He looked at himself in the mirror and smiled. He thought of Mary Alice but decided not to wake her. He even smiled at Victoria as they passed in the hall, knowing that she no longer held dominion over his sex life. Taking the keys from the kitchen counter, he set out. When he climbed behind the wheel of the Volkswagen, the entire scene from the previous evening played across his mind. He could not contain his laughter. Life was good.

As Craig pulled the car onto Interstate 40, he saw a flurry of activity off to the side. Equipment was being unloaded, and men were walking about with purpose. He glanced at the rearview mirror once more as he merged into the flow of high-speed traffic.

Craig was determined not to get discouraged. Everywhere he went, he was given an application and told to fill it out, bring it back, and then perhaps he would be granted an interview. By 3:30 in the afternoon, the passenger seat was full of applications. Craig looked over some of the applications as he ate a Big Mac and decided they were asking him to reveal too much about himself to get a job that would only pay him minimum wage.

As he drove home, Craig fought his emotions. A half-mile from his exit, Craig saw a crane boom rising into the air. This morning, he thought there were only parts being unloaded, and now there it was, reaching for the clouds. What a feeling of accomplishment the men who assembled it must have. Craig wanted more than anything else to share that feeling, so he turned left at the exit instead of right and decided he would seek employment with these men.

Craig pulled his tie off as he drove the VW into the job site. He had no idea how to proceed, but he felt unmistakably drawn to it. He got out of the car and walked toward a trailer.

"Hold on there, Bo," called a man standing beside the crane. "You've got to have a hard hat to go any further. State your business."

"I was looking for a job," said Craig, second-guessing himself.

"Got any Experience?"

"No, but…"

"You wanted by the police?"

"No, I…"

"You scared of hard work, boy?"

"No, sir, I'm not afraid of…"

"Well, quit rattlin' on and come with me," said the man as he tossed Craig a hard hat. "Put that on, or you'll get both our asses in a sling."

Craig put the hat on without adjusting it. The last person to wear it must have had a head the size of a pumpkin because it kept falling over Craig's eyes. He kept pushing it back, but the hat slipped to his nose as he stepped through the trailer's door. When he pushed it back, he was face to face with a man in khaki trousers, a plaid shirt, and dust-covered boots who had a curious grin on his face.

"Boss, this man wants a job. He ain't got no experience, but he says he ain't afraid of hard work. I could use a laborer to help with those footers and leave the rest of the guys to finish up over in Bryson City."

"Put him on," said the man. "My name's O'Connor, and this is Homer Grady, but you better just call him Gus. You'll be working for him. Come on in at 7:00 in the morning, and we'll fill out your tax papers. You'll need a driver's license and a social security card."

With that, O'Connor turned back to his work, dismissing them both. They walked across the lot without saying a word, and when Craig reached the Super Beetle, he turned to Grady.

"Do I need to fill out an application?"

"Hell no. By dinnertime tomorrow, I'll know more about you than you would ever tell me on a piece of paper. Just work hard and do what I tell you, and you'll be fine. I don't give a damn who you are or where you've been. Only one thing I want you to do for me."

"What's that?"

"Spend tonight learning how to adjust that hard hat so you don't get yourself or nobody else killed."

With that, Grady turned and went back to what he had been doing.

Craig climbed back into the car. He had a job. He could not tell Mary Alice who he worked for or how much he made, but he had a job and could look forward to a payday and eventually getting their own place. Although he didn't know it, Craig Cotton was now a bridge builder.

Chapter Eleven

Nowhere were the dog days of summer more prevalent than in North Carolina. The average temperature was between eighty and eighty-five degrees with many days reaching into the low nineties. Combined with almost one hundred percent humidity, and the weather was oppressive by anyone's standard. Some flatlanders who could afford it came to the mountains seeking the respite of temperatures lowered by a few degrees. They lounged in the shade and fooled themselves into thinking the mountain breeze was indeed cooler than their piedmont or coastal dwellings. These people were typically retired professionals or white-collar workers with enough disposable income to insulate themselves from most of the discomforts life throws their way.

On the other side of the coin, the blue-collar workers who struggled in factories and mills had to put up with the heat in the summer and the cold in the winter with no hope of zipping off to a better climate. They worked hard each day and endured. They moved quickly from the plant to home and back, marking time in eight-hour shifts. Then there were the people who worked outside, whose blue collar was marked by a sweat ring. They were cruelly exposed to the weather. For them, there was no shelter or shade, and their lives were completely at the mercy of nature. In the open expanse of a construction site, they could find no escape from the heat and humidity. The men of the Bridge Force fell into this category.

A seasoned outdoor man noticed little difference between ninety and a hundred degrees. Contending with the weather was just another part of the job. But to a man spending his first day as a bridge builder, there was one hell of a difference.

Craig put on his blue jeans, T-shirt, and new work boots and checked the adjustment on his hard hat before letting Mary Alice drive him to work. He felt a little self-conscious about being dropped off until he saw some of the other guys arriving in the same manner. One man drove up on a moped, but no one seemed to notice.

Having Mary Alice drop him off turned out to be a good career move because if Craig had kept the car, he would have quit three times before the end of his first day. As it was, he had no choice but to persevere. By the end of the day, he was sore from head to toe, every inch of his exposed skin was sunburned, and he was soaked in his own sweat. Craig was proud that he had accomplished everything that he had been told to do and had not lingered between tasks, even though his body had cried for relief. When Mary Alice drove up, they were putting the tools back into the trailer. His first inclination was to run for the car and ask her to get him as far away from the job site as possible, but as he came down the steps of the trailer, Grady was waiting for him.

"Kid, you did a solid job out here today," Grady said, laying a hand on Craig's shoulder. "Lotta guys woulda tucked tail and run, but you're pretty tough. See ya in the morning."

"Yeah, see ya."

Craig never thought of himself as tough. All the other guys had been indifferent toward him all day, but now that it was over, they all spoke to him as they made their way to the parking area. Their acceptance and Grady's comments had wiped out Craig's doubts about coming back the next day.

Craig made two decisions as he climbed into the VW: He would continue this job, mainly because he liked the manly feeling that he was experiencing, and he would bring twice as much lunch tomorrow. Sometime during the night, the poison ivy came into full bloom. Craig awoke to a persistent itch. The old Craig would have taken the day off and gone to the doctor for a shot to relieve the itching and help dry up the blisters. The new "tough" Craig knew that if he did not show up on the job, everyone would think that he had quit and couldn't hack the hard work. He had gone too far to turn back. He would not sacrifice the respect of his co-workers or his newfound self-esteem for a rash. He swore to himself that he would make it through the day no matter how uncomfortable he became. Having poison ivy can rarely viewed as good fortune, but Craig's poison ivy indirectly allowed him to become one of the boys.

Nick Hopkins was a loudmouth. His six-foot and two-hundred forty-pound frame gave him a formidable look that bullied most people into putting up with his sarcasm. He was hired as a laborer and was helping Craig do some shovel work inside of a form. He jumped on Craig's case early when he noticed his discomfort. Craig was trying his best not to scratch the blisters. He only dabbed at them with his hand when it became unbearable. Nick talked junk all day and once even tossed some dirt over Craig's head so some would fall down his shirt. He claimed it had been a mistake but laughed in a way that let Craig know he had done it on purpose. By lunchtime, everyone was watching to see how much Craig could take. By quitting time, a deep silence had fallen over the job site, and all that could be heard was Nick's voice. He was having a hell of a time playing with Craig. After stowing the last of the equipment inside the trailer, Craig pulled the door together and put on the padlock. The workday was over, but Nick wasn't quite finished with Craig.

"Hey, itchy," Nick called as he ran up to Craig and put his hand on his shoulder. "Why don't you try a little soap and water tonight?

Maybe you'll be able to stand yourself tomorrow without pawing all day. It might make it easier on me too if I have to work with you."

Craig Cotton had never thought of himself as a violent man, but he had taken all he could take. Trying to remember everything that he had seen on television, he pivoted. He didn't know if he had his fist balled up correctly or not or even where he should try to land the blow, but he put everything he had into it. He felt his knuckles contact Nick's jaw and heard the smack of flesh on flesh. He saw a flash of recognition come into Nick's eyes and made himself ready for the counterattack. It never came. Nick's eyes turned milky, and he collapsed at Craig's feet. Craig's eyes swept the area around him. He saw all his co-workers looking on. Mary Alice watched from the Beetle outside the gate. Having come full circle, his gaze stopped when it came to Grady.

"Well, I guess I don't have a job anymore. I'm sorry for all this, but I couldn't take any more of his mouth."

"Hell, Slugger, I was tired of hearing the som'bitch myself. Anybody who can put up with a case of poison ivy as you've got and listen to his shit till quitting time has always got a job with me. Take care of that stuff tonight, and I'll see ya in the morning."

Grady reached into the truck bed, pulled a cooler out, and dumped its contents over Nick. He began to stir.

"Glass jaws and big mouths don't make good traveling partners, you big ox. Leave the mouth at home tomorrow, or I'll sic Slugger on you again."

From then on, Craig was known as Slugger. He and Nick would work together often, but neither one would ever mention the fight. Mary Alice had seen the whole thing and could hardly wait to get him home.

Chapter Twelve

Mama got tired of waiting on the grounds committee to organize a day of fellowship. The Wilson men fixed the churchyard, and Mama was there to supervise. She made sure we had plenty of tea to keep us going and that nobody else could claim part of the repairs.

"We always fix what we break, and we don't like to owe anybody."

Mama made a fine sight with her feet firmly planted on the sidewalk and her hands on her hips as she took turns shouting orders to us and howdy-dos to the good church members who happened to ride by. As they passed, she would wave and speak, but as they moved away, she would mumble under her breath. The few comments I could hear made me glad the good folks of the church chose to ride with their windows up and that we were the children of a forgiving God.

Chapter Thirteen

U ncle Rodney looked up as he heard Daddy's truck turn off the paved road and crawl down the path to the cabin. He looked like a wild man. His hair was loose and wet with sweat. He wore only an old pair of blue jeans and his trusty brown boots, which anyone else would have discarded years ago. He was splitting wood and stacking it between two trees that seemed to have been grown for just that purpose.

Although it had only been two weeks since Uncle Rodney and Mrs. Amanda met, it seemed like a lifetime had passed. Much to Mama's dismay, Amanda had immediately fallen in love with the cabin and the surrounding land. Uncle Rodney and Mrs. Amanda had moved her things the day after they first visited the cabin, and Uncle Rodney began to get things ready for the winter. He moved into the old Coleman trailer that he used to pull with him when he worked a job out of town. Uncle Rodney didn't much care where or how he lived. He was just as comfortable sleeping under the sprawling limbs of a sweetgum tree as he would be in the finest Southern mansion. Sometimes he was restless and didn't want any wall around him. On such occasions, nothing would do but stay outside. He would put his back up against a tree and sit and listen to the sound of the woods around him. At the least sound, he would turn his head in that direction and not move until he could discern the origin. He missed nothing. I told Jason I thought Uncle Rodney could hear a cricket making up his mind to rub his legs together.

Daddy said it was because of Vietnam, and it was best to leave Uncle Rodney alone till it passed.

Uncle Rodney brought the maul through a sweeping circle and sent wood flying as it sliced perfectly through a large piece of oak. It looked effortless; however, as a veteran wood splitter and stacker, I knew how tough it was. Another swing buried the head of the maul into the stump that he was using to stage the logs for splitting. He let out a yell and ran to the truck, thanking us for saving him from having to continue.

He said, "I've been looking for a graceful way to stop for an hour. I figure you must have sensed my predicament and rode up like three heroes to rescue me."

I loved how Uncle Rodney turned even the most modest circumstances into an event. Jason and I laughed out loud, and Daddy grunted and bit the end off a cigar.

Jason and I tried to be cool, but our eyes kept drifting over to the cooler that Uncle Rodney always kept close when he worked at the cabin. After letting us stew for a few minutes, he walked over to the cooler and made opening it seem like a task. He always had colas of one brand or another in the cooler. "Just in case I run into a couple of thirsty guys," he would say. He tossed us the colas and then reached back in for two beers for him and Daddy. The cola was so cold that you had to pass it from hand to hand to keep from getting frostbite. To us, it was the nectar of the gods, but I longed for the day when I could have a beer with them.

"Ya'll come to see if you could hang ole Rufus? Your poles are leaning against the trailer and the shovel's there too. Dig ya up some juicy worms 'cause Rufus ain't gonna go for no light snack. Takes big bait for big fish."

Rufus was the legendary bass that ruled the pond. So far, Rufus had eluded our best efforts to lure him onto the hook. Uncle Rodney said he had caught him a few times but had felt sorry for him and put him back in the water. It never occurred to me he might have been pulling our leg. I swore that if I caught him, he was bound for the frying pan. As we ran to get the poles and worms, I could already see him on the table. The hundred or so times we had failed so far did nothing to dampen our enthusiasm. Only a few people have been able to maintain that state of dreaming and of seeing endless possibilities as they achieve adulthood. For their name, check any history book.

Time is liquid when you're fishing. Something about the movement of the water, the sun, and the breeze as they take turns playing on your face and the sense of anticipation as you stare at the cork renders any timepiece useless. I don't know if it had been a few minutes or a few hours when my reverie was broken by the sound of the jeep making its way from the road to the cabin.

When I think back and figure out exactly how I transitioned from boyhood to manhood, that day always comes to mind. I looked up and saw the Willys just ahead of a cloud of dust. Amanda Cotton was behind the wheel. I noticed the back of the jeep was full of grocery bags. Without even thinking, I pulled the line out of the water, laid my fishing pole down on the bank, and went to help her with the packages. Rufus would have to wait for another day. As I made my way up the hill, I looked back at Jason but couldn't tell if his eyes or his mouth were opened widest.

In time, I would learn that meaning and purpose, when injected into someone's life, had a way of mentally and physically renewing that individual. In my stumbling and awkward youth, I only knew that Amanda Cotton looked a lot different from how she had when Mama first had her come over for Thursday night supper. She had on brown shorts and a blouse that matched. She wore lace-up boots with brown socks. She reminded me of the ladies who would always come along on the safari in the Tarzan movies. Her hair was in a French braid, and all I could think of was how pretty she was.

I got all the groceries out of the jeep while she put the stuff away in cabinets. I had been inside the cabin hundreds of times and never thought of it as a real house. Uncle Rodney always adjusted himself to the cabin's conditions, but now the place had been altered to its new inhabitants. It looked and smelled clean, and everything was in its place.

Mrs. Amanda asked me to tell Mama that she had been busy at the cabin but planned to come visit in a few days. I responded to all her inquiries and promised to carry the message but was otherwise dumbfounded and tongue-tied.

She finished with the groceries and reached into the refrigerator for three cans of soda. She pulled the tab on one and handed it to me, opened one for herself, and handed me the third with instructions to give it to Jason. I didn't see any reason to tell her we had just finished one, as it would only worry her.

We stepped out on the front porch just as Daddy and Uncle Rodney were coming out of the woods. I ran to the pond so Jason could open his drink before Daddy realized we had been re-supplied. I don't want to seem devious, but the consumption of two soft drinks, one right after another, was not a common occurrence in our family. I neither wanted to lose the opportunity nor be scolded for having taken it. We had just enough time to get Jason's open and sink the first two empties in the pond before Daddy called us to leave.

We climbed into the truck. I took the spot by the window, and Jason sat in the middle. Uncle Rodney stood on the porch beside Amanda as Daddy started the engine. Uncle Rodney made a big deal of waving, bowing, and teasing us about Rufus. We both waved and yelled our goodbyes but were careful to keep the new sodas in a low profile. My belly was about to bust, but I would have no more wasted a drop of that drink than I would have torn a newfound fifty-dollar bill. If Daddy noticed our deception, he never let on. He drove home without saying much and walked directly out to the shop when we arrived. As I passed by, I saw him taking down his emergency bottle of Jim Beam. I was too caught up in my good fortune to think much about it until I heard Daddy telling Mama that Rodney might not return to Florida. Rodney may stay in Cedar Creek and try to find a bridge that needs building in the area. He told her how happy they both appeared and how the place looked civilized. He said this just might be what Rodney needed to settle down.

I was at the top of the stairs. Maybe I shouldn't have been listening, but I was curious to know if we had gotten away with our little coup. I don't know why, but I had two different emotions about what I had heard. I was delighted to hear that Uncle Rodney might stay because life was much more exciting with him around. On the other hand, I secretly looked forward to things returning to normal concerning Amanda's frequent visits to our house and felt saddened to think it might not happen. I didn't hear much of what Mama said, but I think it would be safe to say that we both went to bed with a headache caused by the same thing.

Chapter Fourteen

Some say life is change. Those who are happiest are those who adapt to change. Life brought many changes for my family and those connected with us in an amazingly short period. Witnessing any part of it was educational, but having the opportunity to place all the pieces of the puzzle together as I got older was truly enlightening.

No change was as profound as that which was about to take place in Victoria Pritchard's life. Again, time and opportunity conspired to move the unmovable.

The phone call had come just as they were finishing supper. Mary Alice was doing the dishes, and Craig had gone upstairs to rub more calamine lotion on his poison ivy. Victoria commented sarcastically that Craig resembled those ghastly Aborigines she had read about in *National Geographic,* who covered their bodies with dirt. She asked how Craig had gotten such a case of poison ivy but did not wait for an answer. She didn't really care. The only thing she cared about was how long it would take for Craig and Mary Alice to get their own place. Victoria was feeling more upbeat now that Craig had a job, and they were looking for a trailer to rent. She didn't understand how anyone could live in a rectangular metal box and be happy, but her main interest was her own happiness.

The third ring of the phone broke her pattern of thought. She was annoyed that neither Craig nor Mary Alice had answered it. She moved toward the phone, making sure the weight of her steps could be heard throughout the house.

"Hello."

"Hello. Is this the Pritchard residence? May I speak with Victoria Pritchard, please?"

"This is she," Victoria said, grasping to recognize the voice. The caller was female, and her voice was certainly southern with a drawl that could only be affected with much practice.

"Victoria, this is Jillian Strother. I've just moved to Asheville and couldn't wait to give you a call."

Jillian Strother had been Victoria's roommate at Meredith College. They had been inseparable during their four years there. They had both been scholarly and put their work ahead of any social activities. While their classmates slipped off campus and made their way up Hillsborough Street to meet the young men from North Carolina State College (as it was known then), they concentrated on organizing activities for the Latin club. They joined the movement against censorship of reading material. Victoria and Jillian's mutual love for the works of D. H. Lawrence, Henry Miller, and Anais Nin, whose books were under attack, rallied them to action. They both lived and loved vicariously through the characters of these authors. Sometimes, they would discuss these characters by candlelight well into the night and talk themselves into a fevered state but could not find the courage to initiate and consummate their own liaisons.

They both remained proper ladies throughout school and graduated with honors, promising never to lose touch. Neither could remember which one had failed to answer the other's letter or return the phone call, but soon communication ceased. This call was the first attempt at contact in almost eleven years.

One test of true friendship is that the passage of time does little to dampen the joy of things remembered. With mere acquaintances, you feel awkward when you meet them and try to recount old times. Though both you and your acquaintance lived the events, you each see them differently. You are not close enough to discuss and analyze those shared experiences until you come to a common understanding of what happened, thus the awkwardness. With a true friend, you have the luxury of time. Time is needed to condense each occurrence to its lowest common denominator so that when you meet after an extended absence, you both remember events and people in a mutually agreed-upon way, thus prompting no uneasiness.

With Victoria and Jillian, it was as if no time had passed. They talked of old times and of people from their past. They spoke little of the present, agreeing that it would be best to do so in person. The conversation went on for an hour and a half but seemed like only a few minutes. They agreed to have dinner together the following evening. Victoria would pick Jillian up at eight o'clock. She could hardly wait.

Victoria told Mary Alice about Jillian's call and that they were going to renew their friendship. Mary Alice was happy for Victoria but later laughed as she told Craig all about the two "debutante, bookworm, activist prudes." Her description left Craig with no desire to meet Jillian Strother.

After Craig and Mary Alice left for work, Victoria spent the greater part of the day thinking of the times she and Jillian had spent together. She had failed to ask Jillian if she had married or how her life had progressed after college. Jillian had given her maiden name, but that could have been just for ease of recognition and old times' sake. She realized she knew nothing about Jillian at all, but that did little to dampen her enthusiasm for the night ahead.

The next time she felt any discomfort was when she began to prepare for the evening. She did not know how to dress. She decided on a simple skirt and blouse that was tight enough to show that she had maintained her figure since graduation but in excellent taste as far as business wear went. She was conservative with her makeup, remembering Jillian's distaste for women who "have to paint themselves to be accepted." She teased, curled, combed, and sprayed her hair until it was just right (a point that she could never bring herself to compromise on for anyone's sake). She viewed herself in the mirror and was quite pleased with what she saw. At seven-fifteen, she slipped behind the wheel of her Saab and headed downtown, following Jillian's directions.

The apartment complex, Eden's Gate, was an "adults only community." Victoria drove past the gate and began looking for apartment 14-N. The letters of the alphabet identified the buildings, and there were seven apartments on each of three levels, so Victoria surmised that Jillian's apartment would be the last apartment on the second floor of building N. Feeling competent, she drove directly to the building and parked with ten minutes to spare.

She brushed her hands down the front of her skirt to straighten any wrinkles, made a perfunctory pat on her hair, and rang the bell. She was not prepared for what was to come.

The door opened slowly, and the intensity of the music was a testament to its solidity. Steel guitars and fiddles were engaged in an up-tempo battle that formed a perfect backdrop for the woman standing in the doorway. Victoria was sure she had somehow made a mistake and was at the wrong apartment when Jillian called her name and wrapped her arms around her. Jillian finally released her and moved to the stereo to reduce the volume to a tolerable level.

"Man, I love that song. It really gets the juices flowing," Jillian said as she turned to face Victoria.

The woman facing Victoria was nothing like the Jillian she remembered. Her hair was blonde and hung in spirals around her shoulders. She wore a blouse with pearl overlay buttons and a pair of jeans that must have presented quite a challenge to get on. Some exotic reptiles had given up their skin to become the boots that rose to about mid-calf. Jillian had always been thin as a rail in college, but now her figure and dress made Victoria self-conscious. Victoria had no preconceived notions of what to expect, but she was sure this was not it. It was possible Jillian had been a late bloomer, but Victoria could not accept such a metamorphosis. This could not be the same girl who had dressed in only baggy clothes and railed against makeup and everything false. The makeup she wore now was perfect, but what caught Victoria's attention was Jillian's blouse or more specifically what was inside Jillian's blouse. Late bloomer or not, there was a limit to the development that could naturally take place at any time in a woman's life.

"Come on over and sit down. Damn, Vickie, you look great. I could hardly wait to find you when I got into town."

Victoria cringed at being called Vickie but was in too much shock to correct Jillian. She moved to the couch and took a seat, her mind struggling to accept what she was seeing.

"Jillian, is it really you? I would never have recognized you if we had met on the street. You haven't aged, and, my God, how you've filled out."

"Filled out! Hell, girl, I blew up like a balloon after I got out of school. I've lost seventy pounds. I did most of it myself, but as I got close to the end, I found a good doctor to help me. You know, suck a little out here (she grabbed her thighs and butt) and pump a little in here," she said while cupping her breasts.

Victoria could feel her face flush with embarrassment. This was not going at all as she had envisioned.

Jillian sat beside Victoria, and they began to talk about old times. The discomfort slipped away as they reminisced, although Victoria could not keep her eyes from dancing across Jillian's form. She struggled to accept all the changes, but it was like being back in the dorm if she closed her eyes.

Conversations between old friends are like the roads that run through the neighborhoods of your youth; no matter how they twist and turn, you could never get lost, and they would always lead you right to your doorstep.

As they closed in on the present, Victoria found herself lost in the story of Jillian's post-Meredith days. Her life, with and since Lawrence, seemed a shadow compared to Jillian's adventures. The story of her last marriage (she had mentioned a total of three) to a cross-country truck driver was a fitting prelude to what was to come.

"Anyway, after I gave up my job to travel with the asshole, we stayed on the road continuously. All we did was ride and eat, eat and ride. Every once in a while, we would lay up at a motel and try to kill each other, but as I started to expand, those occasions became few and far between. When I topped two hundred, he topped a little redhead in Tucson and left me to find a way home. All the son of a bitch left me was a love of country music and the assurance that I'd never fall for that shit again. I went to work on myself, and here I am."

"Well, you did a heck of a job," said Victoria with a mix of awe and envy.

"Enough of this old-times shit. Let's go out and make some new times. I know just the place, the Cactus Palace. They got the best beef, the coldest beer, and the hottest shit-kickin' band in Asheville. Who knows, we might get lucky!"

"Jillian, I'm not dressed to go to a place like that. I thought we would just have dinner and talk."

"We've spent too much of our lives talking and sipping wine like a couple of old hags. Let's kick heels and raise hell. As far as your clothes go, I've been every size at one time or another, so I'm sure I've got something to fit you."

"But, I …"

"No buts about it. You trust old Jill to take care of everything."

Victoria did trust her, and Jillian did take care of everything. The outfit was perfect when Jill ("stop calling me Jillian; it makes me sound like a prude") helped her with her makeup and hair. Victoria hardly recognized herself.

As they left the apartment, Victoria felt almost giddy with excitement. The night lay before them like a dream. She felt a certain freedom in stepping outside herself and doing something that would have seemed foreign just a short while ago.

"What the hell," Victoria thought to herself. "Nobody knows me, and I don't know anybody. I can be anything I choose."

As she got in the car, she had no idea just how much of a journey she was beginning.

Chapter Fifteen

The thunder of the Harley-Davidson engine was like a symphony to Troy's ear as he cut through the Asheville night. No sound could compare. The deep guttural growls were so distinct that there could be no question as to their origin. The night air and the speed of the motorcycle combined to produce a tear that streaked the side of his face as he turned to see Alphie McCann riding to his right and slightly behind him.

Troy had ridden directly to Alphie's house when he arrived in Asheville. They had known each other from going on "runs" together. Alphie was the leader of the "Rat Pack," a local gang much like Troy's "Misfits." When Troy explained the situation, Alphie grunted and nodded his head in all the right places. Alphie said that situations like this made having a brotherhood so important, and, of course, Troy could crash with him. Troy, in turn, helped Alphie with repairs in the shop that doubled as the clubhouse. It only took a couple of days for Troy to get settled, and he was ready to begin his search for Mary Alice. He spent a whole day trying to decide how best to go about his task but could not come up with a solid plan. Once again, Alphie came to the rescue.

"Troy, my man, how about we go to the Cactus Palace and have a look? Chances are we might run into your honey right there, and, hell, even if we don't, we might run into something else. The way I see it, we can't lose either way."

Troy hadn't given the plan much consideration at first, but he found himself warming to it after a couple of beers.

Troy heard the unmistakable rumble as Alphie twisted up the power to pass him. As he came by, he showed an open palm pointed downward, the signal to hold the formation, so Troy fell behind him and paced his bike to Alphie's. The brake light of Alphie's hog told Troy they were about to turn.

It was not a dirt road, but it was about the worst paving job Troy had ever seen. The potholes and broken gravel were sure signs that heavy equipment had at one time traveled this road regularly. They slowed their bikes to keep from outriding their headlights, which might prove dangerous as well as embarrassing. The glow of lights against the night sky was the first indication they were approaching their destination. As they rode on, a green neon cactus with a golden crown perched precariously atop it came into view. The words "Cactus Palace" cast light over the parking lot, already full of every kind of vehicle imaginable. Alphie steered to the right and brought his bike to rest at the end of a line of about fifteen other motorcycles. Troy followed suit.

The doors were of heavy wood, probably oak, and braced with metal. The weighty hinges and oversized handle made it a task to pull them open. As the door opened, music spilled out. Troy and Alphie stepped into the pulsating beat only to be met by a bouncer who looked like a refugee from World Championship Wrestling. He carried a wand-type metal detector, which he ran over them one at a time without seeking or waiting for permission. After passing this test, they qualified to pay the $7.50 price of admission and were allowed into the inner sanctum.

Troy was taken back to his days in Chapel Hill. There, he had regularly gone to nightclubs that, although much smaller, operated on the same formula as the Cactus Palace.

The room glowed with neon light made shadowy by the volume of smoke that seemed to accumulate in gray swirling clouds and hover just below the exposed fluorescent tubes. Men and women of every description drank beer and smoked cigarettes as they performed their individual mating rituals and ceremonies. The dance floor was a bed of hardwood surrounded by a sea of carpet. It was alive with undulating bodies paying homage to the band, which provided the rhythm that seemed to drive the whole scene. Three bars, each in a strategic location, made sure that none of the patrons of the Cactus Palace would have to wait long for their favorite brew. Alphie was making his way to the largest of the three. By the time Troy caught up, he had a beer in each hand.

"Hell of a place, ain't it, son," shouted Alphie as he pushed the ice-cold Coors into Troy's chest. "Ain't got many of these up your way, huh?"

Troy shook his head. Hell no, they didn't have anything like this in Cedar Creek. He thought of Paulie's Pool Room, probably the closest thing to a bar in Cedar Creek, and chuckled to himself. They held dances at the American Legion, but his gang wasn't really welcome there. He felt a little out of his element. It had been a long time since Chapel Hill. He secretly decided to stay in the shadows and try not to be too obvious.

Alphie, on the other hand, appeared to be right at home. He seemed to know half the people there. His wearing the "Rat Pack" colors didn't appear to put anyone off. He made his way around the room, shaking hands with the men and receiving hugs from most of the women. Troy followed and acknowledged everyone with a nod as Alphie introduced him. As they returned to the dance floor and bar, three college types got up from a table and headed for the door. Alphie claimed the table.

The band was hot, the beer was cold, and in time Troy came under the influence of both. He found himself tapping the beat of each song with his boot and watching with wonder as the couples two-stepped their way around the dance floor. He had been a dancer at one time but had not kept up with the latest steps. Subconsciously, Troy had thought that dancing and leading a motorcycle gang didn't mix, although, as he watched Alphie dance after dance, he began to reconsider. After four beers, he decided he could learn to dance again. After nine beers, he was sure he already had.

With two more Coors to stabilize his nervous system, he set his sights on a pseudo-cowgirl who seemed inclined to dance with anyone who would ask her. It wasn't that Troy didn't have confidence in his ability to get a dance; he just chose the path of least resistance. She sat at the second table from the corner of the dance floor with two other girlfriends. Troy decided to take the circuitous route and vector toward her at the last minute, giving her little time to think of turning him down.

As he stood to begin his journey, he noticed his head was feeling a little funny. He had not counted the beers but was sure he was not drunk. Hell, he'd just been sitting in one place for quite a while and had probably stood up too fast. The band was already into the song, so he stopped at the bar for one more beer. The song came to an end about halfway through the beer, so he guzzled the rest, not wanting to miss the next dance.

Fate is a cruel and exacting master who makes no provisions for dignity and grace as it drags you headlong toward the inevitable. Troy may have pulled the whole thing off had it not been for two seemingly unrelated items.

First, as he made his way toward the table where his would-be Ginger Rogers waited, he caught a vision in the corner of his eye. Two women whom he had not seen before sat at the table behind and to the right of his destination. Both were beautiful and projected a presence that immediately drew his full attention. The second was a problem of architecture. The hardwood dance floor had been built after the building was complete and sat atop the regular floor, creating an elevation difference of three-quarters of an inch. This was not a logistical problem unless you had consumed twelve ice-cold Coors and had your head turned approximately ninety degrees away from your destination.

The first chords of the new song were being played as the toe of Troy's boot came into solid contact with the side of the polished oak floor. Maybe if any of the circumstances had been different, he still could have salvaged the situation; nevertheless, his momentum hurled him through the air like a "Silver Bullet" (no pun intended). He was totally out of control and flung his arms out to break his fall. Instead, he wiped both girlfriends out of their seats as his upper body slammed into the table. He landed headfirst with nothing to break his fall but the metal table.

Troy had never been one to let a little adversity dissuade him from a goal. The two girlfriends scrambled to get up. The cowgirl pushed her chair back with a look of pure horror on her face. Troy slowly turned his head toward her.

"Care to dance?" he asked and abruptly passed out.

Chapter Sixteen

J illian was up and moving before Victoria had a chance to fully comprehend what was going on. She had seen the man trip and fall, but the whole scene was so foreign to her that she may as well have been viewing man's first landing on the moon. By the time she realized what was happening, Jillian was on the spot dabbing the man's forehead with a damp napkin. The girls at the next table were loud and animated. They were more concerned with the damage done to their outfits and hair than with the prospects of Troy's survival. A crowd gathered, and a multi-layer circle formed around them. Those not fortunate enough to be in the front row stretched as far upward as gravity would allow, trying to catch a glimpse of the action. Several people were knocked off balance as a group of burly "security specialists" forced their way through the crowd. Most of the patrons of the Cactus Palace had no idea what had taken place but wanted to be sure not to miss anything of significance. Rumors of everything from a heart attack to a knife fight made their way through the circle.

Rick, the head of security, was the first "official" to arrive. He assessed the situation and began to disburse the crowd.

"Hey, Alphie," Rick called with a hint of a smile in his voice. "I think you'd better come over and take care of your pal. He seems to have decided to take a nap."

Victoria held her position until all the people went back to their seats, and she could finally see Jillian. She was still holding Troy's head in her lap, and she had a devilish grin on her face. The grin softened into a smile as Alphie came toward them. He walked swiftly to where Jillian held Troy and knelt beside them. Victoria couldn't hear what they were saying, but after a while Jillian rose and walked back to their table.

"Shit, Vickie, I couldn't have asked for it to work out any better. I've been trying to meet that guy, Alphie, ever since I started coming here, and tonight he just sorta falls into my lap. Well, almost."

"What the hell is going on, Jillian? What do you mean? Who's this guy, and what have you gotten us into?"

"Nothing. I haven't gotten us into anything. All you've got to do is drive my car and take Alphie's friend home. He needs to get somewhere and sleep this thing off."

"Why can't you drive your own car, and why do either of us have to play taxi for some helpless drunk?"

"Jesus, Vickie! I can't drive the car and ride Alphie's bike at the same time. That leaves you. Hell, that guy won't be any trouble. He probably won't move a muscle till morning. Come on, Vickie. I've already told you how important this is to me. Give me a break, huh?"

In her heart of hearts, Victoria knew this would not be as simple as Jillian portrayed it. A sense of dread overshadowed every thought she had, but she could not deny that this was a bit exciting, and it was important not to appear too prudish in front of Jillian. In the end, Vickie overcame Victoria.

"OK, what do I do?" she asked, throwing all caution to the wind.

Alphie and Rick carried Troy to Jillian's Mercury Cougar, placing him carefully in the passenger seat. They strapped him in and stood back as if seeking some approval. Troy had not so much as wiggled during the whole ordeal. Victoria moved to the open door and leaned in, pretending to check the seat. In fact, she was checking to see if Troy was still alive. There was no way in hell she was going to ride back to Asheville with a corpse, regardless of how much it meant to Jillian or how dull it made her appear. His light breath on her arm let her know she would at least begin her journey with a living passenger. She moved to the driver's side and started the engine.

Jillian started Alphie's hog and performed some maneuvers around the parking lot, apparently some improvised driving test to assure Alphie that his "first love" was in capable hands. She must have passed, because Alphie fired up Troy's bike and pulled to the front of the Cougar, motioning Jillian to join him.

The night was taking on a playful air. The temperature was pleasant enough to opt for an open window instead of air conditioning. Victoria watched as Alphie and Jillian played back and forth with each other on the bikes. It was almost like watching young animals discovering themselves. She considered the whole night one of the best she had spent in quite a while. She looked over at the man in the seat beside her and could not suppress a smile. She turned up the volume of the radio and sang along with the sultry voice coming from the speakers, and she even got some of the words right. The night wind played around the edges of Victoria's hair, causing the strands to dance like a thousand fingers on her neck. The feel of the powerful engine and the solid response of the Mercury gave her a feeling of total control. In the depths of her mind, she saw herself on the Autobahn, driving unencumbered by limits; she and the car were one with the road. Instinctively, she reached over and turned up the volume on the radio, lowered all the windows, and even slapped old Troy on the knee for good measure.

She never let up on the gas when the road curved sharply to the right. Now, I don't know much about physics or claim any knowledge concerning complex formulas of speed and trajectory or their effect on the pull of gravity, so I'll have to tell what happened in layman's terms.

As the Cougar entered the curve, Victoria leaned to her right. The same forces that made the leaning seem necessary to maintain her balance tossed Troy's limp body to his left. Their heads met at a point approximately in the center of the seat with a force that, as I said, I am at a loss to calculate but sufficient to have an opposite effect on each of them. Victoria remained conscious but became totally disoriented while Troy was shaken awake, albeit in a drunken state. Through it all, the car continued in the direction of the turn. Victoria managed to slam on the brakes while Troy, realizing the situation, wrestled the steering wheel from her grasp. The combination of the two efforts sent the Cougar into a skid. Their bodies were tossed together again and again as they each struggled in their own way to save the situation. When the car came to a halt, they found themselves completely entangled. If an observer had been present, he could not have distinguished whose limb belonged to whom. By some mysterious act, neither they nor the car had sustained any damage.

Victoria had no idea which direction the car was headed. They both tried to free themselves from each other. She felt completely pumped with adrenaline, even if her head throbbed. Although she should have been scared to death, she couldn't help noticing how nice Troy's body felt against her. He was solid, and it had been a long time since she had held a man under any circumstances.

Troy was totally lost. He had no idea where he was, how he got there, or whom he was with, but he didn't mind. He was alive and somehow tangled up with a woman, so it couldn't be too bad.

They heard the roar of the Harleys as Alphie and Jillian rushed to help them. They straightened up and brushed themselves off. As the lights from the Harleys pierced the windshield, they looked at each other for the first time. It was a look with the depth that only having faced death and cheated death can give. They each liked what they saw.

Chapter Seventeen

Each day is a twenty-four hour stage on which to act out the play that is our lives. Comedies, dramas, tragedies, and heroic tales play simultaneously, with as many views of the day as there are people viewing it. Now that I'm older, I think about the complexity of life often, but I believe it was that last Tuesday in August that first made me aware of those complexities.

I could hear Jason moving around in his room as I lay in my bed. I was usually the first one up, but I was determined to linger in bed for a while today. This was the last day of our summer vacation. Starting tomorrow, the alarm would sound at 6:00 a.m., and there would be no ignoring it. This was our last day of freedom for nine months. As I lay in bed, I thought of how I would spend my day. I began a mental list of my favorite activities. The possibilities so polarized me that I drifted back to sleep.

The sound of Mama singing brought me back awake. I thought of Uncle Rodney. Today might be his last day in Cedar Creek. I remember Daddy telling Mama that Uncle Rodney was thinking about staying in Cedar Creek, but since we had heard no more of it, I assumed he would leave for Florida tomorrow as planned. I felt sad at the prospect of life without him. The last few weeks had been exciting, and the time we spent together pleased me as much as it distressed Mama. She had reconciled herself to the situation but counted the days until his departure.

Mama's voice grew stronger and more animated. In her play, tomorrow was her first day of true freedom in three months. In her mind, Uncle Rodney's departure would solve the issue of Ms. Amanda and Rodney's relationship, a problem that Mama had helped create. You see what I mean about different views of the same circumstances.

"Boys, ya'll come on down. We've got to go to the grocery store. We're going to cook out tonight, and I want everything to be here when your daddy gets home," Mama shouted.

The thought of hamburgers or barbecue chicken cooked over charcoal was all it took to get me in motion. I was dressed and down the stairs in no time. Jason was right behind me, and we both went straight to the front porch to wait for Mama. She brought us each a sausage biscuit and a glass of milk, which we devoured like a couple of hungry wolves.

"Ya'll stay right here when you finish your breakfast, so we can go to the store and get back. Jason, you stay on the porch, so you don't get dirty."

Jason rolled his eyes and glanced at me. I knew how he felt. It was just in the last year that Mama had stopped giving me such directions. Basking in my manhood, I winked at him and smiled. I could tell that it got to him. On another day, I would have continued to tease him, but now I had no more time to spend on such things. I had the rest of the day to think about, and a trip to town was a good start to it. A visit to Cedar Creek, for any reason, brought with it the possibility of going to McAdams' Drug Store for ice cream. I might also get to see some of my friends from school.

Mama exercised extreme caution as she drove us into Cedar Creek. After the episode in the churchyard, she seemed determined to prove she was in complete control of her automobile. With hands placed precisely at ten o'clock and two o'clock, she sat bone straight and rotated her head in a fashion that would not allow anything to approach her without being seen. She stayed five miles per hour below the posted speed limit and refused to talk to us or listen to the radio. By the time we reached town, twelve vehicles had lined up behind her, including a school bus on a practice run that had pulled out several times to pass. Horns blew and headlights flashed repeatedly, but Mama would not be hurried. Jason turned around in the back seat, looked out the window, and laughed under his breath. I sat still and stared straight ahead. The last thing I wanted was to make Mama angry with me, thus losing any chance of an ice cream cone. I bore my embarrassment in a stoic manner, which has served me well in many situations over the years. My greatest test was yet to come.

On this and every visit to Worley's Red & White, my ability to stay composed was put to the test. Old Mr. Alton Worley started his grocery store at a time when everyone was enamored by slogans. Lucky Strike cigarettes claimed their name meant fine tobaccos. Wonder Bread built "strong bodies in twelve ways." Even cigar smokers wondered if a gentleman should "offer a lady a Tiparillo." It was a far more innocent time. Mr. Worley was determined he, too, would have a slogan that everyone would associate with his business. He had no way of knowing just how much commotion his slogan would cause over the years.

I prepared myself. I knew I would crack one day, but I prayed it would not be today. I bit the inside of my lip as Mama made her turn from Independence Road onto Dowd Street. I let the sounds of the cars stacked up behind us dominate my hearing as they revved their engines to try to make up for time lost while following Mama for twenty minutes. I didn't want to look at them and somehow betray my embarrassment, but I didn't want to look ahead and take a chance of betraying myself. Just as a moth can do nothing but fly into the flame, I could not keep my eyes from locking onto Mr. Worley's sign. Again, I bit my lip until the slight taste of blood was present in my mouth. Half a block in front of me, the sign proclaimed to the world, "No one can beat Worley's meat." I could feel my control slipping. It came from my belly, and nothing my mind could do would prevent it. I almost spat the laugh; it burst forth with such force. Mama's head jerked to her right, and she saw me staring up at the sign. Her gaze was steady, and I knew my chances for ice cream were melting in its heat. I heard Jason snicker behind his hand. I slipped down in the seat and wished a spaceship would instantly whisk me away to some faraway galaxy.

What I hoped would be a wonderful end to a great summer vacation was quickly deteriorating. I guess in every young man's life, there must come a time when his carnal instincts are revealed to his mother, but I would have preferred to wait a while.

Daddy had never discussed "the facts of life" with me, and every time I thought of such a thing, I was filled with dread. I prayed I would be allowed to pass into adulthood, assuming that I would figure it all out on my own. Those wishes were soon dashed on the rocks.

"I see that I'm going to get your daddy to talk to you, young man!" Mama spoke in the same tone of voice she would have used if she discovered Duchess had slipped into the house and pooped on her lace bedspread.

It is a difficult time in a young man's life when he realizes he has disappointed his mother. The pain is doubled when she lets him know just how disappointed she is. I understood how the lepers must have felt as they walked the streets of New Delhi. I followed Mama at a respectful distance as she gathered the items for dinner. Just a short while ago, I had looked forward to the cookout. Now I faced the evening with dread. Mama would tell Daddy all about my faux pas, and I would spend the final evening of my summer vacation listening to Daddy struggle through an explanation of "the birds and the bees" instead of telling "Uncle Rodney" stories that usually follow an evening spent together. Little did I know, I had nothing to fear.

Just as Daddy was coming out of the shower, we heard the unmistakable whoop that meant Uncle Rodney had arrived. Daddy hurried to meet him before Mama had a chance to speak.

Amanda Cotton came in to help Mama in the kitchen while Uncle Rodney collared Daddy, and they went to the workshop. I had been granted a temporary reprieve. The door to the shop was closed, which was a polite way of telling Jason and me to entertain ourselves elsewhere. After about an hour of talkin' and sippin', Daddy started the grill. I kept clear, hoping that out of sight was indeed out of mind.

There must be magic in charcoal that transforms a hamburger patty or hot dog into a royal feast. Either of the above covered with homemade chili, mustard, onion, and coleslaw, accompanied by Mama's potato salad, and washed down with iced tea, is enough to make a man temporarily forget the fix he is in.

Daddy was unusually quiet the entire evening. I hoped he would wait a few days to talk to me if he wasn't feeling well, but all was explained after we ate.

Uncle Rodney stood up and waved his hands as if he were trying to get the attention of the entire crowd at the Charlotte Motor Speedway and then announced that he would not be returning to Florida but would stay in Cedar Creek and look for a job nearby. Jason and I couldn't contain ourselves. We were so happy. Daddy managed a smile, relieved that the burden he had been carrying since Uncle Rodney's arrival was finally out in the open. I could tell by the look of shock on Mama's face that this was far more alarming than my earlier slip. I knew I had been given a full pardon. Yes!!!

Chapter Eighteen

I guess ya'll might wonder why Mama and Uncle Rodney couldn't quite see eye to eye. I thought for a long time it had something to do with the way Daddy would act when Uncle Rodney was around. Daddy seemed more carefree and willing to take a chance when Uncle Rodney was with him. Except for an occasional Moose Lodge meeting, Uncle Rodney was the only one who could get Daddy to leave the house without Mama or his sons.

Mama was never openly hostile to Uncle Rodney, but an undercurrent of resentment lay just beneath the surface. The only one who seemed unaffected by it was Uncle Rodney. We never spoke of the situation, so naturally our imaginations ran wild. I don't guess I ever would have learned the truth if I had not become reacquainted with Bobby Sessoms between my junior and senior years at The University of North Carolina in Chapel Hill. I was a journalism major and was beginning a summer internship at *The Durham Sun,* an afternoon paper in the city of Durham, North Carolina. Bobby was a sports reporter, and when he found out I was from Cedar Creek, he took me under his wing. After work, we would go out to eat together and sometimes have a few beers. I finally found out the truth of the matter at a place called The Top Hat. Bobby had a four-beer jump on me when I met him there at six o'clock. By nine, we had lost count, and this is the story that he told:

Mama's maiden name was Edna Pauline Raspberry. She was an only child and lived on a farm between Cedar Creek and Asheville.

The farm next to them belonged to my Granddaddy Wilson. He had two sons, Samuel and Rodney.

There were farms up and down the road that varied in size from a few to several hundred acres. One thing that set the Raspberry place apart from all the rest was that it was the only one with a female child growing up on it.

Sam Wilson and Edna Raspberry were the two oldest children on the road, while Rodney had nine other boys his age to hang out with.

Even then, Sam would stay close to home, helping with the chores and tending his little garden. Rodney, on the other hand, would roam the woods. He was especially fond of the creek that flowed through their farm and emptied into a pond on the Raspberry place.

Nobody bothered anyone else. That is until the summer that Edna Raspberry became a teenager. That was the summer that Megan Leary, Edna's cousin, came to visit.

Megan and her family lived in Charlotte. Comparing Charlotte with Cedar Creek would be like comparing buttermilk with brandy; those who have a taste for one will usually not like the other. Such was the case with Megan Leary. She had not come to Cedar Creek of her own volition. This was not a trip to discover nature but an act of desperation by her parents to keep Megan from learning too much about nature. She was definitely "on the farm" under protest.

Megan would have rather spent her vacation in a thousand other ways. As with many big-city girls, Megan had become aware of her power as a female a few years ahead of her country cousins. She had planned on spending the summer whiling away the days with Steve Yates, her thirteen-year-old boyfriend, using her newfound talents to make him jump through as many hoops as she could conjure. With the raising of an eyebrow or the tilt of a hip, she could turn Steve into "Stevie the puppet." Though the dance has been performed millions of times, the awakening of male and female hormones is a wonder to behold unless you are the father of the female whose hormones are awakening.

Megan and Steve never reached the point of doing anything untoward. They didn't have the chance. When Megan's mother happened by Independence Park one May afternoon and saw Megan and Steve on a blanket trying to master the intricacies of the French kiss instead of being in school, she panicked. After blowing the horn to let her presence be known (which effectively broke up the party), she made a beeline home and called her sister in Cedar Creek. All the arrangements had been made by the time Megan walked home from Independence Park. By dinnertime, all of Megan's plans had been dashed upon the rocks, and she drifted between anger and despair. She appealed to her father, but he had been too long in the harness to think he could plow any row but the one he had been instructed to plow. If Elizabeth Leary wanted her daughter to spend the summer in the country, then in the country she would spend it. From that day until the end of the school year, it was as if Megan had two shadows. She was determined she would not like Cedar Creek and would do her best to make everyone have as terrible a summer as she imagined she would have. That was before she met Rodney Wilson.

As you can imagine, June was a testy month. Megan arrived in Cedar Creek with a chip on her shoulder the size of a cheese hoop. The Raspberrys had been forewarned and were equally determined not to let Megan unsettle them. Will and Jesse Raspberry maintained firm control of their new charge but had the wisdom to give Megan enough room to let the steam slowly dissipate rather than gather pressure.

When Megan came to Cedar Creek, Edna saw her as an intrusion into her life. They hardly spoke during the first week. They may never have become friends had it not been for John Steinbeck. Megan discovered the great author by chance at the Charlotte Public Library. Until Steve, nobody stirred her emotions like Steinbeck. His words painted pictures across her mind. She could smell the scents of *Cannery Row* and wept at the travails and injustices faced by the Joads as they made their way to California. When Megan found Edna reading *Of Mice and Men,* they entered their first conversation. The subsequent trip to Edna's room, where she showed Megan her entire collection of Steinbeck's work, cemented the friendship.

In Edna's collection, she discovered a book she had not seen before: *Travels with Charley.* As she read of Steinbeck's journey throughout the United States in his primitive camper with his dog Charley, she came to look at her exile to Cedar Creek as an adventure rather than a sentence. She was living a life much like Steinbeck.

Once Megan relaxed her stand against the Raspberrys, she actually enjoyed herself. She missed Steve but found herself thinking of him less each day. She and Edna were becoming good friends. Edna was so natural and knew so much about the farm and forest, and she was not the prude Megan imagined her to be. They began taking walks, and Edna would tell her about different plants, animals, and rural life. The most surprising event occurred when they finally ventured all the way down to the creek. The creek was twenty-five feet wide and five and a half feet deep where it crossed the Raspberry farm. Edna began unbuttoning her dress as the girls stepped into the clearing bordering the creek. Without a word, she completely undressed and jumped into the water as Megan stood by with her mouth hanging open.

"Hey, come on in, the water's great," said Edna looking back toward the bank.

"Are you crazy? I ain't gonna get naked out here!"

"Nobody's going to see you. It's at least a half a mile to the next farm and then another quarter mile to their house. Come on. You don't get much chance to do this in Charlotte, do ya? It feels great."

Megan was at a total loss for a while. Wasn't she the sophisticated city girl, the adventuress? Edna acted as if being without clothes and splashing around in the creek were the most natural things in the world. She showed no sign of self-consciousness.

"Come on in. I've been swimming here for years, and nobody has ever bothered me. It's great. You'll see."

Megan wasn't sure if it was the heat, the fact that the water looked so inviting, or her determination not to let her country cousin one-up her, but what the heck. Having made the decision, she had to work out the logistics of getting undressed and into the water with a minimum of embarrassment. She stepped to the edge of the woods and disrobed. Holding her clothes in front of her, she moved quickly to the edge of the water, dropped her clothes, and dove into the creek in one fluid motion.

The water was delicious. They were tentative at first but soon were splashing and playing with total abandon. This was one of the greatest moments in Megan's life. She could think of nothing better. Would she have some stories to tell when she got back to Charlotte?!

When it was time to go back, they climbed out of the water. Neither girl seemed to notice the other's nudity. They were just good friends sharing a special moment.

As the last days of June passed, they visited the creek every day they could. There was less and less tension as Megan acclimated herself to rural summer life. By Independence Day, everything had smoothed out, and all was well for a little while.

The Fourth of July was Cedar Creek's day in the sun. Three hundred and sixty-four days a year, everyone in Cedar Creek kept to themselves. I'm not trying to say that we were a snobbish town—anything but. Folks just tended to their own business and left others to do the same. In case of an emergency or a family tragedy, you could count on your neighbors to help you through, but as soon as you were back on your feet, they would recede into the wings until needed again.

The Christmas parade brought out a lot of people, but December in the mountains can be bitter. Many citizens of Cedar Creek chose the warmth of their fireplace over the glitter of the floats and the half-hearted waves of Buster McClure, dressed as Santa, being pulled along Main Street in a plywood sleigh towed by two mules with antlers attached to their heads.

Independence Day was like Mardi Gras, Carnival, and the Olympiad all rolled into one. The only citizens who did not come out on "the Fourth" were those unfortunates who were bedridden, and even they raised their windows to listen to the celebration if they were conscious.

Andrew Addison Park stood in the geographical center of Cedar Creek. Andrew Addison was the closest thing to a hero Cedar Creek could conjure up. He fought with General Robert E. Lee during "The War of Northern Aggression" (also called The Civil War by the uninformed and geographically disadvantaged).

The legend went that Andrew stood beside General Lee until he was severely wounded. After his brush with death, he returned to Cedar Creek and founded Addison Spinning Mill, which was Cedar Creek's largest industry for almost fifty years. It was said that Andrew would continuously walk from one end of the mill to the other, encouraging his employees to new heights of production. That was his legend.

In truth, Andrew was shot in the ass as he turned tail and tried to run from the Bennet place outside of Durham all the way back to Cedar Creek. The rifle ball slanted upward as it entered his left buttock and lodged itself close enough to his spine that it could not be removed. Ole Andy walked all day because it hurt like hell to sit down. They said he even ate standing up and slept on his stomach. The truth is not often pretty, but you can't let the truth get in the way of legend and hero-building.

In the course of time, Andy was immortalized in granite, and his statue stands, bone straight, in the middle of the park that bears his name. He is proudly clad in the uniform of the Confederacy with nary a wrinkle or tear about his derriere where the fateful musket ball intruded upon him. I don't know what we would have named the park if the Yankee that shot him had been a better marksman.

On the Fourth of July, a transformation took place both in town and in the park. Addison Park was a fine place to meander about. It had acres of grass-covered meadows with some fine old trees for shade. Many a love has blossomed there, nudged along by a picnic or the sharing of intimate secrets told in a setting conducive to sharing.

The park had basketball courts, two softball fields, and a clay tennis court for the more athletic crowd. In later years, they added a track for jogging and walking, but in the year of Megan's visit, anyone seen running was assumed to either be in danger or to have just stolen something.

About mid-June, the activity began. The entire park was abuzz as city workers and volunteers erected bandstands and built booths where you could engage in activities that ranged from dunking the principal with a well-placed softball to buying a kiss from the reigning Miss Cedar Creek.

Nowadays, the events are a casual affair with everyone wearing T-shirts and shorts and running around barefooted, but when Edna and Megan were young, things were a bit more formal. Young men wore slacks and shirts, most with a necktie, and young ladies wore dresses, sandals, and hats with large brims to protect them from the sun and assert their Southern belle status. The only people allowed to be barefoot were small children (and then only after eating) and some adults who, after retiring to their picnic blankets for the evening festivities and fireworks, would forget themselves and slip their shoes off to enjoy the sensation of summer grass on bare toes. From the day's frantic activities to the evening's magic, this was Americana at its finest hour.

Jess Raspberry had taken Edna and Megan to Belk's in Asheville for their outfits. They both had chosen a sundress, a hat with bands that perfectly matched their dresses, and a pair of delicate sandals that made their feet appear so fragile it was hard to believe those same feet had been stomping through the woods only a few hours earlier. With great anticipation, they made themselves ready for the celebration.

The ride into town was hot. Air conditioners were not common in most houses, let alone automobiles. The wind that blew through the open window played havoc with their carefully coiffured hair. They each carried their hat to be placed upon their head upon arrival at the park to ensure a crisp look. Once they were at the park, Jesse helped them with their hats and hair. She told them how beautiful they both were. Will Raspberry just stood there, looking at the girls with a worried expression (probably remembering the July Fourth celebrations of his youth and knowing every young man's mind in the park). After the standard disclaimer about how young ladies should act and carry themselves in public, Jesse and Will walked toward the entrance of the park and left the girls to their own devices.

Megan was in for a treat. Her Independence Day celebrations at home in Charlotte consisted of hanging out by the public swimming pool all day and then going with her family to a fireworks display.

If you have never experienced the Fourth of July in a rural North Carolina town, you can't imagine the goings-on. Sights, sounds, and smells bombarded Megan's senses.

The aroma of hot dogs, hamburgers, sausages, and French fries permeated the gentle summer breeze. The smoldering white-hot charcoal added its own smell to the mix as the heat made waves above the grills. Adorned with a large chef's hat and a crisp white apron, members of the local Moose Lodge manned each grill. Their constant chatter and exaggerated movements provided as much of a feast for the eyes as the food did for the stomach. From the sky, the area would have looked like a Technicolor ant farm as people in their brightest colors scampered about.

No matter what level of activity you aspired to, there was something for you within the park. The clang of horseshoes on one side of the park directly contrasted the gentle plop of a cork hitting the surface of the pond on the other.

Once inside, Megan and Edna walked constantly. They feigned indifference to the activities around them to seem sophisticated and above it all. They politely spoke to those they met. Megan first saw Rodney Wilson at the dunking booth, and the rest of the day changed.

Each year, Jamison Dutton, the principal of Cedar Creek High School, would don his bathing suit and a rubberized coverall and climb into what looked much like a tractor seat perched above a pool of water approximately forty-two inches deep. Wire enclosed the pool and seat. Outside the wire, at about the same level as Mr. Dutton's head, a wooden circle about eight inches in diameter was attached to a vertical support, which was fastened to a horizontal support that ran under the seat and held it upright—until a softball struck the circle, at which point it would fall apart, and Mr. Dutton would plunge into the water. Principal Dutton was a great sport and knew something about his present students, past students, and most of his future students. As each one stepped to the line, Mr. Dutton would tell an antidote about that person. Most of the time, it was an embarrassing story meant to amuse the crowd and to make the person try especially hard to hit the target. The harder you tried and the more you aimed, the less chance you had of succeeding. Principal Dutton's theory was that the better the story, the drier he would remain.

The principal's voice drew the girl's attention to the dunking booth, but the sudden quiet made them move closer. The good-humored banter fell to silence when a young Rodney Wilson stepped up to the line.

When the girls edged to the front, they saw Rodney standing there, juggling the three softballs, and Principal Dutton quietly waiting in anticipation, one hand on top of his derby hat and the other pinching his nose as if a foul smell was rising from the tank. Obviously, both the man and the boy knew what was to come. The mischievous grin and the sparkle in Rodney's eyes combined to take Megan's breath as she watched the scene unfold. Time slowed.

Rodney's movements were fluid with no wasted motion. Each time he released the ball, it went directly to the center of the target, as if possessed by some internal guidance system. He made no big show of it and each time waited patiently for the principal to remount his throne. By the time the third ball was on its way, Megan had decided to meet this young man before the day was over.

Edna never realized she was being led through the park. Megan kept the boy in her field of vision all day as he moved from game to game, handling them all with great skill. During the day's premier event, Megan made circumstances work for her.

The three-legged sack race was the only co-ed event of the day. The contest took place just as the sun set and before the ice cream freezers started churning out everyone's dessert. It was an unspoken tradition that if you liked the person you were teamed with in the sack race, you would enjoy your ice cream with them afterward. Many a romance had its seed planted over a bowl of vanilla ice cream with chocolate syrup on the Fourth of July.

Edna told Megan about the sack race and said she hoped she would be lucky enough to be teamed with someone who was not only fast but cute. Megan decided to let luck have no part in her future.

There were two roped-off areas, one for the girls and one for the boys. As they filtered through, the couple that emerged from the line at the same time was declared a team, promptly rewarded with a gunny sack, and pointed to an area to prepare for the upcoming race. The plan was to ensure a random selection of teams. The system designers failed to consider that most of the racers could see and count. Thus, there was always a fair amount of jockeying for position between both sides to stack the odds concerning both athletic ability and romantic potential.

Megan and Edna stepped into the roped-off section for girls at the same time Rodney and his brother entered the male area. Megan quickly calculated and found she was off by one place. She adjusted by letting Edna in front of her. As she approached the end of the line, she noticed another young lady who seemed to be jockeying for the same position. The young redhead was allowing people to move, one by one, in front of her, betraying her intentions. Adjustments would have to be made. The redhead had managed to slip between Edna and Megan and was rechecking her count. The time was at hand.

"Edna, can I ask you something?" Megan quizzed as she grabbed Edna's arm and pulled her back to her side.

The puzzled look on Edna's face quickly turned to shock as Megan seemed to stumble, falling against her and pushing her into the redhead. The redhead was in deep thought, considering how to regain her position between Edna and Megan and was caught by surprise. The weight of Edna falling against her sent her awkwardly through the gate to be paired with Jimmy Grimes. Megan quickly recovered and watched as Edna and Sam Wilson emerged together. Triumphantly, she stepped to take her place with Rodney Wilson. Megan had no way of knowing she had set in motion circumstances that would last a lifetime.

Megan and Rodney introduced themselves and quickly set about getting ready for the race. Rodney eyed the competition as they gathered at the starting line. He obviously took every contest seriously and intended to win.

In a three-legged race, each person places one leg into the gunnysack, and both participants must coordinate the movements of their bound legs. This is best done by holding the sack with your outside hand and wrapping your inside arm around your partner's waist. The results are still precarious at best and ludicrous at worst.

The girls got to change into shorts or slacks to preserve the beauty of their gowns, but the boys were expected to make do. Thus, everyone found himself or herself at the starting line, ready to race.

"Have you ever done this before?" Rodney asked.

"No, but I'm a good runner and swimmer."

"Just follow my lead, and we'll be fine."

The whistle blew, and silence fell over the park. The breeze was blowing, and for the first time Megan felt its coolness on her face. She was also aware of the heat of Rodney's leg against her own.

"On your mark!"

"Get set!"

The gun sounded, and they were off. Megan and Rodney struggled to maintain their balance and find some coordination. Still, they were in second place. They finally came together as a team at the race's midpoint. They started to gain on the leaders, but the finish line was coming up fast. Only a few yards remained between the two teams when Megan felt Rodney's arm tighten around her waist. He pulled her closer and leaned to the right, effectively pulling her outside leg off the ground. With her balanced on his hip, he started to accelerate. He passed the leading team with ten yards to go with Megan hanging on and riding his hip much like a bag of fertilizer. They crossed the finish line to a mixture of applause and laughter. Rodney lowered Megan to the ground, and she could barely conceal her anger.

"I told you to follow my lead, and we would be OK. You don't run bad for a girl. Say you can swim too?"

"You didn't have to pick me up! We could have won without you doing that. I'm a darn good runner and swimmer. Edna and I swim every day at the creek."

She'd had enough of Mr. Rodney Wilson for one day and turned to walk away, but as she was leaving, she felt she had to one-up him in some way. She stopped, turned around, and walked back to him.

"And we don't wear swimsuits!" She placed her hand on his shoulder and gave him a little shove. She stormed away, leaving Rodney to claim the ribbons for both of them.

When ice cream was served, she ate with the Raspberrys. She watched as Edna and Sam Wilson sat together on a separate blanket and enjoyed each other's company. She had not envisioned the evening ending this way, but she could not get past the embarrassment of being carried across the finish line like a sack of potatoes. She was angry but felt sure she had given Mr. Rodney Wilson something to think about.

She had surprised Rodney with her reaction. He had never seen a girl act like that. It must be the way big city girls were. He had eaten his ice cream with Doris Mahoney, the redhead, but he couldn't stop thinking of the city girl, especially the last words she said.

A significant cat had been let out of the bag.

* * *

Sam Wilson first became aware that something was amiss on the afternoon of July 6th. He had been working the garden and was halfway through hoeing a row of butter beans when the notion struck him that Rodney was up to something.

Sam considered keeping Rodney out of trouble at his part-time job. Rodney was always scheming up some stunt or joke that would land him in a pickle. He was fearless and never seemed to learn from his experiences. Most of his pranks were harmless, and some were downright hilarious, but after a while their Papa stopped being amused. Papa would lay a switching on Rodney's legs and then tell him how he could better spend his time learning to tend the land and take care of things so they could later take care of him.

Rodney would bear his punishment and say "yes, sir" in all the right places while planning his next adventure.

Sam was usually aware of Rodney's intention immediately. He could never stop Rodney, but given enough time, he could slow him down and avoid getting Papa involved. All the signs had been present, but Sam was too preoccupied to recognize them. Thoughts of Edna Raspberry had filled Sam's brain. She had always lived down the road, but it was like she had never existed until the picnic. He wondered how he could have been so blind. He had been thinking that if he were more like Rodney, he could find a way to see more of her. Then he realized Rodney had been disappearing each day for several hours. Usually, Rodney would hang around and pester him while he was tending his garden. Sam knew what he had to do.

Rodney came out of the woods just as the sun started its descent. The little cloud of dust that arose as he shuffled his feet across the rows of the field alerted Sam of his return. Sam watched as his brother got to the house, jumped on his bike, and pedaled away without even a word. Rodney had been in a stupor since the city girl snubbed him at the picnic.

When Rodney got back, it was suppertime, and he was the old Rodney. After he ate, he ran upstairs and started his bath without a single threat from Ma. Papa lit his pipe, Ma smiled as she washed dishes, and Sam felt sick in the pit of his stomach.

Sam woke up early the next morning. He dug up some worms, grabbed his fishing pole, and headed for the creek. He followed Rodney's tracks as he crossed the field from the day before. When he got to the creek, he turned upstream and found a place where he could fish and watch the path at the same time. He figured he had a few hours to enjoy his fishing and think about Edna. Sam threaded the worm onto the hook and tossed it gently out into the current. The deep water ran slowly, so the cork didn't demand much attention. When the first bream hit the line, it startled Sam. He lifted the line from the water and unhooked the fish. The next two came rather quickly, and then the fishing settled back down. After a few minutes of watching the cork float, he leaned back on the bank, rolled over on his side, and continued to fish with his fishing pole resting in the palm of his hand.

He dozed off but was awakened by the sound of several voices. He sat up and noticed that his line had drifted up next to the bank. When he pulled it from the water, the bait had been stripped off the hook. He had no idea how long he had been asleep. He jumped behind an oak tree and waited as the voices grew stronger. Rodney was the first to come into sight. Jimmy Talbert, Bobby Sessoms, and Ralph Moore followed him. They were all talking and acting excited. When they reached the creek, they turned right and continued along the bank. Sam rolled up his fishing line and followed the sound of their voices. He must have walked half a mile downstream when suddenly the talking ceased. Sam jumped to the side of the path just in case he had been detected. He held his breath and waited for several minutes. When he felt safe, he eased himself back onto the path and crept along, being careful not to make any noise.

He finally reached the barbed-wire fence that separated Papa's farm from Will Raspberry's. He could tell the wire had been stretched, and the tag of cloth hanging from one of the barbs confirmed his suspicions. He slid through and continued along the narrow path.

Suddenly, he heard a high-pitched scream that pierced the stillness of the woods. Sam broke into a run. He dashed with such purpose that he failed to see a limb that hung low over the path. He ran headlong into it and was thrown off his feet. His head throbbed as he regained his footing and started forward.

He came upon the clearing at a full run. He was in the middle of the circle before he could stop his forward momentum. Blood ran down the side of his nose, and his left eye was beginning to swell shut, but he only needed one eye to take in the whole situation.

Edna Raspberry was standing shin-deep in the water of the creek. She was buck naked and doing her darndest to cover herself with her hands. Rodney, Jimmy, and Ralph were standing in the clearing, laughing and trying to pretend they were worldly men. Megan, the city girl, was in a tug of war with Bobby Sessoms with the girl's clothes acting as the rope. Edna's eyes met Sam's good eye, and to her surprise she dropped her hands. In an instant, the situation's pain and humiliation overwhelmed Sam. He walked directly to Rodney and socked him in the mouth. Jimmy and Ralph were next, and neither of them offered any resistance. Bobby was so surprised that he stopped pulling on the girl's clothes and was immediately rewarded with a swift kick to his most precious possessions. The three injured scamps gathered their immobilized partner and practically slithered into the woods to escape. Sam took his shirt off, walked into the creek, and draped it around Edna's shoulders. He was trying not to look, but he was doing a poor job of it. It didn't seem to matter to Edna. She hugged and kissed him and began to cry. Megan cussed, laughed, and finally jumped back into the water as if nothing had happened. Edna finally stopped crying, and they disentangled themselves. No one said a word as Sam climbed out of the water. He turned to speak but could find no words. He raised his hand in a weak gesture of departure. He turned one more time as he got to the edge of the woods. Edna was still standing in the water with his shirt hanging open. Their eyes met once again. Edna saw a "white knight" who, although injured, had fought for her honor. A romance had begun that would last throughout time.

That night at supper, not a word was said about the incident. Papa did not question his sons about their injuries. Ma shuffled in her seat and looked from Sam's scratched forehead and swollen eye to Rodney's lip that was three times larger than normal, but Papa just shook his head at her every attempt to address the situation. It took Sam a month to get over it. Edna never would.

Chapter Nineteen

The sound came from far away. In the weeks since she had moved into Rodney's cabin, the natural sounds of the country had become soothing to her. How easy to forget the gentle rustling of leaves as they danced about on a morning breeze or the powerful sound of a bumblebee's wings as it hovered while looking for a place to alight and deposit pollen so life could renew out of its efforts. The city had all these sounds, but the manmade intrusion of noise masked them. At first, she found the absence of noise unnerving. Now, she played with the sounds of nature, trying to name them without seeing their source.

A loud pop brought her out of a sound sleep, and she quickly identified it as the echo of wood being split and stacked. She threw the cover off and walked to the window. She could see Rodney across the yard with his back to her. He was shirtless, and his back muscles stood in relief highlighted by the moisture from his sweat. She watched as he placed another log on a wide stump that looked as if it had been left above ground for just that purpose, gripped the ax-like tool with both hands, and raised it above his head. The motion seemed to extend his height by a couple of inches. He slammed the tool down and into the log with a smooth and powerful motion. A ripping sound as the log fell into two halves followed the thump of the impact. The ritual was repeated on each half until the original log had become four pieces. Rodney put the maul aside and tossed all four pieces into a pile.

Amanda gazed at the fluidity of his movements and thought of the timelessness of this task. This could be the twentieth century or the nineteenth century, and the act of splitting wood was accomplished with the same efforts and tools. She saw Rodney as a man completely comfortable with yesterday's ways. He was the most refreshing man she had ever met. His total immersion into the task at hand was contagious. She wanted to be a part of it. Quickly she pulled on her jeans and a shirt.

When he heard the door slam, he turned to see her. His smile let her know he was happy to have her with him. There was no need for words. She began picking up the split sections and tossing them onto the pile. The work was hard but good, and they had produced a large stack of split wood in a short time. Rodney leaned the maul against the stack of wood and reached for his shirt. After putting it on and buttoning it, he reached for her and pulled her to him. The scent of the work and the mingling of their perspiration created a sensual musk. He kissed her lightly on the forehead.

"Good morning. Thanks for the help. The fire from that wood will feel mighty good come December."

"December seems like such a long time away."

"Be here before you know it. You gotta think a couple of months ahead when you live out here. This place demands a lot from a person."

She felt that what he said was true but knew his statement was a declaration of love. Her sense of accomplishment was stronger than anything she had felt in years. The place demanded a lot, but it gave a lot in return. She felt she was beginning to truly love the cabin and the surrounding land. She also knew she truly loved Rodney Wilson.

"Let's get cleaned up and have some breakfast," he said as he took his arm from around her and started walking to the camping trailer at the edge of the yard.

She watched him walk away, then turned and returned to the cabin. She wondered if he would ever advance toward her and what she would do if it happened. He was such a gentleman.

As the water from the shower ran over her body, she remembered the night they had met—how Edna acted toward Rodney all night and her violent reaction at the end of the Scrabble game. She laughed at the thought. She smiled while remembering how Rodney's old jeep had failed to start after he took her home. He had left the jeep parked in the driveway and asked to borrow Craig's old ten-speed bicycle to ride home as if he only had to go a couple of blocks. It was thirteen miles. She had been waiting for him to return the next day when she saw Edna lose control of her car and run through the churchyard. From Edna's actions, Amanda knew she thought things were far more advanced than they were. When she had brought the subject up to Rodney, he had laughed. "Let the old girl think what she will. It's good for her imagination, not to mention her circulation."

She could hardly believe how the people of the church had acted in her husband's absence. If it had not been for Rodney offering her the cabin, she would have had to move back home with her parents. Not a comforting thought. Rodney and the cabin had both been godsends, and now she was completely enamored with both. For weeks she had been on an emotional rollercoaster. Craig's leaving had hurt her deeply, but now she found herself thinking of him less and less. She wondered if she had ever really loved him at all. Still, she was legally married to him, and her growing feelings for Rodney ran counter to her strict Southern Baptist upbringing. The internal debate had been ongoing, but as she reached for the handle of the shower, it was like a light coming on in a totally dark room. She decided to move forward with her life. "Everyone thinks we're living together anyway," she thought as she pulled the towel to herself. She had once heard Rodney say, "Never let anyone accuse you of anything you are not guilty of."

She smiled and said out loud to the mirror, "I will not be falsely accused, Mr. Wilson."

Once made, the decision changed everything. She now felt as free as her surroundings. The "new" Amanda Cotton ignored the folded clothes she had brought into the bathroom and reached for an oversized T-shirt. She pulled it over her head, shook her hair, and stepped through the bathroom door and into her future.

Chapter Twenty

The oak leaves rustled as the early evening breeze moved through them. The smell of rain hung in the air. Shadows from the darkening clouds fell across the trees and deepened the hues of the leaves. Birds and small forest creatures kept up a constant chatter, speaking to one another of the coming storm.

Rodney Wilson looked upon the whole scene and saw nothing but beauty. He had always loved nature and the land and cherished the time he spent with them. Today, there was a special crispness to everything. The greens were greener, and the patches of remaining blue were pure and deep. Even the gray of the clouds looked pillowy and relaxing. The coming rain did not put a damper on his mood; he loved the rain. Life was at once in perfect balance and as upside down as a bat hanging in a cave.

The past two days had been heaven on earth. He wasn't sure what had come over Amanda, but he loved it. He knew they had strong feelings, but neither had chosen to speak of them. He had been unsure how to proceed, considering how her life must have been for the last couple of months. He cared deeply for her and at times almost let himself use the "L" word, but he was afraid of it. He didn't know if saying the word "love" would frighten her off or make her think he used it frivolously, throwing it around like some folks say "hi." Now, he could think in no other terms.

After splitting wood for the winter, they had gone their separate ways to clean up before breakfast. He let himself into the kitchen of the cabin and started making coffee. When she came out of the bathroom, he was startled that she was not dressed. He started to apologize for letting himself into the cabin, but he never got to finish the sentence. They never ate breakfast, skipped lunch, and forgot all about supper. The smell of scorching coffee was the only thing that got them out of bed. They had their breakfast at 3 a.m. the next morning out of necessity. Since then, schedules had walked out the door. It was hard to distinguish the predator from the prey; they both played each part so well. On the afternoon of the second day, Rodney finally ventured outside for the first time. He felt Amanda come up behind him and turned to take her into his arms.

"Rains are coming. I guess we'll have to stay inside once it starts."

"How long do you think before it starts?" she asked as she squeezed his waist and nuzzled the back of his neck.

"Any time now. Maybe we shouldn't wait for it. Let's go back inside."

The storm came but neither Rodney nor Amanda noticed.

Later, as they lay listening to the sound of the rain dance across the cabin's tin roof, they talked about what the future could hold for them. They decided Rodney should get a job near Cedar Creek and that Amanda would stay at the cabin for a while so that they could spend as much time together as possible. If circumstances necessitated, she would get a job as a substitute teacher. Tomorrow, Rodney would call some of his friends in Asheville to inquire if any bridges were being built in the area.

Periods of silence became more prevalent as the rain continued to beat a rhythm on the roof. Neither of them knew which went to sleep first. There wasn't a single question that didn't get answered or a statement that went unacknowledged. The conversation slowed, became intermittent, and then stopped. The cumulative effect of fatigue and contentment took over against all attempts to fight it off. They slept.

Chapter Twenty-one

Victoria pulled into traffic and pointed the car toward Jillian's apartment. The trip was now a familiar one, and she enjoyed making it. She somehow felt different at Jill's. There was a freedom there that she could not explain. It had to be something about the way Jill kept her apartment because the two visits that Jill had made to Victoria's house had been stiff and formal. The personality of the house seemed to dominate in both instances.

It had been two weeks since that night at the Cactus Palace, and Victoria had thought of little else. The circumstances of that evening were so bizarre that she felt as if she may be suffering from culture shock. Despite any misgivings, she had been excited and had felt an unmistakable sense of adventure. The thought of chauffeuring a drunken, passed-out motorcycle bum would have seemed repulsive to her only a short while ago, but now she looked back on it with a wicked sense of pleasure. She had replayed the night many times in her mind, each time thinking of clever things she could have said or cool actions she could have done. She wished she had done anything but sit there as Alphie and Jill unleashed the other man from his seatbelt and took him out of the car. They had taken him into a building that was no larger than her garage. The only saving grace of the entire incident was that the man had quickly passed back out after they had stopped the Cougar, saving her from having to make conversation.

Jill's morning call had set her mind back into motion.

"He's asking about you," she said after the initial hellos. "Troy wants to see you again. Alphie says he calls you 'the mystery angel.' Troy told Alphie he was sorry for what happened. He didn't realize he had drunk so much. He wouldn't have gotten drunk and passed out on purpose, especially with his bike there. He said he sure enjoyed seeing you when he woke up in the car. Alphie has called me twice this week, and he mentions you and Troy each time. They want us to go on a run with them tomorrow."

"I can't run anywhere. Jill, I'd end up in worse shape than, eh, Troy ever dreamed of being."

"No, silly! A run is what they call riding their motorcycles somewhere."

"I've never been on a motorcycle in my life. I don't think I can do it. I'd probably be better off trying to run."

"Come on, Vickie," she pleaded, "do it for me. At least say you'll think about it. Come over tonight, and we'll talk it over."

Now, she was on her way to Jill's. She couldn't tell if what she was feeling was excitement or terror. Victoria knew enough about herself to realize that Jill would probably talk her into going on the "run," so she was already trying to bolster her nerve.

To say she was preoccupied would have grossly understated the situation. She found herself standing at Jill's door and could not remember the drive. As if startled by the revelation, she turned quickly to be sure she had parked the car properly, turned off the lights, and removed the keys from the ignition. She had just located the key ring in the bottom of her purse when the door behind her opened. She was completely surprised and confused.

"What are you doing, girl? I waited as long as I could, but I didn't know if you were going to ring the doorbell or run. Finally, I thought I'd better lasso you while I had the chance."

"I, I, I couldn't remember. I had to think. I, I, hell, I don't know!"

"Come on in. I'll get you a glass of wine."

"Have you got a beer? Have you got a few beers? I think I'd rather have a beer."

"Good God, girl. You look like you've seen a ghost. Sure, I've got a beer. Come on in."

The beer was bitter and cold. It attacked her thirst and seemed to clear her head. Victoria drank the first beer so fast that Jill had to get her a second before she could sit down. She watched as the soothing effect of the alcohol began to win the battle for Victoria's nerves.

"My God, that's good," Victoria said, tilting the second bottle for a long pull. "I didn't even drink this stuff until we went to that club. We used to drink a can or two in college, but I don't remember liking it."

"Only wine was good enough for us back then. God, we drank some cheap wine and thought we were so cool. We were only pompous asses without cause or reason, weren't we?"

Victoria laughed out loud (a natural by-product of two beers consumed in rapid succession). "We thought we knew so much, but we didn't have any idea what was really good."

"I'll tell you what's good: Alphie McCann. I haven't told you, but we've been together for the last couple of days, and it's been great. That's what I called you about. Alphie says Troy has been asking about you. Alphie says he doesn't remember much but is definitely interested in seeing you again and getting to know you."

"I don't know, Jill. I don't know whether he's my type or not, and I've never been on a motorcycle in my life."

"There's nothing to it. You'll love it. Give it a chance."

"I don't know."

"Did you have fun the other night at the club?"

"It wasn't what I was expecting, but it was fun."

"Have I lied to you or misled you in any way since I've known you?"

"No."

"Well, that's it then. We'll go to the store and pick up a few things and you'll be set. They think you're my roommate, and I didn't tell them any different, so you can quit and disappear any time you like. What could be easier?"

The beer was working its magic. What seemed absurd over the phone now had taken on the air of adventure.

"What the hell, I'll go. What do we need from the store?"

Jill walked to the refrigerator and got two more beers. She gave one to Victoria and smiled.

"Here, let's have one more, and then we'll be off to the store. I'll drive."

The shopping trip was like nothing Victoria had ever done before. At Jill's urging, she bought a pair of jeans that were much too tight, boots that were much too high, a bra that was like not having one on, and panties that had a quarter-inch string where the seat was supposed to be. She had spent two hundred dollars and didn't have a thing she would show one of her other friends if she ran into one of them.

"One more stop, and we'll be ready," said Jill as they left the mall's parking lot.

They drove for several miles. When Jill slowed the car, Victoria saw a sign that read "Skeeter's Hog Pen."

Inside, it was like a temple built to worship the god that is Harley-Davidson. There were posters on the walls that depicted motorcycles being ridden across every type of terrain, including the heavens themselves. Mounted on each motorcycle was a virile-looking man. Each rider had long, flowing hair and a full beard. Behind each man was a woman, invariably thin, wearing boots and tight jeans like the ones Victoria had just purchased, and a halter top like the ones Jill was looking at.

"Whoa." Victoria's mind was in a panic. She had not drunk that much beer. The word "no" came to her in every language she had ever heard. Her brain could not reconcile the thought of herself in a halter-top.

Her thoughts must have been transparent because Jill put the halter away and stepped over to a rack of T-shirts.

"This one is perfect," she said, holding one up, declaring that its wearer would "Ride to Live, Live to Ride."

Victoria was so relieved at not having to discuss halter tops worn by middle-aged women who didn't even own a swimsuit that she quickly said yes. She didn't even mind the chaps and vest, each with dangling leather tassels. Ten minutes and two hundred fifty dollars later, they were on their way back to Jill's place.

"I'd better stop and get another six-pack before we get home. You're gonna look great tomorrow!"

"Yeah, okay, sure. More beer."

Chapter Twenty-two

A great philosopher (probably Chinese, probably with a two-syllable name, one first and one last, and probably not talking about motorcycle riding) once said, "The fear of death is worse than death itself," or something to that effect. Victoria was not aware of any such philosophy or philosopher, but she was aware of a dread that permeated her being. Immediately upon waking, she engaged in mental calisthenics. First, she would conjure up a picture of the disaster the day would surely bring. Next, she would devise an excuse to cancel the entire day's activities based on the disaster. Finally, she would dismiss each excuse out of loyalty to Jillian. By the time she arrived at Jillian's, she was both mentally fatigued and resigned to let the day flow around her.

She had left her new clothes at Jill's for fear she might have to open the trunk and, if seen, be questioned concerning her purchases. Now she was into the first two layers of clothing, and it wasn't as bad as she had imagined. The bra gave her a feeling of freedom and allowed a little bounce, which she enjoyed both physically and visually. She was getting used to the thong panties, although at first she had wondered how a quarter inch of silk could feel like a bale of cotton. The T-shirt and jeans were sleek and tight and took a few years off her body. Jill had helped her with her hair, expertly curling it into soft spirals. Jill helped Victoria apply light makeup and loaned her some jewelry made of silver and turquoise. With all the physical preparations completed, Victoria set about preparing herself mentally. She drank two 16-ounce cans of Coors while Jill showered. She turned on the radio, sat on the couch, and let the music of Steely Dan and the soothing effects of the alcohol wash over her.

The wait seemed longer than it really was. Jill had finished dressing and was having her first beer when the roar of motorcycles stopped everything.

Alphie and Troy made a ceremony of parking the bikes against the curb with the front wheels pointed at an angle into the parking lot. Victoria felt all the muscles of her throat contract as the guys dismounted and walked toward the door.

The introductions were brief. Most of the conversation centered on that night at the Cactus Palace. Alphie and Jill did most of the talking while Troy and Victoria sat in embarrassed silence.

Not talking didn't mean Victoria was not taking in the scene. "This Troy is a nice-looking man," she thought. He was over six feet tall and well built with just a slight roundness about his belly (probably the result of many beers). His hair was dirty blond and fell to his shoulders, reminding her of a lion's mane, and there was no hint of thinning. Her late husband always worried about thinning hair, and it happened anyway. Why had she thought of that now? Troy's eyes were a bright shade of blue that looked surreal against his tanned face. A few acne scars appeared on his chin and neck, but they just served to complement his rugged appearance. His faded jeans fit him snugly in all the right places. The T-shirt was a perfect balance with his massive arms putting a strain on the fabric. The tattoos that covered much of his arms drew her attention. She once thought tattoos repulsive, but when viewed as part of a total package, she wanted to examine them more closely. Scuffed black boots with a hole almost worn through the left toe completed the picture.

Victoria's inventory and evaluation were broken when everyone stood and walked to the door. The comfort and assurance she felt only a few minutes ago had drained and been replaced by panic.

Too late to back out. She began inwardly repeating to herself, "I can do this! I can do this!" Jillian caught her eye and smiled with approval.

Following Jill's lead, she stood by while Troy and Alphie straddled the motorcycles and kicked them into life. Each man reached behind himself and lowered a peg on each side of the bike. With a helmet in place, Jill climbed aboard and settled behind Alphie. Victoria lifted her leg but found her foot three inches shy of clearing the seat. Quickly she grabbed the errant leg with both hands and raised it the additional distance. She felt her balance slipping and immediately skip-stepped to avoid falling. Her actions resulted in her falling heavily onto the seat behind Troy. To cover her blunder, she wriggled up behind him, grabbed his waist with both hands, and said, "Let's do it!"

Victoria held her breath as the motorcycle pulled away. She sat stiffly behind Troy as he and Alphie merged into traffic. There was joyousness about the men as one would coax his bike ahead and then fall back as the other took the lead. They were much like puppies playing on the lawn.

After a few miles, Victoria began to relax. Her grip loosened, and she started to flow with the movements of the bike. The engine noise was so loud that it made conversation almost impossible. In the absence of words came sensations. First, she noticed how the wind played against her hair and skin and then how her vision was enhanced without the interference of a glass partition. She could see the tiny details of life. She became intensely aware of the changing smells, the sweetness of the honeysuckle, the clean smell of freshly mowed hay, the acrid smell of exhaust fumes, and even the stench of cow manure as they rode past a dairy farm. She had driven on this road many times but had enjoyed none of these things. She began to perceive what would lure otherwise sane people to straddle a machine that was 40 to 50 percent engine, had more horsepower than most compact cars, and rode with no more personal protection than a hard plastic helmet and a few strips of leather between themselves and the pavement.

The sun was high overhead, and the temperature was in the upper eighties. When they stopped, the sweat beaded up on Victoria's arm, but as they gathered speed, the wind blew against the dampness, causing a cooling sensation that Victoria found exhilarating.

Alphie's arm shot straight out, and he and Troy slowed their bikes. They turned left, accelerated, slowed again, and turned into a parking lot filled with motorcycles.

The building was a plain rectangle house that had been converted into a bar. The most interesting thing about it was the flashing neon sign that promised "Ice Cold Beer." The word "oasis" came to Victoria's mind. She could almost taste the beer. She smiled inwardly as she dismounted the motorcycle and stretched her body. She turned in time to catch Troy looking at her. *What a difference a few days make,* she thought. She had trouble picturing the old Victoria.

The bar was like a cave. The contrast between the brightness of the sun and the darkness inside left everyone momentarily blinded as their eyes fought to adjust. As sight returned to Victoria, she was taken by the starkness of the place. Slat-backed wooden chairs and crude tables were scattered about the floor, which itself was covered by sawdust. The bar was a homemade affair fronted by twelve wooden stools with no padding on the seats. Behind the bar were three old chest-type coolers, each adorned with the name of a soft drink that was not present in any of them. The walls were strewn with various Harley-Davidson paraphernalia, all tightly screwed or bolted on. The only beverages available were an assortment of domestic beers and wine coolers. The only way to get one of those beverages was to approach the bar, order from the biggest, thickest, ugliest human Victoria had ever been in the presence of and pay cash on delivery. No checks, no credit cards, no tabs, strictly pay as you go.

The bar was crowded, and everyone was having fun. Victoria had not seen so much leather in one place since her visit to the stockyards in Chicago a few years back. She was surprised by how comfortable she felt. Her rational mind told her this was not the place for a woman of her standing. These were the type of people she used to cross the street to avoid. Her conservative nature said she should be at home working in her garden or reading. Despite all, her heart told her she was doing fine. She was having fun, and she was comfortable. Putting all thoughts aside and living in the moment, she laid her hand on Troy's arm and said, "I'll have a Coors and see if they have any peanuts."

Victoria's newfound love affair with beer became deeper and more meaningful when enjoyed after a motorcycle ride in eighty-plus-degree weather. The conversation was easy, and the company was good. She was glad Jillian had coaxed her into coming. She found herself casually touching Troy often. As they sat there and drank, each couple drifted off into their own conversation.

"I know Asheville is a big place," said Victoria, "but I can't understand how I've never seen you before." In fact, she could not remember if she had seen Troy or not. If she had, she probably would have ignored him until recently, but it seemed the thing to say at the time. The beer and the events of the day pushed her to assume the persona she and Jillian had fabricated for her.

"I don't get to Asheville that much. I live in Cedar Creek. I just came over for a while and am staying with Alphie while I'm here."

"I have a sister who used to live in Cedar Creek. What brings you to Asheville?"

"Uh, I came to find someone, but that doesn't seem too important anymore." Troy put his arm around Victoria and pulled her close to him.

Victoria's heart was racing. She would like to know a lot more about Troy, but she sensed that now was not the time to pursue it. Besides, she was enjoying the moment. How many movies had she seen that included a scene like this? How many times had she shed tears while watching, not knowing if they were tears of joy for the character of the film or tears of despair for her own life in comparison? No matter. Right now, today, she was in the arms of a man whom she found extremely attractive in a place filled with the air of adventure. For the day, she was living a life in which she was free to act in any fashion that suited her. She nuzzled against Troy's shoulder and enjoyed the smell of a real man. Her eyes closed for a split second, too late to prevent a tear from slipping under the lid. She sighed happily. A vision of Mary Alice came into her mind. For the first time, she did not have any negative thoughts toward her sister. She only hoped Mary Alice was as happy as she was.

Chapter Twenty-three

Mary Alice reached up to scratch her ear. It had been itching for the last fifteen minutes. *Someone must be talking about me,* she thought as she pulled the Volkswagen into the driveway of Victoria's house. She was ecstatic as she worked the key into the lock and felt the resistance of the deadbolt give way to permit her to enter. She removed the key and brought it up to eye level. "Won't be needing you much longer," she said. She felt elated over the morning's activities.

After dropping Craig off at work, she went to look at a trailer for rent. She had seen the ad in the paper and called the number on a chance. She and Craig needed a place of their own, and she made it her business to find one. Her expectations had been quite low as she drove to meet the leasing agent. The advertisement had been brief and gave no description except that the "mobile home" had three bedrooms and two baths and was on a private lot.

Her meeting had taken place at a convenience store, and after fifteen minutes of question and answers, she must have passed some invisible test and was awarded the right to view the house. This behavior would have provoked rage at one point in her life, but that was before she had lived with her older sister and was trying to nurture a relationship under adverse circumstances. Now she found herself relieved rather than indignant and gladly followed the agent to the house.

The "private lot" turned out to be ten acres and the mobile home turned out to be a doublewide with as much room as Victoria's house. The furnishings were stylish and relatively new. The agent told Mary Alice that the owners of the home were forced to move to New Jersey because of a promotion in the husband's career. It was perfect, and the rent was reasonable, considering it was furnished. They could handle the rent on what Craig made. She couldn't wait for the end of the day so Craig could see it for himself.

* * *

Craig looked up at the sun and wiped the sweat from his brow. He felt good. In fact, he felt better physically than he had in his life. His skin had a healthy glow, and his arms and legs were taking on some shape. He had always been the skinny kid that everyone picked on, but now he was developing some muscles.

The work had been exhausting at first, and there had been times when he wanted to walk off and find somewhere to rest. As the days passed, his body and mind adjusted until he looked forward to the work and felt he was learning something. He had diligently purchased one tool every payday and made it his business to learn how to use it properly.

Gus noticed how hard Craig had been trying to learn and assigned him to work with James, a black carpenter. James appeared to be about sixty years old, but the talk was that he was closer to seventy. He was never in a hurry and never made a mistake. He taught Craig all about the forms they used, how they were made, how they were set, and how to take them down so they could be used again. Craig also got an ear full about how things had been in bridge building throughout the years. Craig sought out James at every opportunity and reveled in his knowledge. Some of the other laborers thought Craig was crazy.

"Why do more than you have to?" They would chuckle and joke to each other but never said anything to Craig after the way he handled Nick Hopkins. Craig was still known as "Slugger" on the job. Nobody called him by his name.

James came for Craig at ten a.m. and asked him to help build some new forms. Craig was on top of the world. The times he was helping James were coming more frequently, and his labor duties were fewer. They worked for a couple of hours and then took lunch together.

During lunch, James had recounted a story about a fellow he used to work with by the name of "Mr. Willie," who, like James, was black and had never done anything but build bridges. James' story was about an incident that happened in Williamsburg, Virginia. They had been sent to help finish a bridge. The company had set up a camping trailer for James and Mr. Willie to live in. They were not charged rent, but they were responsible for anything that took place that would damage the trailer.

"I won't too worried about it myself," said James as he pushed a three-inch thick sandwich into his mouth and cleanly bit it in half. "I knew that I ain't gwine mess it up, and Mr. Willie was older 'n me. I got to Virginia on Monday and went out to the job site with Mr. Virgil, the foreman. Mr. Willie was coming up later and going to the trailer. I figured he would be set up by the time we knocked off. Come quittin' time, Mr. Virgil said he would drop me off. Mr. Willie's Buick was out front when we got to the trailer. Mr. Virgil said he needed to see Willie for a few minutes and asked if he could come in. "Sure," I said. I was proud of the trailer and had got there early Monday to clean it. I wasn't ready for what I saw when we got to the door. As I opened the door, my feet got tangled up in newspaper. That was strange cause I'd just swept the floor before I left for work. Mr. Virgil was right behind me, and we sounded like a herd of mice in a gift-wrapping factory. When we were both inside, Mr. Willie sat in a rocking chair with nothing on but his long-handled drawers and a baseball cap that said CAT on it.

His old brogans were beside the chair. All across the floor was a single layer of newspaper placed like a make-do carpet cover. Boy, was I wrong. Mr. Willie rocked back and forth a coupla' of times and let fly a big ole wad of tobacco juice that arched halfway across the room and landed somewhere between the garden news and advice to the lovelorn. He wiped the sleeve of his long handles across his lips and grinned. 'How you gentlemens today?' He grinned and let go another gush. I could see my money flying across the room with that tobacco juice."

They both laughed. James would only tell a story to a certain point and then fall silent. He seemed to take great pleasure in having the listener pry the rest of the story out of him with questions. It was his way of seeing who was paying attention and who really cared about his stories. Craig was his favorite because he seemed to hang on to every word and ask countless questions.

"How'd it turn out, James? Did that tobacco juice cost you a lot of money?"

Just as James was about to answer, the alarm went off, and lunch was over.

"Go to the trailer and get us some double-headed sixteen-penny nails, and I'll tell you."

Craig was approaching the tool trailer when the door to the office opened, and a kid of eighteen or nineteen came out. "Thanks, Mister," the kid said. "I'll see you tomorrow."

Craig gathered the nails and was heading back when the office door opened again.

"Hey, Slugger!" Gus yelled. "Can I see you for a minute?"

Craig turned and walked back to Gus. Most days, not much was said between Gus and the guys on the job. He usually assigned jobs to the lead carpenters, mason, and laborers each morning and left it to them to get things done. The only time he got involved was to correct a mistake or to fire someone when needed. Even though Craig hadn't done anything wrong, he felt a knot in his throat as he approached Gus.

"You see the kid that just left?"

Craig nodded.

"That's your replacement."

Craig's head fell, and the bottom dropped out of his stomach. "But, Gus, what did I do?" Craig was obviously stunned and confused.

"Hold on, Slugger. I ain't getting rid of you. The truth is, you've done a damn good job since you've been here. I've noticed you buying some tools, and James says there's something to ya. I have a new carpenter starting tomorrow, and he will need a helper. That's gonna be you. Starting tomorrow, you ain't a laborer anymore; you're a carpenter's helper. That'll mean another dollar an hour. Bust your ass and learn from this guy, and there'll be more."

"Thanks, Gus, I…"

"Shut up and get those sixteens back down to James."

When he got back, James was grinning from ear to ear. He had known all along. Craig never found out how the story about Mr. Willie ended. They spent the rest of the day talking about carpentry and Craig's new job. James gave Craig some tips about how to anticipate what a carpenter needed so he wouldn't have to ask for everything. James also told Craig he was proud of him. Craig swelled up like a balloon. Gaining the respect of a man like James was far more rewarding than the extra money.

The day wore on and when it was finished and all the tools were put away, Craig stopped James on the way to the gate.

"Thanks, James. Thanks for all the things you've taught me."

"You're mighty welcome, Slugger. Keep on, and you'll make a good bridge man. Pay attention to the new man; he'll teach you a lot. He's a good man. Yes, sir, that Rodney Wilson is a hell of a good bridge man."

James slapped him on the back. "And whatever you do, don't spit no bacca juice on the floor."

Craig laughed and turned toward the gate. He saw Mary Alice waiting outside. She saw him coming and smiled. He fell in love all over again. He could hardly wait to tell her the news.

"I've got great news!" they both said as he opened the door.

Mary Alice went first and told him about the trailer and then Craig told of his new job and the raise that came with it.

They laughed and played all the way home. The play became amorous and escalated until they were both at a fevered pitch. They ran inside when they turned into the driveway and saw that Victoria was not home. They made love on the floor of Craig's room to keep from ruining the sheets since bridge building was such dirty work. Afterward, they lay in each other's arms and visualized their new future. Everything in the universe seemed to have aligned perfectly.

Chapter Twenty-four

The end of the summer brought many changes to the lives of our select group of folks in Asheville and Cedar Creek. Whether the changes were good or bad would depend on who witnessed them and on which day. Washington Irving once wrote: "There is a certain relief in change, even though it be from bad to worse; as I have found in traveling by stagecoach, that it is often a comfort to shift one's position and be bruised in a new place."

At no time in a young man's life does the shifting come more rapidly nor the bruises more constantly than in his teenage years. With so much to get used to and so many rites of passage to endure, it's no wonder a guy can get bewildered and dumbfounded. Thus, at fifteen, I found myself totally out of sync as a freshman at Cedar Creek High School.

In our county, three junior highs fed into the one countywide senior high. The transition from being an upperclassman in a junior high where you knew everyone to being a member of the freshman class comprised of two-thirds strangers was humbling. Add that to contending with large sophomore, junior, and senior classes, and any freshman might feel downright unnerved. I felt like the ultimate peon. As a freshman, you were fair game for anyone's ridicule. I was especially prone to receiving comments thanks to a case of severe acne that was, at least in my view, showing signs of clearing, although that must not have been so obvious to others.

Almost all males and females have some facial blemishes when they reach puberty, but I must have arrived later and stayed longer than most in that stage of development. I once likened my face to a ripe strawberry, but that was probably unfair to the strawberry. I tried all the scrubs, lotions, and cover-ups available to no avail. They either made me look like fresh roadkill, a dew-covered strawberry, or some two-bit actor made up to play a mud-encrusted swamp monster. I never went to the doctor. We didn't know there were doctors for such things back then. Mama's answer to the whole dilemma was to tell me I looked fine and was, in fact, quite handsome (a mother's love) while at the same time admonishing me not to squeeze them for fear of permanent scarring. Daddy would say, "It could be worse." Jason acted as if he didn't notice my affliction until he became angry with me, at which time he would refer to me as "crater face" or "zitzilla." It was a trying time. I felt my greatest claim to fame was that I could probably terrorize any mirror in the world.

Another impending change was my transition from passenger and pedestrian to driver. At the magic age of sixteen, I could obtain a driver's license in North Carolina. Attaining the age does not qualify you for the license. You also must pass a written test and perform certain skills in a driving test. To prepare for this and teach safety, you must take and pass a driver's education course. Some people took driver's ed, which was offered as an extra-curricular course at the high school from private driving schools. That was my only option.

The joke went that they were going to cancel sex education in Cedar Creek because they needed the car for driver's ed. The faculty of Cedar Creek High School did not enjoy this jest. (At least none of them ever admitted to laughing, but then I never saw them laugh at much else either.) Mr. Sam Alt, driver's education instructor, wrestling coach, dean of boys, and general badass for all occasions held the joke in special contempt.

Although I had never met him, I had heard many stories about Mr. Alt. Some stories said he instantly knew when you were trying to lie to him. He could make you confess to any misdeed. I even heard he could read minds and know if you were planning anything that did not strictly follow school rules. Jimmy Ross, who goes to our church, told me that he and Tommy Watson were skipping school last year, and Mr. Alt was waiting for them in the woods beyond the football field. Jimmy swore that nobody besides Tommy and him knew of their plans. Anyway, Mr. Alt caught Jimmy as he was coming down the hill. Tommy turned and ran back to school. Mr. Alt marched Jimmy back to school and directly to Tommy's algebra class, where he pulled Tommy out and took them both to the office. Tommy thought Jimmy had snitched on him, but Jimmy swore he didn't. Neither Jimmy nor Tommy knew how Mr. Alt figured out their plans to skip and the path they would take, but they had three days of suspension to think about it. Jimmy said he never tried to pull any other foolishness at school. What was the use with a mind reader patrolling the grounds?

With great apprehension, I made my way to driver's ed. The classroom was located in the basement under the gym. As I passed Mr. Alt's office, I looked through the open door and saw a wooden paddle about sixteen inches long and five inches wide with holes bored along its length hanging on the wall behind his desk. For a moment, I considered walking wherever I wanted to go and forgetting about my driver's license. If it had not been for my male hormones doing jumping jacks and the thoughts of all the possibilities that can come as a result of having a license, I would have turned tail and run out of school and back to the safety of Mama's kitchen.

The classroom was stark even compared to Cedar Creek High's other rooms. I believe the room had been converted from an old athletic equipment storage room. A coat of off-white paint barely disguised the chips and cracks in the wall. Scars and scuff marks covered the floor. Obviously, some custodians had tried to clean it but, in the end, had waxed over the marks and leave them as a testimonial to the glory days of the room. There were twelve student-style desks aligned to face a blackboard that had been hung on the front wall. Even the blackboard was not a permanent fixture. It was hung using some braided wire and would move about when Mr. Alt used it to illustrate some of the finer points of automobile manipulation. A teacher's desk and a lectern stood at the front of the room. Behind the lectern, Mr. Sam Alt, standing at parade rest, glared at the seats.

I had been led to believe Mr. Alt was some superhuman giant when he was actually not a tall man at all. He was a rotund individual who stood about five feet seven inches tall and who at one time may have had a good physique. His hair was dark and worn in a flattop. His torso made up the greater part of his height, and his legs looked like stubs, hardly long enough to perform the tasks they were designed for. My first thought was that this is what Fred Flintstone would have looked like if he had spent twenty years teaching high school.

"Take a seat, young man. No, one of these up front."

My first plan of the class had been foiled. I took the second seat in the first row beside a boy named Roland Crews and, seconds later, counted my blessings as the most gorgeous creature I had ever seen walked into class and was instructed to take the seat next to me. I could hardly believe my luck. I'm sure my peripheral vision improved at least two hundred percent over the next forty-five minutes.

The rest of the students arrived en masse and filled the remaining chairs without having to be assigned. Throughout the introduction to the course and a history of the invention and development of the internal combustion engine and its use in the modern automobile, I continued to look at the angel beside me. Her every move was poetry.

She had shoulder-length blonde hair and wore a simple sweater and skirt. She sat with her legs crossed, and her skirt ended four inches above her knee. I surveyed every inch of her exposed leg.

She had on flat shoes made of deep brown leather. I would try to look away and pay attention because I knew from his reputation that Mr. Alt was a no-nonsense kind of guy, but every time she would shift in her seat or swing her leg, I was drawn like a moth to the flame.

At the end of the class, Mr. Alt got out his roll book and, starting with the seat to my right, asked each person in turn for their name. I was sitting on the edge of my seat when it came her turn.

"D-D-D-Diane M-M-Mullins," she said in a whisper.

"What did you say, young lady?" Mr. Alt asked.

"D-D-D-Diane M-M-Mullins," she said again, faintly.

"Speak up!" Mr. Alt demanded.

"D-D-Diane M-Mullins," she shouted out. "I-I-I st-st-stutter, s-sir."

Except for Mr. Alt and me, the entire class broke into laughter. Suddenly, I knew how a mass murderer must feel the moment before he unleashes a barrage of automatic weapon fire on a group of noonday burger munchers. I saw her head drop in embarrassment.

I don't know what came over me, but before I could think, I jumped to my feet and turned to face the rest of the class. "Just shut the hell up," I yelled at the top of my voice. I don't know how it happened, but somehow my right hand settled on Diane Mullin's wrist and continued to rest there.

"Mr. Wilson, if you would return to your seat, I'll see if I can't handle the discipline of this classroom. And, by the way, keep your hands to yourself."

Another burst of laughter gushed forth, but the ice-cold glare of Mr. Alt quelled it instantly. I sat down quietly and started contemplating how my life was about to end. I had done the unthinkable; I had interrupted Mr. Alt's class. Disaster was imminent. Mr. Alt continued to take roll. When he had completed the roll, he assigned driving groups. My heart was momentarily bolstered when he announced that Roland, Diane, and I would comprise one group of drivers. I thought I saw her smile.

"Class dismissed—with the exception of Mr. Wilson."

That same heart came into my throat, making it almost impossible to breathe. I watched as Diane and the rest of the class filed out of the room, each eyeing me with various amounts of pity.

"I don't know what you've heard about my classes, Mr. Wilson, but I will not tolerate that kind of outburst in the future."

I gulped and braced myself.

"However, what you said needed to be said, and it was brave of you to take on the rest of the class. Don't do it again. Let's go home."

I was numb. I felt as if I had put my head into the mouth of the lion and survived. I stood on weak legs and made my way to the door. On my way out, Mr. Alt put his hand on my shoulder and said, "You really should come out for wrestling, Sir Lancelot."

The hall was empty as I walked to the gym door. I saw Daddy waiting in his old Ford F-150, and a surge of relief came over me, which brought with it a single tear. I climbed into the truck's cab and watched as Daddy pulled from the curb into traffic. I felt safe.

"Daddy, what do you know about wrestling?"

Chapter Twenty-five

The reopening of the school had simplified Mama's life. Mornings were hectic, but that was largely due to her worrisome nature.

Her morning started at 4:30 a.m. when her alarm clock would chirp like a flock of rogue guinea hens. She would pull herself out of bed and go quietly to the kitchen to make coffee. If anyone were privy to observe this ritual, their heart would surely break as they watched Mama come down the stairs. She would move one foot down the step and then bring the other to rest beside it. This was the one time during the day when she would let her body acknowledge that age and weight had finally had an effect on her.

Once in her kitchen, she felt rejuvenated. She cast aside any afflictions once she reached the nerve center of the Wilson household. Like a general in his combat information center, from her kitchen she would prepare her troops to face the battles of a new day.

The male waking process in the Wilson family was slow and gentle. As my life goes on, some of my most vivid memories center on school day mornings. If I were allowed to hold one intangible thing in my hand and tell old Mr. Webster, "Take a picture of this and put it in your dictionary beside the word family," it would be those school day mornings long ago.

Our coffee maker gurgled, spit, and hissed as it brewed. Mama and Daddy were not educated, sophisticated, or properly enlightened enough concerning the devils that dance around in a cup of coffee to know that young men should not partake, so Jason and I got a cup every morning too. If you find yourself terrified at the thought of two young boys being subjected to the archvillain that is caffeine, you should have seen the hunk of lard that Mama put in her biscuits. Lard, flour, salt, and buttermilk, none of which seem especially savory, combined to create the most wonderful aroma. Nothing can coax a man out of bed more quickly than the smell of biscuits, coffee, eggs, and sausage cooking. By the time we were dressed and down the stairs, the food was on the table, and Mama had washed her hands to eat. Nobody could touch their food until all were present. I often suspected Mama of grazing a little while she was cooking because she never seemed as hungry as the rest of us. We ate like a pack of hungry wolves while she nibbled and inspected each of us. Once we had passed muster, she gave Jason and me our lunch money and Daddy his lunch box. With a quick peck on the cheek, we were sent forth to meet the day. Having become an expert at putting the house back in order after the departure of three messy men, she would invariably find herself finished with the housework by midmorning. This was when Mama was most dangerous.

Most women would love to have some free time. They could read books or do some volunteer work. Some might take a class to learn a new skill or expand their knowledge, but Mama would spend her days surfing from one talk show to the next.

Mama was an upright, church-going woman who would never be caught watching that type of show, but with Daddy at work and us at school, there was no one to catch her. She was forced to abstain during summer vacations, but with school in session she could catch up at her leisure.

The first program featured urban grandmothers who saw their golden years as the perfect time to have certain regions of their anatomy pierced and decorated with metal studs and rings. These nouveau hip seniors, whose more sedate counterparts were often referred to as "blue hairs," had taken that description as a starting point and from there had exploded into a full range and spectrum of colors. Those five septuagenarians' craniums exhibited more colors than a gallery full of LeRoy Neiman paintings. They were dressed in black Lycra with enough leather and metal thrown in to give them the look of a popular subculture usually made up of persons in their twenties. The theme of the show was "Generation X-tra."

A man or woman in conservative dress sat to the right of each of the featured guests. Even a cursory inspection would tell you that these were the sons and daughters of the hipsters. To the left of each sat a young male or female dressed in the same manner as their grandmothers. Off to the side was the ever-present doctor, psychiatrist, psychologist, or other expert used to offer credibility the show never quite achieved. The premise of the program was that the grandmothers had become intrigued watching their grandchildren evolve into this hip lifestyle and, through experimentation, had found a new sense of freedom and youth themselves. They did not see their age as an impediment. As a side effect, they had become closer to their grandchildren and even escorted them to venues they could both enjoy. Of course, this was a dilemma for the middle-aged, conservative children who found they were battling the generation gap on two fronts. The banter was heated and animated with one orange-plumed granny affecting a split to illustrate how great she felt. The good doctor assured everyone this was truly a normal phenomenon, and everyone should relax and flow through these changes.

Bullshit! Mama thought as she watched the display. Normal indeed! She was reminded of a bumper sticker she had seen that read, "I only hope I live long enough to be a burden on my children." Looking again at the television, she was struck by the full realization of that sticker's meaning. *Where do they get these freaks?* It never occurred to her that no one would bother to dig up the bait without a fish to catch.

The next hour passed unnoticed as Mama watched a once overweight star of cult movies handle the delicate subject of having a foot fetish and the havoc that such a thing can wreak upon the life of its practitioners when allowed to go unchecked.

Next came Mama's favorite, although she would never admit it. She could always count on this show for pure excitement and titillation. The host resembled the sort of man you would think of as an insurance agent or used car salesman. He would lead his audience and guests along an emotional rollercoaster while trying to convince them he was on their side. At the show's end, he would editorialize how his subject matter related to the bigger scheme of life. In fact, what he produced was a combination of World Championship Wrestling and the sideshows of Ringling Brothers Circus. There was always fighting, yelling, finger-pointing, chairs turned over, and intervention by a team of offstage tough guys. Every other word was covered by a bleep administered by a censor with nimble fingers. The host would drag his forearm across his brow, shuffle his papers, and look embarrassed that we had to endure such a display of human weakness. However, he was not embarrassed by what these antics did for his ratings. He was "the leper with the most fingers."

Mama found herself in such an agitated state that nothing but a tall glass of tea and a bologna sandwich would allow her to go on. It was good that the news came next, so she would not miss anything while eating.

After lunch, Mama watched the show that would push her into action. This program was one of the calmer in the talk show genre. It would usually address issues that more of the public could deal with. Mama watched as each guest was introduced. The lady host of the show led her guests through their story. Each had the common theme that the husband had abandoned them for another woman, devastating the person left behind. The first had become an alcoholic while trying to cope. The second had gained sixty-five pounds in the aftermath of her abandonment and subsequently had a heart attack. So low was the self-esteem of the third that she turned to prostitution. They talked of the shock, the period of denial, and finally the sinking into despair that led to each of their personal afflictions. Finally, the camera panned to an empty seat at the end of the row of destitute castoffs. The host looked directly into the camera and adjusted her red-framed glasses. She told the story of a religious couple who worked together to build a church from nothing until it became a success and an icon of regional worship. As she recounted the sacrifices that such a task demanded, a tear begin to form behind the lenses of those oversized spectacles. Just as things were about to smooth out so they both could enjoy the fruits of their labor, a new organist was hired. It seemed her organ playing was adept on many levels, and thus she enticed the husband to forsake all and join her on the road, where she hoped to form a country and western band. He would be the manager. The dutiful wife was left behind to take care of the flock and further the mission of the church.

"Joyce was supposed to be here today to tell her story," the host said while removing her glasses and dabbing at her now wet cheeks. "She was found, just this morning, dead, an apparent suicide. Her note said she had tried to recover but could no longer keep up the charade. She apologized for not being here today. Joyce Harrington died at age thirty-one from a broken heart. She could fool everyone else, but she could not fool herself. We'll be back after these messages."

Mama's head was spinning. She repeatedly wrung her hands as she considered the possibilities. Her throat was dry, and her skin felt clammy.

"Amanda, oh my God," Mama whispered aloud. She grabbed her keys and ran out the door without turning off the TV.

Chapter Twenty-six

Ping, clunk, smile! This succession of sounds in the yard behind Rodney and Amanda's cabin evoked the grin. Little BBs hitting the dead center of an aluminum beer can produced the ping. The clunk followed as the can hit the ground behind the fence on which it had previously set. The smile was the instantaneous reaction across the face of Amanda Cotton as she watched the beer can fly and land. This kind of unabated joy is most commonly associated with children as they make their discoveries before years of cynicism serve to take the edge off life. Only slowly mastering an activity that was foreign and mysterious a short time ago could bring such joy to an adult.

Amanda had always been afraid of guns. When she first saw Rodney cleaning and oiling the several he owned, she told him of her aversion. He smiled and said her reaction was normal and healthy for someone who didn't understand firearms. Rather than letting it drop, he explained how guns had played a significant role in the history of our country. He said these weapons were only hazardous in the hands of dangerous people and those lacking the understanding of their power and place.

"Dangerous people will continue to be dangerous with or without a gun," Rodney said. "These people will wreak havoc even if they have to do it with sticks and rocks. Of course, folks who don't understand guns can do a great deal of harm by mistake. Guns have to be respected and handled with much thought. Knowledge brings about respect; fear is the mask of ignorance," he added. With that, he sat about teaching her to understand and use a pistol.

To make the education safer and less intimidating, he purchased a BB pistol that was the exact replica of a Colt U.S. Army issue .45 calibers. It had the appearance and feel of the real thing. Her fear gave way as she learned to fire the pistol, and in no time she was enjoying the new activity. No matter how she tried, she could not outshoot Rodney, but after he went back to work, she had a plan. Each day, she would practice her shooting until she thought she could beat him and strategically challenge him. Her plan also served the purpose of taking her mind off how much she missed having him around on a daily basis. She sat the eight cans back on the fence and counted the number of steps back. She turned and took careful aim. Supporting the pistol with both hands, she drew in a breath and gently squeezed the trigger. There was a muted sound and the first can flew into the air. She almost laughed out loud. It took three more shots to send the second can flying. She hit the next three with one shot each and then a sudden gust of wind blew the last three cans off the fence.

"Oh heck," she said and started walking toward the fence. Clouds had been moving in all morning, and the wind was beginning to pick up. Amanda stepped behind the fence to retrieve the cans. She held the gun down alongside her leg the way Rodney had shown her and bent to pick up the cans. Just as she bent over, another burst of wind was suddenly upon her, this one carrying dirt and grit. The quickness of the wind caught her with her eyes wide open and filled them with sand. She swiftly closed her eyes, but it was too late. She straightened up, gave in to her reflex, and dragged her hand across her eyes. If she had let her tear ducts do their job, she would have been all right, but her hand had only made things worse. She found herself almost blinded by the combination of tear flow and abrasion. Holding the BB gun in one hand and feeling her way with the other, she started to work her way back to the cabin.

* * *

The feeling of dread and purpose had eased somewhat as Mama drove toward the cabin. Her internal dialogue told her she was probably overreacting. Mama was always one to believe in her intuition, but the drive over was diminishing the panic she felt. She had calmed down considerably as she applied the brakes to turn into the driveway of the cabin. She could see Amanda standing beside the cabin. Something was wrong. Mama's senses piqued as she saw Amanda stumble. She brought the car to a stop and cut off the engine. It was when she opened the door and stepped out of the car that she saw the gun. She knew she had been right. What a fool she had almost been to second-guess herself. She had always thought of herself as psychic, and now her suspicions were confirmed. There may even be a hotline in her future: 1-900-CALL-MAMA.

Amanda turned toward Mama and blinked her eyes wildly. Tears ran freely down her cheeks. She waved her left hand frantically and stumbled forward while holding the large pistol in her right hand down by her side. Mama could clearly see that Amanda was distraught. Her face was soaked with tears as she wandered aimlessly in despair. Amanda's foot bumped solidly into a limb that had fallen from the old oak tree beside the cabin. Her weight shifted as she pitched forward. She had to bring both hands up to maintain balance.

Mama saw the gun being raised to Amanda's head and knew what she had to do. With no thought for her own safety or consideration for her health, Mama broke into a run. She quickly closed the gap between them. Now, she was only a few feet from Amanda, but the gun was still in an upward trajectory. Mama launched herself with a vision of Kate Jackson as one of "Charlie's Angels" playing in her mind. Mama hit Amanda squarely in the chest. And they both tumbled to the ground, knocking the breath out of Amanda.

She started to gasp, trying to get some air into her lungs. Amanda's body cushioned Mama's fall, so she took the gulps for air as further proof of Amanda's despair. She quickly regained control and moved up, straddling Amanda's body. She reached for the weapon and twisted it out of Amanda's hand. Gaining control of the gun, she threw it as far as she could.

"It's all right, honey," Mama said as she collapsed onto Amanda. "Mama's here. You don't have to worry. Nothing can be bad enough for this."

Amanda Cotton was not fully aware of what was going on. She was certain of two facts. First, she had been attacked and bowled over, and, second, somehow in the melee, her eyes had cleared up. She was faced with the sight of Edna Wilson perched squarely upon her stomach. Amanda was bright, pretty, and witty with a firm grasp of reality. However, she had never faced a frontal attack by a middle-aged, overweight woman whom she considered a friend. She felt both dazed and confused.

"Oh, Honey, I'm sorry. I didn't want you to hurt yourself."

"I couldn't see a thing. The wind blew dirt all over my face. I was trying to get inside to wash my eyes. Where's my BB gun?"

No one could accuse Mama of being the most nimble-minded person in Cedar Creek, but she had already accumulated enough facts for doubt to start gnawing at the back of her brain. In all her time of watching TV docudramas, movies, and tabloid news shows, none had ever featured a suicide where the intended suicide victim wanted to remove a mote from their eye only to replace it with a bullet. Also, probably nowhere in recorded history had anyone ever taken their own life with a Daisy BB pistol.

Mama dislodged herself and slowly stood. She offered her hand to Amanda. They brushed themselves off. Amanda found the BB gun and wiped it clean on the legs of her jeans. She fired two pellets to be sure it worked. Mama stood by with a great emptiness in her stomach.

"It seems to be working fine," said Amanda as she stared down the barrel of the gun. "Rodney just bought this for me. I was practicing."

"Let's go inside and clean up," Mama said, assessing the damage to both her and Amanda. "I think I have some explaining to do."

They walked to the cabin. Yes, she would have to explain, Mama thought. *That damn Rot-ney has set me up again.*

Chapter Twenty-seven

Rodney spent the first two days filling out paperwork and getting settled into the new job. Rodney studied the blueprints and until he had a full understanding of how this bridge was to be built. For the most part, all bridges followed the same path to completion. There were subtle differences due to soil conditions, the amount and nature of the traffic, and laws and ordinances put in place by wise-intentioned local and state legislators. Rodney also spent those two days becoming reacquainted with Miles O'Conner and Homer (Gus) Grady. They had worked on several projects together before Rodney decided to take his skills to a warmer climate. They caught up quickly and traded war stories and talked of old times.

Gus pointed out "Slugger" to Rodney on the first day.

"He's going to be your helper when you hit the slab. Slugger doesn't have a lot of experience, but he's a good boy. I think he may have had some trouble before he got here. He doesn't have a lot to say about his past, but what the hell? James says he's a fast learner and will do anything you ask him to do."

Rodney didn't care much about a man's past. In his years on the bridge crew, he had seen a few come in, work like hell, and sooner or later not show up or get led off the bridge in handcuffs by one law enforcement agency or another. Hell, he didn't care to discuss every activity he had ever been involved in either. Vietnam and bridge work had taught him to call a guy whatever name he wanted to be called, not ask too many questions, and take the relationship for exactly what it was. If you were lucky enough to get a helper that truly wanted to work and learn, then you were already ahead of the game. Rodney would have no trouble honoring Slugger's privacy. Jungle logic. Besides, there wasn't a much better endorsement for any man than to have Miles O'Conner, Gus Grady, and James Washington on his side. Rodney watched Slugger from the trailer window whenever he got the opportunity. He liked the way he moved. Tomorrow, they would become a team. Everything seemed set to go right.

* * *

Daddy was waiting for me after school. He worked until 2:30 p.m. each day. By the time he got to his truck and drove to school, he had just enough time to light a cigar before the bell rang. On the days I took driver's ed, he had to wait a little longer. If he minded, he never let it show.

I came through the large oak doors just in time to see a cloud of steel-blue smoke rise from the driver's seat of the F-150. I was a teenager and we were supposed to rebel against anything our parents held dear, but for the life of me I couldn't do it. I loved the fact that Daddy picked me up every day and that we had some time alone. We might make the whole trip without a word, but the space was available if we needed it. I loved the way Daddy looked as he drove his truck with one hand on the wheel and the other arm propped on or stuck out the window, depending on weather conditions. Above all, I loved the smell of his cigars. The pungent aroma still smells like home after all these years.

We used the time on the ride home that day to discuss the pros and cons of a fellow such as myself trying to become a member of the high school wrestling team. Daddy was in favor of doing what I thought would be best. He confessed he knew little about the sport as it pertained to the high school and college variety.

We had watched Championship Wrestling on TV. Although we thought it was fake and even talked about it being fake, we each had our favorites. We squirmed in our seats and convulsed our bodies right along with the participants of the match, physically taking some of the impact of the blows upon ourselves to help our heroes persevere. We would even yell at the TV, trying in vain to get the attention of the inept referee. He always seemed to have his attention glued to some unseen event on the opposite side of the ring while our hero was being double-teamed or beaten with a foreign object the dastardly villain had concealed in his trunks.

Daddy said he didn't think high school wrestling was anything like the stuff on TV, but we might have trouble convincing Mama of that. He told me he trusted me to make the right decision and that if I wanted to go out for the team, he would handle Mama.

When we pulled into the driveway, Jason was standing on the porch. As the truck slowed, he came running to meet us. He climbed on the running board on my side and whispered into the cab, "Mama's wearing pants. Had 'em on when she picked me up."

This may not sound much like a revelation to the uninformed, but to us it was a bombshell. Mama was the type of woman who believed a proper Southern lady would never go out in public in such informal attire. Pants were for doing yard work or particularly unsavory chores around the house. When it was time to leave the house, one would change into a proper dress or at the very least a skirt and blouse or sweater. Mama was a holdover from another time, a victim of too many vintage films and novels of a bygone era. Everyone else's mother wore slacks all the time, but that didn't matter to Edna Wilson. To hear that Mama had picked up Jason from school in slacks was quite shocking.

"Um?" said Daddy.

"Um?" I said.

"Um?" said Jason.

It was Sunday before we saw Mama in a dress again. The cuts and bruises were mostly healed by then, but the practiced eye could still pick them up. Maybe nobody else noticed, but after seeing Mama in slacks for five straight days, our eyes were drawn to her legs like a tongue would be drawn to the space vacated by a newly pulled tooth. I'm sure Daddy knew the truth behind those bruises, but nobody offered to share that with either Jason or me, and we knew enough about self-preservation not to ask.

Chapter Twenty-eight

Mary Alice moved about the rooms she and Craig had occupied since arriving in Asheville. As she cleaned, she thought about their new home. The move was only two weeks away. Every time she let her mind drift, she became excited. She couldn't wait for them to have a place of their own. *Privacy at last.* She thought back to the episode in the Super Beetle and laughed. Things had seemed so uncertain then, and it appeared that Victoria was doing everything she could to make it worse. Now everything was working out. Even Victoria was acting like a different person.

At first, Victoria stayed home all the time and never missed an opportunity to goad her or Craig. Victoria had let them move into her home because she didn't feel she had much choice. Their shared blood had been Mary Alice's only ticket into Victoria's home, and Victoria never missed a chance to reconfirm that fact. If there had been any alternative during those first weeks, they wouldn't have chosen to live with Victoria, but there was none. Mary Alice knew it must be worse on Craig, but he never complained. They had both settled into their life, just waiting their turn. Now, it had come.

Mary Alice moved from her room into the kitchen. She had made a habit of cleaning the entire house to get and stay on Victoria's good side. The kitchen showed no signs of use. For the past few weeks, the house had been unquestionably easier to clean. Victoria rarely ate at home anymore, and even her laundry had been much lighter. In fact, Mary Alice wondered how her sister could function on so few clothes. Then, it dawned on her that Victoria was spending less and less time at home. Recently, it seemed she and Craig were alone a good many nights and had the run of the house.

Now that Victoria was on her mind, Mary Alice realized the sharp remarks had all but ceased, and Victoria acted much happier than when they arrived. What had caused the metamorphosis? Mary Alice was mesmerized by her thoughts. What had happened in Victoria's life that would bring about such a shift in her attitude? Such changes were usually brought about by a defining moment. Most often, those were of a religious or amorous nature. Stunned by this revelation, Mary Alice took a seat on the couch and began to analyze the possibilities. Victoria had not shaved her head and started passing out literature at the Asheville airport, nor had she started preparing to relocate to the jungles of some third-world country where she might take part in some suicide pact or alien space excursion. Mary Alice ruled out the cult factor. She had not noticed an influx of holy books. There were no copies of the Koran, the Talmud, the Bhagavad Gita, and no dog-eared copies of *The Watchtower* lying around, the reading of which might inspire a nagging sister to become a compassionate convert. The only holy book she had seen was the family Bible that Victoria displayed on the coffee table, and she had just wiped dust from it yesterday. Religion was out.

Love, yes, only love, could account for Victoria's behavior. Even the tartest lemon can be made into nectar when it meets sugar water. The instinctive nature of amore would indicate the involvement of two people. That opened a whole new line of thought. Who? Who could be the mystery man in Victoria's life?

Mary Alice hadn't realized how deep in thought she was. The phone rang twice before it interrupted her concentration. She jumped and ran to answer it.

"Hello," she said into the receiver, surprised at how out of breath she was.

"Hi, Mary Alice. It's me, Vickie."

Mary Alice was taken by surprise. She didn't know whom she expected to hear on the phone, but the fact that it was Victoria certainly took her aback. It momentarily escaped her that her sister had referred to herself as Vickie.

"Victoria, how are you?"

"Great. Listen. I'm going to be spending the night at Jillian's tonight, so you and Craig have fun."

"Yeah, okay, thanks," Mary Alice stammered into the phone, trying to regain her composure.

"Look, why don't we meet tomorrow for an early lunch, just you and me? We'll get a bite to eat and then go shopping for your new house. Spend the day together—on me. Do the sister thing."

"Okay."

"Great! See you at Antonio's around elevenish. Got to go. Bye."

The phone went dead in her hand. She was unaware of the dial tone, and it was only the incessant beeping that brought her back to the present. She tried to process all the information she had just been given. Suddenly, her sister was going by the name Vickie, spending the night with a woman she had known in college, wanting to spend time with her younger sister, implying she would finance the outing, and suggesting they shop for her new house. Do "the sister thing." Damn! They had never done "the sister thing." Then it hit her like a ton of bricks.

"Victoria and Jillian, oh my God!"

* * *

Troy reached in and gave the idle screw a quarter turn. The engine smoothed to a low guttural growl. He reached for the throttle and gave it a twist. The distinctive roar of a Harley-Davidson V-Twin filled the shop. He couldn't help but smile. Across the room,

Alphie was detailing his own bike. He looked up and nodded his head in appreciation. Troy knew he was an asset to the shop. Alphie had stepped back and let him take over most repairs, calling him more of a maestro than a mechanic. They had settled into a groove, and that concerned Troy.

Troy liked to think of himself as an outlaw, even if he was the small-town variety. His life in Cedar Creek had been one of riding a lot, working a little, and having Mary Alice around when he needed her. Not exactly an enlightened existence. When she left, he felt he must pursue her, punish her in some way, and save face. Now, Troy couldn't remember why he had wanted to chase her, how he had planned to punish her, or even why saving face was so important. He was not a violent person and would never hit a female in any case. Since coming to Asheville, so much has changed.

A wrench landing at his feet pulled Troy from his thoughts.

"Hey, bro, what's on your mind? You look like you're a thousand miles away," said Alphie as he wiped his hands on a shop towel.

"I don't know. I was thinking about Cedar Creek and the guys back there. With me in Asheville, I wonder how they're doing," Troy lied.

Alphie had to think for a minute. When Troy first showed up, Alphie had seen him as an intrusion on his life. The only reason he had let Troy stay was out of a feeling of brotherhood from one biker to another. But Troy had proven to be a godsend around the shop and was turning into a good friend. Alphie was getting used to not having to do much work, so he sure didn't want Troy leaving now. He felt Troy was probably tired of living in the shop, but he only had a one-bedroom apartment himself. Alphie chose his words carefully.

"Yeah, I know what you mean. It's tough being away from your bros, but it's been good having you around here. You sure helped me out of a bind. How about that old girlfriend of yours?"

"Oh, her. Tell you the truth, I hadn't thought about her too much lately. I guess I'm still wondering why I'm sticking around."

"Shit, man, you know why you're still around. I'll tell you in one word: Vickie."

They both laughed. Alphie felt a little relief when he saw Troy nod his head in agreement.

"I guess you're right. I really like her, but it just feels strange."

"She likes you too, bro. Jill keeps me updated. Hell, if you hadn't come to town, I'd never have met Jill, and you wouldn't have met Vickie. I'd say you were good luck for both of us, even if it did take a rocky start."

They both laughed again at the mention of Troy's drunken night.

"All joking aside," said Troy with a serious look on his face, "I'm having a great time, but I need to do something. I don't want to keep taking advantage of your hospitality. I need to either get back home or find somewhere to live. I want to spend more time with Vickie, but I can't ask her to come back to the shop with me. No offense, 'cause I really appreciate you letting me crash here."

"None taken. Look, I wish you would stay here. I appreciate you helping me out with the work, but the truth is I've been thinking about it lately. I could use a full-time mechanic, and I can't think of anyone better than you. Why don't I put you on a full-time salary, and then you can afford to get an apartment? Hell, I've been thinking about getting a bigger place myself. If you want, we could get a place together, maybe even over where Jill and Vickie live. Wouldn't that be great? All of us living right there together."

"Cool, man. I'll mention it to Vickie tonight. Maybe we could go look the place over tomorrow."

Troy felt much better. If things went right, he would go back to Cedar Creek, pick up the rest of his things, and let the guys know he was moving to Asheville to be with a righteous biker woman. That should reinstate their respect for him. To hell with Mary Alice and her Bible thumper. That was another life. Before long, he and Vickie would be neighbors. Then it would be "Damn the torpedoes, full speed ahead."

Chapter Twenty-nine

"**S**hit, shit, shit, shit, shit."

Victoria paced back and forth across the living room of Jillian's apartment. It was 12:30 a.m., and Jillian was wide awake—almost. The slamming door had shaken her from a sound sleep. By the time she got from the bedroom to the living room, Victoria had already gotten to the refrigerator, extracted a cold Coors, tore the tab cleanly from the top, and downed two-thirds of it. Now, she just paced incessantly, muttering the single syllable word.

"Vickie, what the hell's wrong? I've never seen you like this. Did Troy do something? Slow down and tell me what happened," Jillian pleaded, not really knowing what to do.

"The whole thing is going to hell in a handbasket," said Victoria without ever missing a step. She downed the rest of the beer and strode to the refrigerator for another. Savagely tearing the tab from the beer, she tilted her head back and let the liquid flow, her throat working at a pace that defied reason.

"Please, Vickie! For God's sake, tell me what happened before you get too drunk to talk."

"I wish I were drunk! I wish I could pass out. Hell, I wish I could disappear. I had a bad feeling about this all along, but would I listen to myself? No-o-o-o-o-o. What the hell am I doing?"

"What the hell are you doing?" Jillian demanded. She considered herself to be a compassionate, caring, and understanding woman, but now she was starting to get a little pissed off. She had been sleeping in her own bed in her own apartment when she was ripped from a nice dream by an out of control, ex-roommate, who seemed hell-bent on guzzling all her beer and wearing a rut into her practically new shag carpet.

Victoria finished her second beer and headed for the refrigerator for a third. Before she could reach the door, Jillian launched herself toward the kitchen and got between Victoria and the icebox.

"You can have another beer—as many as you like. I'll have one too. Hell, we'll drink until we're all out and then go get some more and drink them too, but first you've got to tell me what's going on."

Victoria looked at Jillian as if she had just come into the room. "I don't know what to do now," Victoria cried and collapsed into Jillian's arms. Tears rolled down her cheeks.

Jillian helped her to the couch. She sat and waited until the waves of tears subsided, and Victoria had a few minutes to compose herself. When Victoria looked up, Jillian held out a tissue for her. Victoria dabbed at her eyes, blew her nose, and proceeded to lay the whole thing out for her.

She told of Troy's plan to stay in Asheville. He said he was going to work for Alphie full time and relocate so they could keep seeing each other.

Jillian could not for the life of her see why this news was so disturbing to Victoria. It was not until Victoria told her that Troy and Alphie planned to become roommates and rent an apartment in Eden's Gate that the source of the despair became apparent.

"Shit, shit, shit, shit, shit," Jillian said. "Okay, okay. This will not be a problem. We can work it out."

"I should have told the truth from the beginning."

"There's no need for anything that drastic," Jillian said, rubbing her forehead. "We'll think of something."

Victoria seemed spent. She went limp on the couch and stared at the opposing wall. Jillian stood, walked to the refrigerator, took out a beer, and drank it. She reached inside, got two more, and returned to the couch.

"Don't die on me now, girl," she said, shaking Victoria and handing her the Coors. "We've got to make this work for us."

Chapter Thirty

The road between Cedar Creek and Asheville was a two-lane winding affair. Like every other road in the state highway system, it had been assigned a number. The people of Cedar Creek just called it Asheville Road. Most people would just follow it mechanically, thinking only of the shopping, entertainment, or work that waited at the end of the fifty-minute drive. Rodney Wilson was not like most people.

Rodney loved the road and always had. When he was younger, there had been countless adventures at its end. In his late teens, he and his friends would pile into their cars and blast down Asheville Road every weekend. The lights looked brighter, the beer seemed colder, the music sounded louder, and the skirts were worn just a little shorter in Asheville. Many of the defining moments of his youth took place there.

After Vietnam, he never felt like he was back in the world and safe until he was on Asheville Road, heading from the airport back to his daddy's farm. Although it had been February and the temperature outside was below twenty degrees, he had rolled the window down on the passenger side of his brother's truck. Seeing the pines, cedars, and majestic oaks along the way had given him a feeling of relief so great that it had loosened his tears. He stuck his head out the window into the wind in an attempt to mask them. It had not worked. When he pulled his head back inside, the tears continued to flow. Not a word was spoken. Sam just looked ahead and silently followed the Asheville Road into Cedar Creek. A glance to his left had shown Rodney that Sam's cheeks were also streaked with tears. "It's good to have you home," was all Sam said during the whole trip.

Now, Rodney once again traveled the Asheville Road. Each morning, he rose, had his time with Amanda, and headed out for Asheville before sunrise. By 7:30 a.m., the road was cluttered with the white-collar crowd that chose sleepy little communities like Cedar Creek in which to raise their children but opted to drive to Asheville each day for better jobs and wages than were available in smaller towns. By leaving before daylight, Rodney missed all the congestion. It was between seasons, so the traffic was sparse. A few weeks earlier, he would have had to dodge tractors as the farmers navigated toward their fields for the day's work, but now the crops were in, and the farmers prepared for their next big activity: deer hunting. Soon, Asheville Road would be lined with pickup trucks, and Rodney would have to watch for deerhounds and overzealous hunters, either of which might run out from between two trucks and into his path without looking.

Rodney smiled as he thought of the farmers turned deer hunters. Invariably, these were some of the hardest-working men on the planet. They started each year with the odds against them. Each year, drought, flood, infestation, or legislation could lay low their labors, but they fought and persevered. At the end of the season, they would sell their crops, pay off their accumulated debts, and set about putting some fresh venison on the table and in the freezer. From October through the first week in January, they would drive their $50,000 trucks to the woods, where they let loose their pack of eight to ten $400 hounds, take out their $1,000 rifles or shotguns, and wait for the dogs to run a buck into range. At the end of the day, they would gather at a common location (usually a store that sold beer and soft drinks) and talk about how much money they had lost on their last crop.

Rodney looked out the window and chuckled. Life was sure a hoot. The laugh brought thoughts of last night to mind. When he arrived at the cabin, a bruised Amanda Cotton was waiting. The story she told was so crazy he would not have believed it if it had not involved his sister-in-law. With her, anything was possible. He shook his head as he recalled some of Edna's exploits. She was a handful, but she was a good woman. Sam was a rock, never ruffled by anything that happened. Rodney envied Sam and secretly hoped that one day he would find something like his brother's contentment.

His thoughts accompanied him most of the way to Asheville. He loved the solitude of his morning rides, he loved the breeze, and he loved the road.

The lighted sign for Jackie's Grill came into view just over the horizon. Like he did each morning, Rodney would stop and have a plate of eggs, grits, and bacon with biscuits, jelly, and coffee. Then, he would drive the last two miles to the bridge site and work like hell for eight hours. Today, he and Slugger would work together for the first time. He wondered what the day would bring as he strolled into Jackie's and took a seat at the counter.

* * *

Mary Alice dropped Craig off at the job site gate. He had been both excited and apprehensive at the thought of his first day as a carpenter's helper assigned to work with what must be a local legend, Rodney Wilson. As she turned around and headed to the street, she saw the black Ford pickup pulling in. By bringing Craig to work every day, she had come to recognize all the vehicles that belonged on the lot. She could almost take roll each morning by the cars and trucks parked there. She had seen the black truck for the first time on Monday and took for granted that it belonged to Rodney Wilson. Usually, it was parked and empty by the time she and Craig arrived. Her curiosity got the better of her. She slowed as she saw the truck door open. The man who got out was of medium height and build. His most striking feature was his salt and pepper ponytail. He reached into the bed of the truck and lifted out a tool belt much like the one Craig had bought a few weeks ago, only more worn and weathered. He walked toward the gate. As Mary Alice released the clutch and edged forward, their eyes met. He reached up and tipped the brim of the gray hardhat he was wearing. It was the briefest of encounters, but she would think of it for days to come. He was handsome, but she felt no physical attraction to him.

It was an eerie feeling. She felt, no, she *knew they had something in common.*

* * *

The sleep she had managed to get had been fitful. Victoria and Jillian had "brainstormed" until 3:00 a.m. They never came up with a solution, but they devised a plan to buy them some time. Now, Victoria was trying to get ready to meet her sister for lunch. She was sluggish and wished she had not made the plans, but what the hell? This would be the ideal way for Victoria to handle one problem with the plan. She had two weeks before Mary Alice and Craig moved into their new house, two weeks to either come up with a true solution to her problem or figure out another lie that would be big enough and good enough to cover the first.

She looked in the closet for something to wear. She was faced with a couple of her older outfits, the type the old Victoria would wear. She pulled first one, then the other, from the closet, looked at them, and put them back. She was so much into her new life that the clothes from her old one were a drag and really brought her down. As she pulled a lavender two-piece from the closet, the rack hung on a pair of faded jeans causing them to fall to the floor. She bent over to pick them up. The denim felt good to her. Even with her brain fogged from lack of sleep, she remembered how she looked in them and the reaction she got from Troy as he looked her up and down. Other guys were more aware of her too.

"What the hell?" she said aloud to her reflection in the mirror. "Maybe it's time Mary Alice met Vickie!" She tossed the suit back into the closet without replacing it on the rack and lay down on the bed to pull on the jeans.

* * *

Mary Alice chose a blue print dress with a flowing skirt that struck just below her knees. She would rather dress in a more casual manner, especially if she and Victoria were going to do any shopping, but she would not chance the ire of her sister. She reminded herself that Victoria was a throwback to a time when people dressed to eat and would never be seen in public looking "sloppy." After all, Victoria was paying.

The traffic around downtown Asheville had been terrible, and then she had trouble finding a parking space, so by the time Mary Alice got to Antonio's, it was 11:20 a.m., and she was late. Things were not starting out well. Victoria would surely blast her for not being punctual. There would be no excuse. Mary Alice braced herself for the worst and entered the restaurant.

The transition from a sunny sidewalk to a dimly lit restaurant caused Mary Alice a moment of blindness. When her eyes adjusted to the difference, she found she still could not trust her eyes. Standing at one of the window tables was Victoria, waving and smiling. This would not seem like a strange happening to the uninformed. In past times, Victoria would have remained seated and let Mary Alice either search her out, only making her presence known by clearing her throat at a strategic time or leaving word with the maître d' to escort her guest to the table upon arrival.

"Little Bit, over here," Victoria said while waving her hand.

Now, Mary Alice was thoroughly confused. She had not been called "Little Bit" since her mother had passed away (God rest her soul), and the last time Victoria called her that was before leaving for college. Once away from rural North Carolina, Victoria had become much too sophisticated to address anyone by a nickname.

Mary Alice made her way to the table, trying to sort out the sensory overload. The person at the table looked like Victoria if her sister had entered modern times like everyone else. She wore jeans that accented her figure, which Mary Alice had to admit wasn't half bad. Her shirt (you really couldn't call it a blouse) was a western affair with accented pockets and pearl overlay buttons. Her boots were also western style and slightly scuffed. She had pulled her hair back into a French braid. Her makeup was tastefully done but heavier than Mary Alice had ever seen on her sister.

Victoria leaned over, kissed Mary Alice on the cheek, and said, "Sit down, honey. I was beginning to think I told you either the wrong time or the wrong restaurant."

Mary Alice was once again stunned that Victoria was kissing off the fact she was late or even taking the blame upon herself. She was flabbergasted when the server appeared, and Victoria ordered a beer.

"Victoria, I …"

"Mary Alice, I've found in the last month that I've been a prude and a bore most of my life. I'm trying to change. Call me Vickie."

"Okay, *Vickie*, but you've got to give me a chance to get used to all this."

"I know it's got to be a shock to you, but let me assure you, I'm not crazy. I just suddenly feel alive. The first thing I want to do is apologize for the way I've treated you and Craig. I understand now how you feel."

There it was. Victoria had all but admitted that she was in love. Mary Alice didn't know how to feel. On one hand, she was happy for her sister. She deserved to be happy too. On the other hand, Mary Alice wished it had been someone other than Jillian. In her heart, she knew it shouldn't make a difference, but it was going to take some getting used to. She didn't know how much Victoria was willing to talk about, so Mary Alice decided to follow along, not pushing the issue. If Victoria wanted to talk about it, fine. If not, she would respect her privacy.

"Vickie, we appreciate you letting us stay with you. I know it has been an imposition."

"That's what I wanted you to think, but that was just my selfishness and probably a little jealousy too. If it weren't for you, I probably wouldn't be where I am today."

Victoria didn't know just how true those words were.

The waiter returned with their drinks and took their order. Victoria, who usually was a salad and half-a-sandwich person, ordered a prime-rib hoagie with fries and another beer. Mary Alice ordered a club sandwich. Victoria lifted her glass and drained half of the beer when the server left the table. Mary Alice had to stifle a laugh as she watched her sister acting so out of character. The conversation changed to general subjects. They laughed and joked and even poked fun at some of the more starched patrons of Antonio's. Mary Alice found herself genuinely having fun. For the first time in years, they were acting like friends. When their meals came, they both ate silently, savoring the food. Even the silence felt good. It had been a long time since they had been together and not felt like they had to force conversation. Victoria finished first, ordered another beer, and pushed her chair slightly away from the table.

"Some wonderful things have happened to me, Little Bit," she said, leaning back to the table and speaking in a soft voice. "I don't really want to go into a lot of details right now. We'll talk more about it later. I hope you understand. I've got a favor to ask of you."

"Sure, I understand, Vickie. I'll do what I can," Mary Alice replied, thinking, here comes the catch.

"I'm going to be moving in with Jill for a while. I know your house will be ready in two weeks, so what I want you to do is stay in my house just like you've been doing. The favor is to not tell anyone about this. If anyone should call, take a message. Tell them I'm on vacation. Take care of the house and truly make yourself at home."

"Sure, we'll do that. What's going to happen when we move?"

"I'll have some things worked out by then. Don't worry. I'll be fine.

A deep feeling of compassion swelled within Mary Alice's heart, and it was all she could do to hold back the tears. What a battle her sister must be waging, wrestling with her sexuality. She had read studies on the subject in *Cosmo* and *Elle*, but now it was happening in her family. She knew from the articles she could best help by being supportive and letting things come out in their own good time. She was, after all, a modern woman.

"Be strong, Vickie," she said and reached for her sister's hand.

Victoria saw the hand coming and thought Mary Alice was reaching for the dessert card. She handed Mary Alice one card and picked the other up for herself. The waiter reappeared as if on cue and took their order for a shortcake and coffee.

She's slipping back into denial, Mary Alice thought as she watched the server come through the kitchen door with their desserts. *Don't push; be supportive,* she reminded herself.

Victoria picked up the tab for lunch, and then they drove to the mall. Neither said anything more about Victoria's *situation.* Victoria bought Mary Alice some towels and bath clothes along with two pairs of jeans and some shirts for herself. When Mary Alice had to visit the restroom, her sister was not outside when she came back out. Mary Alice looked all around and then walked to the main concourse. She saw her sister rushing back toward her from the lower end of the mall.

"I've got to go, sweety," Victoria said as she met Mary Alice. "I'll call you in a few days, and maybe we can get together then. Oh, yeah, here's a little something for tonight." With that, she handed Mary Alice a bag and kissed her on the cheek.

"I had a great time," Victoria said, rushing down the mall.

"Me too! See ya."

She looked into the bag her sister had given her. The words "Victoria's Secret" were printed on the outside. What was inside made her blush and think of Craig. "Craig, oh my God," she said aloud. She looked at her watch and realized she only had thirty minutes to get across town and pick him up from work. She ran for the car.

He would have a good time tonight, and she would keep "Victoria's secret."

Chapter Thirty-one

Love has been likened to many things. In songs, we have been told "Love Is a Rose," "Love Is a Many-Splendored Thing," and even "Love Is a Drug." In *Venus and Adonis,* Shakespeare told us that "Love is a spirit all compact of fire." Love has been called a mystery, a trap, and a disease. I personally think of it as a virus. It is invisible, suspended, lighter than air, and moves about silently. It enters your being undetected, lying dormant, incubating, gaining strength, and then one day, boom! You break out in a sweat, you fluctuate between chills and fever, and you can't think straight. By the time you realize you've been infected, you're too far gone to do anything about it. There is no prevention; there is no cure. In the luckiest of cases, two people are infected simultaneously.

I'm not trying to pass myself off as some expert on the subject of love. I'm anything but. Even though I know something about the subject, most of my knowledge has been secondhand. Like most, I am far better at advising other people concerning their lives than I am at living my own. Even with what I know of the "bug" that is love, I can say without hesitation that I wish I had been bitten more often.

Love manifests itself in many ways. You can see someone every day for many years, and then one day it's like you're looking at a different person. There is no explaining it. It can hit you as you look at them across a desk at work, in the aisle of a supermarket, across the dance floor of a club, or even at church. For me, the first time was in the back seat of a driver's education car.

Three times a week, we got to really drive. Roland Crews, Diane Mullins, and I would join Mr. Alt in the rust-speckled Chevrolet Caprice for a spin around the streets of Cedar Creek. The car must have been specially made for driver's education because neither before nor since have I seen a Chevrolet Caprice with a manual transmission and an extra set of controls on the passenger side. The class consisted of approximately thirty minutes of driving time for each student. All we had to do was listen to Mr. Alt and do exactly as he said.

I was lucky. Daddy had let me drive around the farm, and Uncle Rodney would let me drive his jeep sometimes (even on the street on those rare occasions when Mama and Daddy weren't around). Everything we owned was straight drive, so the transmission of the Caprice was nothing new to me. Diane caught on pretty fast and, after a few days, could control the gears, except when faced with a stressful situation. Roland was another matter. The clutch was nuclear fission, time travel, and astrodynamics all rolled into one to Roland. He would stand a better chance of landing the Concorde on the deck of an aircraft carrier than he would of getting the Caprice rolling without a jump, a lunge, or choking it down altogether.

Mr. Alt would say, "Roland, give it a little gas, release the clutch until you feel the friction point, and then slowly continue to release the clutch and give it the gas."

Roland would say, "Yes, Mr. Alt," and then rev the engine like a drag racer waiting at the lights, pop the clutch, and send us into another wild ride.

"Sorry, Mr. Alt."

Despite his reputation, Mr. Alt never became angry with Roland. He would calmly tell him it was okay and that he thought Roland was very close to getting it. Mr. Alt took it as a special project to teach Roland the intricacies of the manual transmission and the coordination it took to make it work properly. He devised a plan.

Diane would always drive first and take us away from school. Next, I would drive since I had the most experience and could get us along the secondary roads out of town. Then, while in deep country, Roland would take the controls. If things went according to plan, we would encounter no other traffic. If we were lucky, Roland would get the car rolling and keep it on the road. In that case, Mr. Alt would let him continue on a straight path with as few interruptions as possible. The second Roland completed his mandatory time behind the wheel, Mr. Alt would have him pull over and change places. Mr. Alt would drive us back to school while Roland, in the passenger seat, would place his feet on the second set of pedals and try to get the feel of the combination clutch and gas movements. I thought it was great that Mr. Alt would go the extra mile for Roland. I was also ecstatic that I got to spend Roland's driving time and the trip back to school with Diane.

I didn't know if I should thank Mr. Alt, Roland, Cupid, or Mr. Solstein's bull for what happened next. We were out on Smith Level Road, and Roland was struggling as usual. He had finally gotten the Caprice rolling and had worked his way through the gears. We were cruising along at thirty-five miles per hour with no traffic in sight. Mr. Alt was orating on the intricacies of parallel parking and its place in modern society. Diane was taking notes, and I was thinking about my future as a high school wrestler. I was at the point in my fantasy where I had just won the state championship, and all the girls at Cedar Creek High had decided to forget my acne or that acne was really cool when it was on the face of a state champion.

I never saw the bull. Diane later told me she saw it out of the corner of her eye and knew it had no plans to stop. The first thing I knew of the situation was when Roland applied the brakes without depressing the clutch. He twisted the wheel to the right to avoid a collision. The bull was safe, and we were safe, but the Caprice began to buck and jump about. To this day, I believe I saw a look of envy in that bull's eye at the movements of the Caprice.

We were all wearing seat belts, so only our upper bodies were tossed about. Sometime during the melee, either Diane or I had reached for the other's hand (we never could agree on who did what). When Mr. Alt took control of the car and started back to school, we were still holding hands. As we pulled into the parking lot, her hand was still in mine. Only getting out of the car broke our grip. From that day forward, we would slowly work our hands to the middle of the seat and timidly entwine our fingers. Not a word was spoken, no future plans were made, but we knew we were a couple. It took another month for us to discuss the subject, but once it was breached, neither of us could wait to spend time with the other. By Christmas, our love was in full bloom. If I had been a rich man, I would have bought Roland Crews a brand-new Chevrolet Caprice, one with an automatic transmission, of course.

Chapter Thirty-two

For Victoria, waking was a slow, luxurious process. Tiny strands of consciousness would work their way into her brain. She would hold them there, savoring them. This was purely a cerebral exercise, so she would not let her body move from its sleeping posture. As she became more awake, she would stretch, not a full-body stretch all at once but a progressive extension starting with her neck and then moving each body part separately. Once this task was accomplished, she would flip over (she always slept on her stomach), stretch her whole body one last time, open her eyes, and greet the day. Her regimen always tossed the covers from her queen-sized bed, but she didn't care.

She was almost through her movements. Victoria relaxed the tension in her calves and felt her toes drag along the sheets as she pointed her feet toward the end of the bed. Her toes found some resistance where the top sheet was tucked under the mattress. It felt odd, but she thought she must have scooted down in the bed overnight. She gathered herself and shifted her weight to the right. With force, she rolled over and shot both arms into the air. She opened her eyes in time to see a strange light fixture suspended from the ceiling. In her confusion, she failed to realize she momentarily had balanced on the edge of the bed. The act of flinging her arms straight away from her body had somehow delayed the inevitable. She felt the balance evaporate and dropped to the floor.

She hit the carpet solidly. Her eyes scrambled to focus. Instead of her queen-size, four-poster bed, she looked up at a single bed on a frame with neither a headboard nor a footboard. She now remembered where she was. This was not the way she envisioned her first full day at Jillian's beginning.

"Vickie, are you all right?" Jillian asked through the closed door. The noise must have summoned her.

"Yeah, I'm fine. Just got my feet tangled in the covers. Sorry."

"Come on out. I've got something to tell you."

Victoria followed a mental checklist to assure herself everything was in place and still working. Finding everything okay, she struggled to her feet.

"I don't know if this is a good idea or not," she thought as she surveyed the small room that would be her home for the next two weeks. Three walls were bare. There were two frames hung side by side on the other wall. One contained a picture of an eighteen-wheeler in the parking lot of a truck stop in Taos, New Mexico. Jillian and her ex-husband leaned against the front of the truck. They were both dressed in western-style clothing and smiling. In the other frame was a decree of divorce, ending the marriage. When Victoria asked Jillian about the set, Jillian told her she kept them as a reminder of the difference between how things may seem and how they really are. The only furniture in the room was the bed, a dresser with a small mirror, and a table with a slat-backed chair. The closet, hidden behind sliding doors, held her new wardrobe, including the clothes she bought when she and Mary Alice were at the mall. It was livable, but it was small. She was used to living in a twenty-two hundred square foot house furnished exactly to her taste. Even with Mary Alice and Craig there, she had enough room to maintain her privacy and live as she chose. No one would have heard if she had fallen from her own bed even if they had been in the hall. Jillian had heard her fall all the way in the living room.

A feeling of dread and gloom came over Victoria. She sat back on the bed and lowered her face into her hands. How would she make it for two weeks? What was she trying to prove and to whom? Just as the despair enveloped her, she heard a motorcycle from the street and thought of Troy. It would have been better to tell the truth from the beginning, but she was way past that now. *What the hell,* she thought as she pulled on her housecoat. *I'm in it, and I'm glad. Anyway, I've got two weeks to work it out. The world can change in two weeks.*

She opened the door and went into the living room. Jillian sat on the couch, reading the paper. She looked as fresh as a new snow. Victoria didn't know how Jillian could always look like she had just come back from a day spa. Her makeup and hair were perfect, and her outfit was impeccable. Even her boots were polished. Who sits around home with boots on? Victoria wondered.

"I'm glad you're up. I was just about to wake you. The guys are going to come over in two hours. They have something to ask us; well, you really. I'm not sure what it's about, but it seemed important."

"Two hours. Oh my God! Why this morning? Jeez, I'll have to hurry!"

"Go ahead," Jillian said, walking to the kitchen to get them both a cup of coffee. "I'll fix us something to eat while you shower."

There wasn't much time to relax, but ninety minutes and two pieces of toast later, Victoria found herself sitting on the couch, looking and feeling pretty good.

The knock startled both women. They had been listening for the roar of the bikes, which usually preceded the guy's arrival. Troy and Alphie came in and each proceeded to greet and lightly kiss the girls. They seemed nervous and ill at ease. They chose to sit together on the couch, leaving the loveseat to Jillian and Victoria. Now, they were all ill at ease.

"Y'all want something to drink, a beer or a Pepsi?"

"No, thanks," Alphie said. "We can't stay long. We've got to get back to the shop. We need to ask you something, and if you don't want to do it, say no."

Victoria didn't know about Jillian, but all her defenses were on alert and her imagination was working overtime.

Troy spoke. "Vickie, it's really you we have to ask."

All eyes were on Victoria, and it was all she could do not to stand up and run. *It's just my first day out of the house; give me a break,* Victoria thought.

Troy obviously had been the designated talker and was anxious about playing that role. He was wringing his hands and had little beads of sweat across his forehead.

Victoria wondered what kind of diabolical, illegal, immoral, murderous plot she was about to be asked to take part in. She didn't know why, but she thought of dear Lawrence and of the rose bushes in her garden that must surely need pruning.

"You know we want to move to Eden's Gate. The problem is we don't think they would be too crazy about renting to a couple of bike guys. We know we're okay, but most people won't give us a chance to show it. What I'm asking is if you will go with me to the office. We could pose as a couple. I've been thinking of getting a haircut and trimming my beard anyway. With you and your classy looks, I feel like we would be a shoo-in. It would mean a lot to us, to me. Don't answer now. We've got to get back to work. I'll call you later, and we can go out to dinner and talk about it. Okay?"

Victoria didn't know what to think, so she remained silent. The word fraud came to mind, but so did the word prejudice. She knew what Troy was saying was true. This was just the sort of thing she and Jillian had debated in college. Now she was being given the opportunity to help strike a blow for the oppressed. She had to admit the idea appealed to her on an intellectual level, but how about the practicality of the situation? What could happen to her if she did it? Could she and Troy pull it off? How deep into this charade was she willing to go? She smiled and nodded her head.

The guys took that as a positive sign. Troy rose and came over to Victoria. "Thanks," he said as he kissed her. "I'll call you later."

After they left, Jillian got herself and Victoria a beer and sat down across from her.

"Tell me why this won't work," Victoria said after taking a swallow of the Coors.

"Hell, girl, it just might work if you want it too. They don't know you at the office, and you're not officially a resident here. Just don't sign anything."

"No, I won't sign anything. I don't guess it will hurt to help them. I can't believe people would keep them out just because they ride motorcycles. It's almost my civic duty to help. You're either part of the solution or part of the problem, right?"

"Yeah, I guess," said Jillian, thinking how naïve Victoria was. She didn't doubt that Troy and Alphie would do the right thing, but in her travels she had seen some screwed-up stuff left in the wake of bikers. It would be nice to have them around. Why worry Vickie with details? "What are you going to do today?"

"Let's go shopping. I want to pick up a few things for my room, but let's have another beer first so I can think this through."

Jillian started toward the refrigerator, smiling. "Girl, you're hooked. What's there to think about?"

Chapter Thirty-three

Craig took it as a sign. He had thought about it for three days now, debated the pros and cons, and still came away unsure. Now, he was given an opportunity to take the step, and he felt sure it was okay to proceed.

When he was introduced to Rodney Wilson, he liked the man immediately. Rodney had looked him straight in the eye and said, "How ya doing, Slugger?" No laughing at his nickname, which he had come to like, no explanation necessary, no questions, just "How ya doing?" They had gone out to the job site and started to work. When Rodney needed something, he would explain in detail what he wanted and how to accomplish it. Rodney made no challenges to or assumptions about his knowledge (or lack thereof) of carpentry. When he accomplished a task, Rodney would smile, tell him he did well, and ask if he had any questions about what they had done. Consequently, Craig found himself learning a great deal, enjoying his work, and developing a profound respect for Rodney.

They had been together for about an hour when Rodney went for his pouch for the first time. He pulled it out of his rear pocket, reached into the black bag, and pulled out a cluster of tobacco leaves. He rolled the tobacco between his fingers, forming a small ball, and put it into his left cheek. Just as Rodney was rolling the pouch back up, Gus walked up. Rodney handed him the bag, and Gus took some leaves and started chewing them.

"Thanks, Rodney. I don't get to 'chew' as much as I used to. I have to stay in the damn office all day, and it just ain't the same."

Gus stood around for a few minutes, talking and chewing, and then left. Craig knew that many people around the bridge, especially the old-timers, chewed tobacco, but the fact that the two men he admired most both chewed got him thinking. He had never entertained the thought of doing so, but it couldn't be all that bad. He knew there were some health concerns involved, but a little couldn't hurt. Thus began the debate.

He had all but decided to go ahead but didn't know how to go about it. He didn't want to ask Rodney for a "chew." What if he didn't like it, or it made him sick? He couldn't take a chance of looking bad in front of Rodney. Mary Alice brought him to work every day, but he couldn't ask her to stop by the store so he could buy tobacco. She might think he was crazy or fuss at him. He had to find a way to get the tobacco on his own and have time to try it in private so he would be the only one to see any adverse effects. That's why he saw what happened as a sign.

"Hey, Rodney," Gus said as he approached them. "Can I borrow Slugger for a few minutes? We're about out of gas for the generators, and I can't leave the office. Could you spare him long enough for him to take the truck to the station and fill up the cans? He shouldn't be gone over a half hour or so."

"Sure, Gus. How 'bout it, Slugger? Ya wanna go?"

"Yeah, I'll be glad to go," Craig said, thinking this was the chance he had been waiting for. This was surely a sign it was okay to proceed with his experiment.

"Thanks, Slugger. You're the only one I feel I can trust to go and come back on time and sober," Gus said with a laugh.

Craig loaded the gas cans into the old International flatbed and, armed with the company credit card and a burning desire, headed for the store. Upon his arrival at the store, he went directly inside and found the tobacco rack. There were lots of brands to choose from, but he picked out a black pack with the name Manchester on the front, Rodney's brand. After purchasing it, he went outside to fill the cans. While the gas was running into the first can, Craig opened the pouch and stuck his nose into it. The smell was pungent but not unpleasant. He tentatively reached in and secured a few leaves. Rolling them into a small ball like he had watched Rodney do, he placed the tobacco in his mouth. He was ready for whatever happened. He waited.

He felt some numbness along the inside of his cheek and a slight burning sensation on his tongue but nothing other than that. As he slowly began to chew the tobacco, saliva gathered in his mouth. He looked around to be sure nobody was watching him and spit into the trash can. He felt great. He followed the pattern until all the gas cans were filled and then went inside to pay.

"Will that be all, sir?"

"Um," said Craig, not knowing how to talk around the tobacco.

"Forty-three dollars and thirty-five cents, please."

"Um," said Craig handing the clerk the credit card.

"It'll just be a minute, sir," said the clerk as he turned to process the card.

Craig felt saliva building in his mouth. He didn't know what to do. He saw his reflection in the mirror on the wall behind the counter, his cheek bulging. Beads of sweat were forming across the bridge of his nose.

"Sign here, please," said the young lady as she laid the multi-part form on the counter.

Craig's hand was shaking as he picked up the pen and wrote his name.

"Thank you," said the clerk, laying his copy of the sales receipt on the counter. She looked at him strangely.

He looked at the mirror and realized the cause for her concern. Two brown streams of tobacco juice forced their way out of the corners of his mouth and ran down his chin. They were joined there by rivulets of sweat that ran profusely down his face. There were drops of both, precariously hanging from his chin, ready to drop on his shirt. He snatched the sales slip with one hand and clamped the other to the bottom of his face. He began backing through the door. Once outside, he turned and ran to the truck or rather the trash can beside the truck. Once he got there, he bent over the can and opened his mouth, expelling what felt like gallons of tobacco juice. Relieved, he sat down on the running board of the truck. After a few minutes, he reached inside and got a shop rag he had brought with him. He dabbed his face and then wiped his chin.

He probably should have taken the episode inside the store as a sign, but, as with so many of us, he only saw the sign that told him it was all right to do what he wanted to do.

This tobacco chewing can be some serious stuff, he thought as he started the truck and headed back for the job. *It's pretty good, though; I'll just have to be careful.* He drove on, knowing he could truly be one of the guys. By the time he got back to the job site, the discomfort he had faced at the store was already fading from his memory. Little did he know there were still tobacco chewing hurdles to clear.

Chapter Thirty-four

Two days passed without further mishap. Craig was really getting the hang of tobacco chewing. He had hinted to Mary Alice that he had tried it and it wasn't bad. Of course, at first Mary Alice said it was a disgusting habit, but after a little thought she mellowed to the idea.

Mary Alice knew Craig had been through a lot and was just now feeling comfortable about their new life. Things seemed to be going their way, so she wasn't going to let something as small as Craig chewing tobacco put a kink into their life. After all, with what she had been asked to accept with Victoria, chewing tobacco was nothing. At least it was a manly activity.

Rodney, too, noticed Slugger chewing tobacco. He chose to say nothing. He had always believed a person should be able to accept or reject his or her own vices without outside influences, the exception being if a person's vices caused physical or emotional harm to an innocent bystander.

What Slugger lacked in technique he made up for in enthusiasm. He chewed all day. There is nothing more zealous than a new convert. The only time he was without a chew was during lunch.

Rodney and Craig worked on building and setting the forms for the footing of one of the bridge's columns or stems as the crew called them.

There wasn't much for carpenters to do during a pour, but they had to be present in case additional bracing was needed or anything went wrong with the forms. Usually, they would help with the bucket. This left the lead man on the concrete crew free to signal the crane operator. They heard the truck rev its engine and knew the process had begun. Craig put a fresh chew into his mouth.

"Hey, Slugger," Rodney said as they waited. "Be sure to put some tobacco juice in with the concrete. It'll make the bridge stronger and part of you will always be in there."

"Yeah, okay," Craig said with a smile. The idea appealed to him. It was the first time Rodney had acknowledged Craig's new practice. He took it as a form of acceptance.

Everyone stood clear until the concrete foreman signaled the bucket into position. Craig moved quickly and grabbed the handle, taking responsibility for the dumping. He pulled the handle, and the concrete flowed into the form.

This scene replayed itself twice before Craig decided to make his contribution. The level of the concrete had risen to the point the guys inside the form now had to work from the outside. When Craig dumped the fourth bucket, he let go of a stream of tobacco juice that arched and fell into the form. Rodney saw it, and when Craig looked his way, he was grinning from ear to ear. Rodney gave him a thumbs up. He admired the kid's enthusiasm. He knew instinctively that he had a good partner.

As the form filled, they needed to keep the bucket a uniform distance from the concrete already inside the form, which meant the bucket was raised higher off the ground. As a result, the men who handled the bucket had to climb up and balance themselves on the two-by-four forms while handling the bucket. Since most of the form was below ground level anyway, the men only had to steady themselves two and a half feet above ground.

Craig, Rodney, and the concrete foreman climbed onto the form as the bucket was brought into position. Craig grabbed the handle, and Rodney helped position the bucket. The concrete foreman signaled the crane operator. They dumped a portion of the concrete into one corner of the form, and the foreman signaled the crane operator to slowly move the bucket to another corner to finish emptying it. As they walked along the top of the form, Craig decided he would add a little more essence to the concrete. He took a sidestep and let go of the bucket with one hand. Bending slightly at the waist, he took aim. Rodney stepped away from the bucket, anticipating the move to the other end. The concrete foreman was away from the bucket so he could keep eye contact with the crane operator. He signaled the operator to take the bucket to the left. The operator nudged his controls, and the crane edged to the left. The energy was relayed down the cable and the bucket moved with Craig attached to it by one hand.

The motion of the bucket plus the precarious position he was in conspired to make Craig lose his balance. He struggled to regain his footing but found himself losing the battle. He had to let go of the bucket and leap to the ground to keep from falling into the wet concrete. This was not a dangerous move, but when taken suddenly and without time for thought, it had the same effect as a gun backfiring. When his feet hit solid ground, the tobacco juice he intended to add to the concrete was taken down his throat, preceded by the wad of tobacco in its entirety. Craig gathered himself and immediately climbed back onto the form to complete the pour. His throat was filled with a burning sensation, and his eyes began to water, but he was determined to complete his task.

Everyone had seen what happened. They knew Craig had swallowed his tobacco, but nobody said a word.

The bucket was on its way back now. Craig's stomach began to rumble. He felt light-headed and a cold sweat that differed from the perspiration of the work crept over him. Everyone watched;

nobody spoke. When the next bucket stopped, Craig grabbed the handle and made the pour. Once again, he was reaching critical mass. When the pour was complete, he heard his name.

"Hey, Slugger, you okay?"

He could not answer. Holding his hand up in a gesture he hoped would be interpreted as "wait," he then calmly walked away from the form and into the portable toilet nearby.

They could all hear the sounds of agony. Wave after wave came and went. Everyone around the form looked from man to man. Some smiled, some shook their heads, but nobody spoke. Soon, the noises subsided, and the door to the toilet opened. Craig came out, wiping his face with a towel. Everyone quickly shifted their eyes, but they still watched his approach.

Craig walked to the form and looked inside. The concrete finishers were smoothing the surface of the pour. Craig leaned against the form and removed his hard hat. Taking the towel from his back pocket, he wiped the top of his head. He replaced the hat, reached into his other back pocket, and pulled his tobacco pouch from it, making ready for another chew.

The concrete foreman walked over to Rodney and positioned himself where he thought Craig couldn't hear him.

"Damn, Rodney, yo boy got style."

"He's tough, all right."

Craig had heard the exchange. It counteracted his sickness. He was determined not to wimp out in front of Rodney. He felt a hand on his shoulder.

"Let's get going, Slugger. We've got to get another one ready to pour."

Craig pulled himself up and walked with Rodney away from the form, fighting the nausea but feeling on top of the world.

Chapter Thirty-five

Victoria's day was passing without incident. She had settled into the routine and honestly enjoyed Jillian as a roommate. In the years since Lawrence's death, she had always lived alone. As time softened the loss of her husband, it also dulled her memories of how nice it was to have someone around to talk with. Simple interactions with another human being had given her life a fullness she had not known for quite a few years. She felt a small sadness that she had not allowed herself to interact more with Mary Alice in the time they had shared her house. She had been too stubborn and self-absorbed to allow herself even to be civilized to the young couple, even though it was obvious they were in need. She vowed to make it up to them.

She had bought some things to personalize her room and had become comfortable in the small space.

She was concerned at first about Troy and Alphie's request that she take part in the charade to help them get an apartment, but after some thought and further discussion with Jillian, could see no real harm in it. She notified Troy of her willingness, which made him happy. He said he would come by, take her to lunch, and they would plan the ruse.

She was now dressed and waiting for his arrival. Once again, no roar of the motorcycle engine warned her of his arrival—just a knock on the door. Victoria walked to the window and peeped through the crack in the drapes. Standing at the door was a man in a blue pinstriped suit. She could not see his face or the front half of his body. The drapes and her angle of view had him sliced in half vertically. She almost ignored the knock, figuring it was a salesman canvassing the apartment. Then she remembered the "no soliciting" sign posted prominently by the front entrance. Besides, Troy would be along any minute, and when she opened the door for Troy, the salesman would know she was dodging him. She put on her most stern expression and opened the door, intent on dissuading any sales approach posthaste.

Troy stood in the door, clean-shaven, neatly trimmed hair, and dressed like a Wall Street trader.

"Well, what do you think?" he asked, holding his arms out to the side and turning in a slow circle.

The transformation took her aback. She had never noticed how close in size and shape Troy was to Lawrence. She knew that was where the similarity ended, but still it was there. She wondered if somehow that was what had drawn her to Troy. For a second, she was being the old Victoria, trying to analyze everything. Just then, she saw her own reflection in the mirror beside the door and dispensed with the analysis. *What the hell. She thought, I don't care what caused it. I'm just glad it happened.*

"You look very handsome," she said, meaning it. "You'd better come inside before all the girls in the place come after you."

She thought she saw him blush but was unsure because his cheeks looked pink and tender from having shaved his beard. She had considered Troy ruggedly handsome since she met him. Now he seemed attractive in a more refined way but with an edge of roughness running just below the surface. She found this very sexy.

"Thanks again for agreeing to help us with the apartment. You're a lifesaver."

"I don't think you'd have any trouble anyway, especially looking like you do today."

"Thanks, but this ain't the real me, and I'm afraid it would show, but I know everything will be okay with you there."

It was Victoria's turn to blush. "I think I should change into something that looks a little nicer if I'm going to lunch with you."

"That's not necessary. In fact, I've got my jeans in the truck and can change."

"No, sir. I want to go with you just like you are. I'll only be a minute."

She slipped into her room and changed into the only dress she had at the apartment. She would have to go to her house later and get something different to wear to the apartment manager's office tomorrow. She changed her hair, adjusted her makeup, and went back into the living room.

"Damn, you look good," Troy said after letting go with a wolf whistle. "We look like a couple of citizens out to paint the town."

"Let's go eat," Victoria said, riding on a wave of elation. No one had whistled at her in a long time, and she could tell by the look in his eyes Troy meant it.

Troy stood and offered his arm. She took it and they walked through the door and down the steps to his pickup truck. The thought struck Victoria that they must look like a couple of high school kids on their way to the prom.

They drove downtown and decided to eat at Vincent's Tap Room, a local surf and turf restaurant with good lunch specials. It was not the kind of place they would normally go for lunch, but Troy seemed hell-bent on trying his new persona.

After being seated, Victoria excused herself and started to the ladies' room. She had to cross the lobby to reach the facilities. As she stepped into the lobby, she heard her name being called. She looked toward the voice and saw Helen Conklin walking toward her. She glanced back at Troy and saw that his back was to them. She stepped out of the doorway and his line of sight. Helen was a member of the same garden club as Victoria and a widow as well. Helen hugged Victoria the way socialites hug each other.

"I thought that was you when you came through the door. I almost came over to your table, but I wasn't sure enough in this light. We've missed you at the meetings, but now I understand," Helen said and gave a naughty wink. "Who's that handsome hunk you're with? I thought I knew all the eligible bachelors around here, but I don't recall him."

"He's a very dear friend of mine from out of town," said Victoria, not wanting to divulge too much information.

"Why don't you introduce me to this old friend?"

"No!" Victoria replied a little sharper than she intended. "He's recently gone through some changes, and I don't want to put too much on him. This is the first time I've been able to get him out like this."

"Oh," said Helen, buying the half-truths. "I'm sorry. Maybe I can meet him later after he's had some time." Like most people, Helen saw the lives of others as a reflection of their own, so it was natural to project the tragedies of her life onto those she came in contact with. "Will we see you at the meeting next week?"

"I don't think so. I may be out of town."

"I see-e-e-e," said Helen slyly. "I don't think you're telling the whole story, but that's okay. We'll talk later. Bye-bye."

Victoria stepped back so she could see Troy and still watch Helen go through the door and across the street. She felt agitated at having run into Helen but relieved she was able to contain the situation. If Helen had come to their table, her cover would have been blown. It was at that moment that Victoria realized how much Troy and their relationship meant to her. What had started as a lark had taken on new meaning, but it took a near miss to make her see it clearly. She would find a way to tell him about herself. She knew they could not survive with her lying about who she was.

Yes, she would straighten everything out, but first she had to help him with the apartment.

When she came out of the restroom, Troy was turned in his seat, looking for her. She smiled and waved. She had been away from the table for several minutes and he looked concerned. She walked back into the dining room determined to enjoy the food and the company of a good man and to formulate a plan to get Troy the apartment he wanted.

* * *

Mary Alice was just finishing their laundry when the doorbell rang. She knew she looked a sight. Walking to the door, she pulled the old apron off and attempted to get her hair out of her face. She saw her reflection as she passed the mirror in the hall and sighed in resignation. She opened the door and found Victoria standing on the other side.

"Hey, Little Bit."

"Victoria, I mean Vickie, did you forget your keys?"

"No, I've got them right here. I didn't want to barge in on you."

"Vickie, this is your house."

"Not for the next two weeks. I told you to take it over, and I meant it."

Mary Alice didn't know what to say. Could this really be her older sister? She had to be completely turned around, or this was the worst case of alien impersonation she had ever heard of.

"I just needed to run by and pick up some clothes for an important meeting tomorrow. Come on upstairs with me. I've got something to talk with you about."

Throughout lunch, Victoria had thought of her relationship with Mary Alice. She remained attentive to Troy, but her sister kept popping into her mind. During the drive over, she thought of ways she could make up for how she acted when Mary Alice and Craig moved in. The idea that came to her also presented a good way to finally tell Troy the truth about her life.

"Honey, I want to tell you how bad I feel about the way things were when you first moved in with me."

"Think no more about it. Everything's okay now, and that's all that matters."

"Okay, but I've got a great idea. You and Craig are going to be moving into a place of your own in a little over a week, but right now you don't have much to move. What I want to do is throw you a moving party. We can invite anyone and everyone to come and bring you a present. Doesn't that sound great?"

"But we don't know that many people."

"You let me worry about that. We can have it right here. I'll take care of everything. All you have to say is okay. I think it will be wonderful."

Mary Alice could see that Victoria was really excited about her idea. She would have to talk it over with Craig, but she didn't see any reason not to do it. Besides, they might meet some new people. Maybe she could get Craig to invite some people from work. The more she thought about it, the better the idea seemed.

"If it's okay with Craig, then it's great with me. Thanks, Vickie," she said and reached over to hug her sister.

When they broke their embrace, Mary Alice saw there were tears in Victoria's eyes, although she was smiling widely. Victoria went quickly to her closet and picked out a cream-colored suit. She next chose shoes and accessories to complete the outfit. She put everything into a suitcase she retrieved from a utility closet. Mary Alice watched as her sister picked up the case and headed for the steps.

"Besides," said Victoria as she reached the bottom of the stairs and opened the door, "I'll be bringing someone very special with me, and I think it's time for everyone to know about it." She was out the door and gone before Mary Alice could formulate a reply.

Mary Alice would really have to talk to Craig now. She would have to warn him that their moving party was also going to be Victoria's "coming out" party.

Chapter Thirty-six

Craig was awake before the alarm on the clock radio sounded. He reached over and turned it off. Mary Alice remained asleep. He watched for a few minutes as the covers rose and fell with her rhythmic breathing. She appeared at peace with the world. She never seemed to let anything bother her.

Last night she told him about Victoria. The things she said had surprised him. His own life had changed so much; how could he be anything but empathetic? Craig told Mary Alice it was vital that they support Victoria and be ready to stand beside her if there were any negative reactions. They agreed the party was a good idea if that was the way Victoria wanted to handle it. They laughed at the idea of a moving party and receiving gifts from people they had never met but agreed Victoria could pull it off if anyone could. Mary Alice's eyes had filled with tears. She hugged him and told him he was the most understanding man that she had ever met and that she loved him very much. Looking at her now, he knew he loved her as well.

Glancing at the clock, Craig realized he only had fifteen minutes before he had to get up and get ready for work. He considered waking Mary Alice but decided to let her sleep. He had an uneasy feeling in the pit of his stomach. He knew how an escaped convict must feel. His life with Mary Alice was great, especially since their privacy had been restored. It was a dream come true, and soon they would move into a place of their own, but the way they had begun still troubled him.

For the past several nights, he had dreamed of Amanda—not all night, just snippets of scenes from the past.

As he lay there thinking, he knew they had not been right for each other. His feelings for Mary Alice in no way resembled how he had felt about Amanda. He and Amanda had to make so many decisions without experience or frame of reference. Still, she deserved an explanation. He knew his life could not be complete until he apologized and explained things to her. Then he and Mary Alice could marry. If Victoria could face her situation so bravely, so could he.

He tossed the covers aside and rolled out of bed. Turning, he bent and kissed Mary Alice on her temple. She stirred but did not wake. He knew he had to set things right.

* * *

At lunch, he ate quickly and then walked across the street to the convenience store. He saw two phones attached to the side of the building. First, he dialed the number of the parsonage in Cedar Creek and got a recording informing him the number had been disconnected. Next, he dialed information and asked for a listing in the name of either Craig or Amanda Cotton. When that failed, he asked for a listing in the name of Amanda Stewart or Louise Stewart, Amanda's middle and maiden name. No listing, new or old, existed for those names. He hung up the phone and stood looking at the side of the building. He had mixed emotions about not being able to reach Amanda. He looked at his watch and realized he only had five minutes to get back to work. He and Rodney were forming the stems to be poured atop the footings they had previously poured, and he didn't want to hold Rodney up by being late.

As he crossed the street, he realized he was acting impetuously and without talking with Mary Alice about it. Suddenly, he was glad he had not been able to reach Amanda. Tonight, he would discuss his feelings with Mary Alice. If she had no objection, he would write a letter to Amanda, explaining everything and asking for her understanding. He would make two copies of the letter. One he would send to the old address in Cedar Creek and the other to her parent's home in Kingsport. Surely, one would reach her. Soon, he, too, would be in the open. With a plan formulated, he felt a burden lift from his shoulders.

Looking into the parking lot, he saw Rodney rise from the tailgate of his truck and put on his hard hat. Craig reached into his back pocket for his pouch of tobacco and quickened his step.

* * *

Just after lunch, Victoria picked Troy up at the shop. They drove in her Saab to Eden's Gate and parked in front of the office. She wore a cream-colored outfit, and Troy wore his suit. They looked like a couple of yuppies. Troy got out of the car quickly and came around to open Victoria's door.

As they entered the building, a woman in her early twenties greeted them. She had blonde hair cut in a bob and green eyes that sparkled behind her stylish glasses. Her nose was perky and turned up slightly on the end, either a gift of nature or the work of a talented surgeon. Below her nose, there was nothing but a smile.

"Welcome to Eden's Gate, y'all. My name is Lou Ann Street. How can I help you?"

As Lou Ann elongated the last word of her sentence, her eyes fluttered, and she rose onto her toes. Victoria decided that Lou Ann had probably seen every episode of *Designing Women,* maybe even had them taped, and if so had watched them continuously. Troy seemed ill at ease.

"We would like to inquire about an apartment," said Victoria, taking the lead. "I'm Victoria, and this is Troy Jacobs." Victoria purposely avoided saying her last name, letting Lou Ann assume it was Jacobs. "We're just moving into the community and are looking for a nice place in a good location."

Victoria let just a bit of snobbery sound in her voice. It was not lost on Lou Ann.

"Well, y'all came to the right place. Eden's Gate is an upscale adult community featuring one and two-bedroom homes. It's convenient to the major business centers, the hospital, and the mall. You'll love it here."

Victoria wished she had picked up a brochure on the way in so she could read along. "It seems nice enough on the outside. Could…"

"You see a model?" Lou Ann said, finishing the sentence. "Sure!" she replied, once again stretching the word to its maximum and oozing syrupy charm.

She went to the desk and picked up a set of keys. When she had them, she pirouetted in a fashion that allowed her full skirt to wrap half again around her legs, flashed her best Cheshire cat grin, and said, "Y'all follow me."

Victoria took Troy's arm as they followed. The whole time they were walking, Lou Ann kept up some babble, which was probably part of a memorized spiel. They made a show of looking at the apartment, opening closets, inspecting cabinets, and even commenting on the wallpaper in the bathroom. Lou Ann was content to let them browse. Through the door of the bedroom, Victoria could see her standing by the window, rising on her toes as she checked her notes to be sure she had left nothing out.

"Well, what do y'all think? *Isn't it beau-u-ti-iful?*"

"Yes, it's quite lovely," said Victoria. "What do you think, honey?"

Troy, who had been in a daze, did not realize the question was meant for him until Victoria said the word honey again. He looked at her slowly and said, "Yeah, uh, it's fine."

Lou Ann took Troy's slow reply as indifference. She wished she had time to review the part in her sales kit about handling objections and closing the sale. This was just her second week on the job, and she desperately needed to sign a lease agreement.

"I know Eden's Gate is for you," said Lou Ann, remembering a line from her training. "We've got a one-bedroom and a two-bedroom unit available. You all seem perfect, so if you want the unit, I can probably get it approved to reduce the deposit and give you half off the first month's rent."

Troy had little experience with this type of phony deal-making, so her spiel had the effect it was designed to have on him. He started to jump at the deal, but a gentle squeeze from Victoria pulled him back.

"That sounds very nice, Lou Ann. If we decide in the affirmative, when could we move in?"

"That unit will be ready in a week and a half."

"Oh, my," said Victoria, letting a little uncertainty creep into her voice.

Lou Ann felt the sell slipping away. "Look, folks, I *really* feel this is the place for you. Let's go back to the office. If you like we can waive the whole deposit for right now. Just write me a check for fifty dollars, and the place is yours. We can settle the paperwork and the rest of the financials after you move in."

"Okay, Lou Ann, you sold us," said Victoria feeling pretty good about the deal she had just forged. She had saved Troy and Alphie a good deal of money, secured their apartment without a background check, which would have shown some inconsistencies, and now had ten days to figure out everything else. Not a bad day's work.

All that had taken place was not lost on Troy. He hadn't said much, but he had watched Victoria maneuver Lou Ann, and she had done it all for him. He had never really had an advocate before, but it was more than that. He felt he was falling for her and secretly wished it was she who would be sharing the apartment with him instead of Alphie. As they walked back to the office, he slipped his arm around her waist and gave her a squeeze. When she turned, looked up at him, and winked, he felt his legs turn to rubber.

Back at the office, Troy signed the agreement and gave Lou Ann fifty dollars in cash. They all shook hands and said their goodbyes.

Lou Ann watched as the couple walked to the Saab, and the gentleman opened the door for the lady. When the car was out of sight, she jumped up and down with glee. "Yes, yes, yes," she thought. "That was one tough sale, but I made it. Before long, I'll be just like Julia, Mary Jo, and the rest of the girls, lounging on my sofa, sipping mint juleps, and watching the money roll in. Lou Ann Street, super salesperson!"

Chapter Thirty-seven

y eyes opened slowly. On weekdays, the hellish noise of an alarm clock or Mama's incessant calling from the kitchen below rudely tore open my eyelids. But today I rose naturally like a human was designed to awaken.

Between the last week of August and the first week of June each year, Saturday was the only day of the week when such a luxury as awakening in one's own time was possible. Monday through Friday, we had to go to school and to church on Sunday.

School wasn't so bad. There was still a lot of crap to put up with, but since meeting Diane, I had something to look forward to. I closed my eyes and tried to visualize her face. Ah, yes, beautiful. What could a girl with a face like hers see in a guy with a face like mine? I didn't know, but I was certainly happy we were together. I'd call her, and maybe Daddy would drop me off at her house for a few hours if it was okay with her parents. I had done this once before, and we had a great time. We walked around her yard, sat on the porch swing, and listened to some tapes on a portable radio. Her daddy was cold toward me at first, and I noticed he watched us through the window for the first two hours.

He had nothing to worry about because my daddy had already lectured me about how important it was to act like a gentleman, especially in the presence of a lady. He told me how proud he was of the way I'd turned out and always to remember I was carrying the "Wilson name." He convinced me of how happy we both would be if I carried it with pride and honor. Without his having to say it, I knew that a coin has two sides. If I did anything to dishonor the Wilson name, we would both be miserable. Of course, his would be a mental discomfort, while mine would carry a lot of physical discomfort along with the shame. To state this in layman's terms, if I screwed up, he'd beat my butt. My daddy was not a strong proponent of the "time out." Anyway, my gentlemanly skills were honed to a razor's edge.

Finally, Mr. Mullins came out on the porch and gave us permission to walk down to McDaniel's drugstore to get a couple of milkshakes. He even tried to slip me some money, but I told him I could take care of it. I was glad I'd put five dollars in my pocket before leaving home. I had no idea I would need it, but a man feels better about himself if he has some folding money on him. It was the best milkshake I had ever tasted. On the way back, we held hands, and when we turned the block to Diane's house, she stopped on the corner and gave me a kiss, our first. I was filled with excitement, but I must admit to peeking out of one eye just to be sure that neither her daddy nor mine had mysteriously appeared to thwart our moment of love.

For the rest of the afternoon, we were left alone, although I swear I felt eyes on us from time to time.

When Daddy came to pick me up, Mr. Mullins came out, and they shook hands. Mr. Mullins told Daddy that I seemed to be a fine young gentleman. I took this as a sign of approval and proof that our kiss had gone undetected. Daddy didn't ask me any questions about my date, and I didn't volunteer any information, but when I got home, he slid a hand onto my shoulder and let it rest there until we were in the house. I thought I saw a tear in Mama's eyes when I went into the kitchen for a glass of milk, but I couldn't be sure since she quickly turned to the stove upon my arrival.

I looked at the clock, which read 8:42 a.m. Mentally, I calculated I would need to wait one hour and eighteen minutes before calling Diane. I rolled out of bed to face the day.

I opened my door to go the bathroom and take a shower just in time to see Jason run into it.

"Come on, Jason," I cried as I banged my fist against the door. I could hear him laughing.

"You snooze, you lose" was all he said before the shower coming to life drowned out any other sound. Foiled, I returned to my room.

Through the window, I could see the top of the trees swaying in the wind. I unlocked and raised the window. The breeze that rushed under the sash contained a hint of autumn. The warm days would soon give way to the shorter, cooler days of fall. A flurry of multi-colored leaves blew past my window, acting as an exclamation point to my thoughts. I left the window open just because I knew that soon I would not be able to.

My books lay on my desk across the room. I momentarily thought of doing some homework but quickly put that out of my mind. Instead, I walked over and picked up my algebra book. From it, I extracted a group of three pages stapled in the top left-hand corner. This was the handout Coach Alt had given us yesterday at the meeting of those interested in trying out for the wrestling team. The first page contained a brief history of Greco-Roman wrestling, culminating with a description of the modern sport as practiced in high schools and colleges. The coach had talked about it being a discipline of both the body and the mind. This appealed to me. He said that although we were a team, we were a team of individuals. We would compete individually, winning or losing our bouts on our own merits. We would face opponents of our own size, thus making mental and physical preparation tantamount to our success. I liked that idea too since I was too short to play basketball and too small for football. I was just cocky enough to believe I could more than hold my own against anyone my size. I guess that was the Wilson/Raspberry blood coursing through my veins. I felt this might be my sport.

The next page listed exercises designed to get the would-be wrestler into shape. Some were obvious, such as pull-ups, push-ups, running, and some basic weightlifting. Then, there was a series of stretches illustrated by stick figures. I found this a little confusing, but the coach said to look at them, adding that he would show us each posture as he called them at the first practice. This was my first introduction to yoga. He also said we would lift weights together as a team. I began to feel excited.

The third page shared a list of equipment we would have to furnish. Most of the items were standard stuff that I already owned, but the last two caught my notice. As the coach finished the meeting, I found my eyes drifting back to those two articles, the same two that later drew my attention that Saturday morning: athletic supporter with pouch pocket and protective cup in your size. I had no idea what my size was or how to go about measuring it, and I certainly didn't want to ask Mama or Daddy for help in the matter. The last requirements were two pairs of black leotards. I had always equated leotards with pantyhose and never thought of either as manly wear. Maybe there had been a mistake. The only image I could conjure up was of me standing in the middle of the gymnasium in front of the whole student body, wearing a pair of black pantyhose with a protective cup protruding from my nether regions. That vision brought cause for great concern.

The sound of Jason's door slamming pulled me away from my bizarre mental image. I stuffed the list back into the book, determined to find a solution. As I made my way to the door, a blood-curdling yell came through my window. Uncle Rodney. I rushed to the window and saw his pickup coming down the driveway. He was perched in the driver's seat with his head sticking out the window. Ms. Amanda Cotton sat beside him. I ran to the bathroom, cursing Jason for making me late.

I probably set the land speed record for showering in the rural South. A sailor at sea would have been proud of my efficiency. I almost gave way to the temptation of getting dressed without drying my hair, but vanity got the better of me. I was still young and anxious enough to want to run down to see Uncle Rodney but was old and vain enough to want to present myself favorably to Ms. Amanda Cotton. After dressing in a crisp pair of blue jeans and a pullover knit shirt with the tail left fashionably outside, I went downstairs.

The aromas that wafted up the stairs were enough to send a growing fifteen-year-old male who had nothing to eat in sixteen hours into a frenzy. The smells of bacon frying in the pan and biscuits baking in the oven permeated my senses, and it was only a short stretch of the imagination to believe I could smell eggs, grits, and sliced tomatoes. The thought caused me to pause halfway down the stairs. Once again, Uncle Rodney had managed to make himself available for one of Mama's home-cooked meals.

As I stopped to savor the moment, I heard Ms. Amanda talking to Mama.

"When we leave here, we're going to the mall in Asheville. A guy Rodney works with is having a housewarming party next Saturday, and we have to pick up a gift for him. But listen to this, Edna. Rodney doesn't even know his name or anything about him. They call him Slugger on the job. When I asked Rodney about him, he only said he was a nice guy and a hard worker, which is fine, but it doesn't help me know what to buy him. This Slugger is moving into a new house with his girlfriend whom Rodney knows nothing about either. So, Edna, what would you buy for a guy named Slugger and the mystery lady for their new home?"

"Just like a man," said Mama, flipping the bacon. "I guess you'll just have to buy something generic that will fit in any house, or you could get a gift certificate."

"Rodney doesn't want to get a gift certificate. He says it's too impersonal."

"Too impersonal, huh? Like working with a man every day and not knowing his name."

They both laughed. I thought Mama showed great restraint. Usually, given that much ammunition, she would have gone into a dissertation covering all of Rodney's faults and shortcomings, but now she just said, "Good luck, honey."

I walked down the remaining steps and paused at the kitchen door.

"Good morning, Mama. Hello, Ms. Amanda."

"Hey, Scooter," said Ms. Amanda with a smile.

"Scooter, why don't you go down to the shop and tell the men breakfast will be ready in about fifteen minutes? I want them here to eat while it's hot."

"Yes, ma'am."

As I walked across the yard, I could see Daddy and Jason out in the pasture, opening a few bales of hay for the cows. I smiled to myself, thinking that Jason got what he deserved by cutting me off to the bathroom. If I had gotten there first, it would be me out there working. Uncle Rodney stood by the fence, watching. I decided to ask him about the items on Coach Alt's list.

"Uncle Rodney, can I ask you a question in private?"

"Sure, Scoot. What d'ya need?"

I told him about the articles on the list and my uncertainty about them.

"Turn around, Scoot. Let me have a look at ya."

I turned slowly around and then stood facing him. I was a little embarrassed but nothing like I would have been if I had asked Mama or Daddy.

"It seems that a medium jockstrap would be about right. You're probably wearing medium tights too. You know they make some just for men nowadays. I think we should get you a large cup though."

I always enjoyed talking with Uncle Rodney, especially on the occasion when we got to speak alone. I was glad to hear there were tights made for men, but it especially made me feel good that I might qualify for a large cup.

"I'm mighty proud that you're going out for wrestling. That's a real man's sport. Tell you what. I'm going to the mall today, and I wish you would let me buy you those things."

"Thanks, Uncle Rodney, but don't tell Ms. Amanda, okay?"

"Okay," he said and slapped me on the back. I suddenly remembered why I was sent down there in the first place.

"Daddy, Daddy," I yelled, trying to calculate how long since I left the house. "Mama said breakfast is ready."

Daddy and Jason stopped what they were doing and walked across the pasture. As they came through the gate, I gave Jason a push and grinned at him. He returned an icy glare that told me he understood the consequences of his earlier actions. It warmed my heart.

As we walked to the house, I wedged myself between Daddy and Uncle Rodney. Jason walked on the other side of Daddy, his rubber boots making a squishing sound with every step. I looked up at Daddy and Uncle Rodney, then across at Jason. The "Wilson men" were on the way to a great breakfast. My problems had been solved. I felt like the luckiest man in the world.

Chapter Thirty-eight

The coffee systematically dripped into the waiting pot. Victoria sat at the counter, watching the liquid fall. She started a mental countdown, which would reach zero when she sipped her first fix of caffeine of the day. For years, she had limited herself to decaf, but along with the other changes in her life, "one hundred octane" coffee had also made a comeback. Now, as she waited, she wondered why she had ever switched to decaf. So many things about her previous life had come into question. She thought of it as the difference between merely living and having a life.

She smiled as she recalled the previous day's activities. After she and Troy left the office at Eden's Gate, they went to lunch to celebrate. Troy looked so handsome. He thanked her over and over for helping him get the apartment. Although he had to wait to move in, he was excited. They spent the rest of the afternoon walking around Asheville, holding hands, and making small talk. Troy expressed an interest in going to the mall.

"I noticed that Belk's is having a sale, and I might need to pick up another dress shirt just in case," he said.

She remembered thinking he was getting comfortable with his new mode of dress. They went shopping, and Victoria helped him pick out four shirts and a couple of pairs of slacks. She insisted she be allowed to pay for them as a present. He seemed genuinely pleased. After shopping, he told her he needed to go back to Cedar Creek to get some more of his things and asked if she would like to ride along. She declined, saying she also needed to do some things. It was after six p.m. when he retrieved his truck, and she returned home.

Back at the apartment, she began making preliminary plans for Mary Alice's housewarming. She also had to figure out the best way to tell Troy about her other life. She hoped it would not create a problem. What had started as a lark was now becoming serious, and her continued deceit gnawed at her conscience. After a while, she retired to her room and fell asleep. She didn't hear Jill come in.

The last gasps from the coffee pot let her know it was ready. She took two cups down, intending to pour one for herself and one for Jillian. She thought she would take the coffee into Jillian's room and surprise her with it. She was getting ready to pour the second cup when she heard a key rattle in the lock on the front door. Startled, she looked over to see Jillian come through the door. She obviously was not returning from a morning errand but an all-nighter. She had made an admirable attempt at fixing her hair, but she had done so without the array of tools necessary for a complete job. She had slept in her makeup, the option she had chosen over washing it off and exposing herself to the harshness of the "morning after" light. While not looking slept in, her clothes appeared as if they had spent the night in a heap near the bed in which their owner slept. She was barefooted and carried her shoes in her hand.

Recognizing the situation, Victoria poured the second cup of coffee and held it out in Jillian's direction. Victoria thought she saw a flush of color work its way across Jillian's cheeks.

"Thanks," said Jillian as she accepted the coffee. She took a sip and waited. She felt the liquid work its way into her system. Although it was a shock, it was also renewing.

"Good morning," Victoria said, wanting to hurry past the awkwardness of the moment. "Do you want some breakfast?"

"Sure. Let me take a quick shower, and we'll go out for breakfast. That way, we won't have to clean up, and I can tell you all about last night."

In only thirty minutes, Jillian emerged from her room, looking fresh as a daisy. Victoria was amazed and rightfully surmised that this was not Jillian's first time dealing with this situation. As they drove, Victoria told Jillian about her day with Troy. When she related how excited Troy was that he and Alphie would get the apartment, Jill remained silent. Victoria had little time to think about it as the Pancake Kitchen appeared on the horizon.

Nothing else was said as they parked, walked inside, and were seated. After they ordered and were served more coffee, Victoria looked at Jill and asked, "Is anything wrong?"

"No, nothing's wrong. In fact, everything's great. I guess you've figured out that I spent the night with Alphie. That was our first all-nighter—not because we haven't been, eh, active, you know. It was just the first time it worked out that we could stay together. Things are really working out for Alphie and me. I swore I'd never get involved again, but this seems different. Do you know what I mean?"

"Jill, I think I know exactly what you mean. My problem is that my relationship with Troy is built on lies. Troy has no idea who I really am. I'm afraid he'll never be able to forgive me after he finds out."

"That's nonsense. I know Troy really cares for you, so I don't think anything else will matter."

"I hope you're right because I'm going to tell him everything. He was just so excited to get the apartment so he and Alphie could move closer."

Again, Jill looked away and moved uncomfortably in the booth. Victoria's curiosity was piqued.

"What is it, Jill?"

"I don't know how to tell you this, so I'll just say it. Alphie is having second thoughts about moving in with Troy. It's nothing to do with Troy; it's just that we've been talking about living together.

If he moves in with Troy, that can't happen for a while. He doesn't know what to do. He hasn't said anything to Troy yet, but I think he will. How do you think Troy will take it?"

"Oh my," Victoria replied, thinking once again about Troy's excitement. "I don't know. With Alphie's news and what I've got to tell him, I don't know how he'll react."

"We talked about Alphie moving in with me and giving his apartment to Troy. Do you think he'll go for that?"

Victoria was stunned. She had no idea things could get so confused so fast. Suddenly, the totality of the situation hit her. She was also being asked to move out. She had planned on returning to her house after Mary Alice and Craig moved into their new place, but now there was no option. She could not blame Jillian. In fact, she was delighted for her because she now knew how it felt to want to spend every minute of your life with another person. She had given up any hopes of a relationship after Lawrence's death. There was a time in her more selfish life when Victoria would have become angry or hurt by being asked to move but not now. She no longer had the choice of continuing the charade. Now, she felt only happiness for her friend and a determination not only to tell Troy the truth but to make sure that they, too, would be happy.

"Jill, I'm so happy for you. Don't worry about a thing," she said and reached out to touch her friend's hand. "Now tell me all about last night."

They devoured the food when it came. Jill was a tell all kind of person and she did. By the time they left the Pancake Kitchen, they were laughing like they used to in college and making plans for a double date later that evening.

* * *

Mary Alice moved about the kitchen in a methodical way. She was so familiar with the place that it almost seemed like her own. She placed the glasses, which had been turned upside down to dry, in the cabinet above for storage. Silverware in the drawer next to the refrigerator, plates in the china cabinet, bowls underneath the counter beside the range, and pots underneath the range. As she cleaned up after lunch, a task easily completed without thinking, her mind was anything but idle. Today she was on an emotional rollercoaster.

Since moving to Asheville, she had allowed herself to become insulated from the reality of their situation. She hardly ever thought of Cedar Creek and her life there. Living in a trailer, working as a waitress at Sybil's, and dating a motorcycle bum was not the kind of life that got you on A&E's *Biography*. Craig had been a pleasant diversion. When he suggested they run away together, she jumped at the chance, even swallowing her pride to ask Victoria for a place to stay. Craig turned out to be so much more than she had originally thought. She had allowed herself to live in the present, disregarding the past.

Yesterday, when Craig came home from work, he seemed preoccupied. Recognizing this, she gave him room. After dinner, they settled on the couch as they were in the habit of doing, but instead of turning on the TV, Craig said they needed to talk. He started out by telling her he loved her and how much he looked forward to them moving into their own place. Next, he shared that he had tried to call Amanda and had decided it was a mistake to do that without talking to her first. Still, he felt it was time to clear the air so they could go on with their lives with nothing hanging over their heads. He told her of his idea to write a letter, saying that sooner or later there would have to be contact if for no other reason than to obtain a divorce. He then asked her to marry him once everything was final. She told him she thought it was a good idea when, in fact, it scared the hell out of her.

Mary Alice could not sleep. She drifted in and out of consciousness. Each time she awoke, she looked at the clock only to see that fifteen minutes had passed. Finally, she fell asleep around four a.m. When she woke up at seven-thirty, Craig was already out of bed. She found him at the desk, working on the letter. She felt emptiness in the pit of her stomach all morning. Just before lunch, he emerged with the finished letter. He asked her to read it. Doing so, she had not been able to contain her tears. Now he had gone to mail it as she cleaned the house. Her fears and insecurities began to subside, and for the first time in her life, she began thinking of herself as somebody's wife.

Chapter Thirty-nine

Privacy is an illusion, and anonymity is an illusion within an illusion. It's like the child who stands behind the slim trunk of a pine tree with his forehead pressed against the bark, thinking he is hidden. Only his own vision is obscured. Many times, we think our activities and the conditions of our lives are our own. We follow our chosen paths daily, free, so we imagine, from the encumbrances of public knowledge or opinion. In the end, we realize we have been playing our game on the center court. Most of us would find it quite unsettling to realize just how much others know about our lives.

Amanda Cotton was not thinking of privacy or anonymity on Tuesday morning. Her mind focused on the gusting wind that whipped about the yard. The breezes had a cool edge, and although the temperature was in the mid-seventies, the promise of winter was unmistakable.

She wiped a gloved hand across her brow, pushing an errant strand of hair out of her eyes and tucking it behind her ear. Leaves fluttered to earth with each gust and were chased by escapees from one of the piles she had already gathered. Subconsciously aware of the futility of her quest, outwardly she remained determined to keep up. With so many trees, she knew it would be a monumental task if she waited for the last leaf to fall before she began raking. Besides, she reveled in the way the cabin and yard were coming together. She felt a real sense of accomplishment, and Rodney was continually complimenting her achievements.

When she was a little girl in Kingsport, she helped her father with the leaves each fall. They raked them into little mounds and then burned each pile. As they burned, she and her dad stood by, leaning on rakes and watching, making sure the fire stayed under control. Sometimes, they would rake up a large heap, and her father allowed her to jump into them. She remembered the total abandon she felt as she flung herself into the cushiony pile of leaves. The thought was too enticing to resist.

She worked furiously until she had pulled six of the smaller piles into one large hill. She walked purposefully over to the large oak tree and leaned her rake against it. With the unbridled freedom of a child, she took three large strides and launched herself. The leaves seemed to rise to meet her, cradle her gently, and lower her softly back to earth. She laughed out loud.

She did not see the mail truck slow down and turn into the driveway. There was no reason to suspect it was coming. Although it passed by each day, Rodney kept a post office box in Cedar Creek and received all his mail there. Now, the mail truck pulled to a stop as she lay splayed in a bed of fallen leaves.

"Good morning, Mrs. Cotton," said Fred Thomas as he climbed out of the truck, pretending not to notice that she, a grown woman, was playing in the leaves.

"Good morning, Fred," she replied, pretending not to notice he was pretending not to notice. "What brings you out here?"

"I've got a letter for you. It was sent to the parsonage. Billy Whitman, who has that route, knew you weren't living there anymore, so he gave it to Mary Schultz to take back to the post office because she always finishes her route before him. Mary was going to put it in Rodney's box so he could pick it up tonight, but she looked at it and thought it might be important. Anyway, I saw Mary at Hardee's, and she asked me to drop it off out here, so here I am. It's from the preacher."

At first, what he said didn't register with her. She stood up and brushed herself off. He held the letter out to her, and she took it without glancing at it.

"Thank you, Fred," she said with a smile.

"You're mighty welcome, Mrs. Cotton," he said. He turned and walked to the truck. As he reached it, gripping the wheel and preparing to pull himself inside, he turned and smiled. "That sure looked like a lot of fun. I haven't jumped in leaves since I was a boy. Bye."

"Bye, Fred," she said as he put the truck in gear and headed back down the driveway.

After Fred turned back onto the road, she remembered the letter. She turned it over and looked at the face of the envelope. Her heart skipped a beat, and her breath caught in her throat as she read the return address. It only had one line, a name, C. Cotton.

Amanda stuffed the envelope into the rear pocket of her khaki trousers. She returned to her raking, meaning to finish the job. She absentmindedly swiped at the leaves as her mind raced at breakneck speed. Finally, she gave up and went inside.

She placed the letter on the table, still unopened. Then she circled the table. She regarded the letter like a wary wolf would look upon a piece of fresh carrion, not knowing if it was a gift of happenstance or bait for a cleverly disguised trap. She walked repeatedly from the window in the living room to the one over the sink in the kitchen. On each trip, her eyes were drawn inexorably to the letter. She had thought of Craig often, though not as much since moving to the cabin. Her anger and embarrassment had subsided quickly, perhaps too quickly, and had been replaced by indifference. When Rodney came along and their relationship flourished, her apathy had slowly been replaced by what she knew was love. Any warm feeling can pass itself as love until the flame of real love licks you. She had realized a while back that she had never really been in love with Craig Cotton. Still, she once had thought she loved him, and they were still married.

Finally, she sat down, took the envelope into her hands, and slid her finger between the flap and the top. Slowly, she ripped the envelope open and removed the letter. She read:

Craig Cotton

2064 Lakeview Rd.

Asheville, N.C. 28804

Dear Amanda,

First, let me say I'm sorry. I'm sorry I left without talking to you. I know it was the wrong thing to do, but when it happened I was so confused that I didn't think about right or wrong. That's no excuse, but I hope you will accept it as a reason.

You have every right to hate me and tear this letter up without reading it, but if you will bear with me, I would like to explain some things that I have come to realize as true.

I have lived most of my life according to a script. A script written by me before I had the experience or the frame of reference to write such a script, and endorsed by my parents, my pastor, and the small group of friends who thought they knew who I was. In this script, a young man grows up in a strong, strict, Christian home. He studies hard, goes to college, enters seminary, becomes ordained, and preaches. Along the way, he meets the right girl, gets married, has a family of his own, and lives happily ever after. I know now that this was the wrong script for my life. I'm sorry I lured you into my illusion.

Please don't get me wrong. I thought we were doing the right thing. Our marriage added a dimension to my life that I will always treasure.

In time, I realized I was not being honest with you or myself. I made what seemed like some foolish decisions and became involved with someone else. In doing so, I saw the absurdity of my life and took the coward's way out: I ran away.

I have learned that sometimes things that start out for all the right reasons can turn out to be wrong and that some things that start out for all the wrong reasons can turn out to be right. I hope you can understand.

I will not ask for forgiveness because I don't think I have the right to ask. I only ask that you try to understand why I did what I did. I pray for your happiness.

I can be reached at the above address for any correspondence. I will take care of the cost of any legal proceedings and agree to any settlement you suggest. Again, I'm sorry.

Yours truly,
Craig

She folded the letter and set it aside. After what seemed like a long time, she reached for it again. Unfolding it, she saw the smudged ink where her tears had fallen. She reread it. She thought of Craig and then of Rodney. Her thoughts of Rodney renewed her tears. She imagined how Craig must have felt as he penned the letter. His letter had served to confirm what she had come to believe.

She did understand and wished she could tell him. She would write to him next week, and they would work on the terms of a divorce. She felt no animosity toward him, only relief that he was well and that soon they would both be free to pursue their respective futures. She put the letter away and went back outside. One more leap into the leaves was what she needed right now.

Chapter Forty

Victoria's fingers drummed against the steering wheel in an endless rhythm. She was on her way to pick up Troy.

After her breakfast with Jillian, her life had shifted into another gear. The rest of the weekend passed in a blur. Physically, she responded to whatever stimuli were directed toward her, but mentally she was in another place.

She replayed her life, skimming over her childhood and adolescence, discounting her college years, lingering on her marriage, choosing not to spend much time on Lawrence's death and her subsequent period of grief (it still hurt in a place deep inside her), and finally taking a slow frame by frame look at her life from that time until the present. No lightning bolts of insight emerged. She felt no anguish at opportunities missed and no regrets. What came was the unerring knowledge that the hourglass of her life was steadily seeping sand. She had an overwhelming sense of urgency to set everything right and get on with it.

Unfortunately, knowing what to do hardly ever arrives with a set of instructions, so she had spent the last four days going over various scenarios of how to accomplish her task. Her ideas ranged from sophomoric to soap operatic, but in the end she settled on a simple, direct approach.

Now she sat on the side of the road, engine idling, finger drumming, looking ahead into the next block at the garage where she had arranged to meet Troy. Things had worked out the way things have a habit of doing. Craig and Mary Alice were going to spend the evening at their new home, cleaning and preparing to move in. This would give her the window of opportunity she needed to introduce Troy to her other house and life without having the added pressure of having to introduce him to family.

She saw movement at the garage door. Troy emerged, and she pulled away from the curb simultaneously.

She saw the smile come on his face as he recognized the Saab approaching. *God, he's handsome, she thought as* she stopped in front of the shop. He was dressed in jeans, but instead of a T-shirt, he wore one of the Oxford shirts they had bought at the mall. He opened the door, got in, and leaned to kiss her. She turned to receive the kiss and, upon its completion, noticed that a new pair of leather deck shoes had replaced his old boots. He looked more like a lawyer dressed for a casual outing than the ex-leader of an outlaw motorcycle gang.

"Hey, gorgeous," he said as he settled into the Saab's passenger seat. He had become accustomed to her driving and seemed perfectly at home as her passenger.

"Hey, Troy. Thanks for meeting me. I've got something to talk about with you and something to show you." Even as she spoke, she felt her stomach tumble.

Troy sensed the tension. He hoped he had done nothing to upset her. Glancing at her from the corner of his eye, he saw her jaw was firmly set, her eyes fixed straight ahead, and her knuckles were turning white from the pressure of her grip on the steering wheel. He decided to let her direct the conversation if and when she wanted to say more.

They rode in silence for what seemed like an hour but was, in fact, only ten minutes. She slowed the car and turned into a driveway.

Troy saw a two-story house built out of white stucco accented with contrasting wooden trim. It reminded him of a house he had seen in a magazine article about Britain. There was a name for the style, but he couldn't think of it. The lot was spacious and looked well taken care of. There were flower beds, lawn sculptures, and even a small water garden.

Victoria stopped the car and got out without saying a word. Troy followed suit. They walked to the upper end of the driveway, through an opening in the hedge, and onto the patio at the rear of the house. Troy expected Victoria to ring the doorbell, but instead she reached into her purse, pulled out a key, and opened the door. They entered a spacious kitchen, which was neat, clean, and orderly. Above an island, in the middle of the kitchen, hung pots and pans, all the same make and in descending order according to size. Troy gazed at the utensils, again thinking of the magazine article, when Victoria turned around.

"This is my house!" she blurted out and then burst into tears. She sobbed uncontrollably and fell into his arms. Waves of despair seemed to wash over her again and again. Troy was at a loss for what to do. He held her, rubbed her back, ran his fingers through her hair, and repeatedly kissed her cheek. It was as if, in an instant, a veil was pulled away to reveal a priceless work of art. How much he cared for this woman echoed through his heart.

They stood like that for some time. When Victoria gained control, Troy said, "I think it's a great house. Have I done anything wrong?"

"No, of course not. It's just that I haven't told you about this before. I've only been Jill's roommate since I met you. My sister lived here, and I stayed with Jill. I wanted you to know everything. I want you to know the real me."

"Vickie, I know the real you. I may not have all the details, but I know the real you. The fact that you would live with Jill and let your sister live in a house like this only assures me that what I know is true."

"I had never ridden a motorcycle before the day you took me on yours. I never used to go to bars, dances, or even drink beer.

I worked in my garden, volunteered at the hospital, and went to club meetings. I'm not the woman you think I am." She talked fast, one sentence running into another as if punctuation didn't exist. All the while, she sobbed. When she finally slowed down, she realized Troy was laughing.

"What is it?" she asked.

"You're incredible," he answered. "You don't think I knew you were a greenhorn with bikes? I had an idea there was more to you than you were showing. I don't care about that. I love you, and the details don't matter."

There, he had said it. It was out and hung like a helium balloon in the air between them. He had said it a thousand times internally. The first time had scared the hell out of him, and now he was terrified again—scared he wasn't good enough, that he had misread all the signs, scared to expose so much of himself.

When she heard the words, a feeling of relief swept over her. What she feared would be the worst moment of her new life had become the most tender. She reached out, took his hand, and led him to the stairs. "Let me show you my room," she said and started up the stairs.

* * *

They talked little on the ride back, each replaying the previous hours and comparing them to their fantasies of the anticipated event. Upon their arrival, they spent another forty-five minutes kissing and playing like a couple of teenagers.

When everything had calmed down and he was getting ready to open the car door, Victoria said, "Troy, I want you to move into my house with me. My sister is moving to a place of her own next week, and then we will have the whole place to ourselves. You don't have to answer me tonight. Just think about it."

"I don't have to think about it. I would love to. The only thing is that I promised Alphie I would move in with him at Eden's Gate, and I'll have to figure out how to tell him."

"Just tell him the truth," Victoria said, remembering her conversation with Jill. "You might be surprised. I'm throwing a housewarming party for my sister on Saturday, and I want you to be there. It will be a good opportunity for you to meet her. I'm going to ask Jill and Alphie too. Will you come?"

"Sure, you know I will. I want to know your family. I'll talk to Alphie tomorrow about the move."

They kissed again. Troy closed the door and watched Victoria drive away. He felt like a passenger on a runaway train. Things were moving fast, but he thought that was okay. Soon, he would be living the life of a "citizen." He had never viewed himself as anything but a biker. He read all the literature, attended all the big meets, walked the walk, and talked the talk. Now, it seemed, he was on the way to a "normal" life. What the hell! It felt pretty good. He smiled and walked inside.

Chapter Forty-one

Thursday was normally a hectic day in the motorcycle shop. Nobody wanted to be without his or her bike on the weekend, and to most riders the weekend started on Friday. Monday was usually slack because everyone was recuperating from the previous days and trying to act like responsible citizens. Tuesday, they started to filter in. The heavy repair jobs, things broken on the last ride, came first because they usually took more than one day. Wednesday brought light repairs and tune-ups because the bikes had to sit overnight to cool before the tune-up could be done. They usually did routine maintenance, oil changes, and new tires on Thursday. Bikers arrived in a flood and kept the shop jumping all day. Alphie's shop was no exception.

It took an hour and a half to write up the work orders on the bikes that were waiting when they arrived. After getting everyone on their way with assurances that their trusty iron would be returned to them by Friday, Alphie made coffee while Troy went to the doughnut shop for a dozen glazed. Actually, it was a dozen glazed and a cinnamon roll, but the cinnamon roll was for the ride back to the shop. They ate noisily while they divided up the day's work. They started work when the box was empty and the coffee pot contained only a stain.

The day had moved along swiftly. Troy meant to find time to talk to Alphie, but none availed itself. A heaviness anchored in the pit of Troy's stomach. At first, he passed it off as the result of six doughnuts and a cinnamon roll, but the feeling got worse instead of better as the day progressed. Troy knew he would find no relief until he spoke with Alphie.

Troy glanced at the clock and was surprised to read 4:45 p.m. He was almost finished adjusting the valves on a Sportster, his last job of the day. Alphie was working on a Yamaha. Troy thought of the days when a Harley man wouldn't be caught dead working on a Japanese motorcycle. Some diehards still wouldn't, but it was mainly because they couldn't keep up with the technology. Alphie was a great mechanic. Troy also considered himself good, but Alphie had taught him a lot in the short time they had been working side by side. That made it even harder to tell him they wouldn't become roommates. He knew it was time to do the deed.

"Hey, Alph. You about ready to finish up?"

"Yeah, just got to put this tank back on. Take me about five minutes."

"How 'bout we go for a little ride when we're finished? I've got something I want you to see."

"Sure, why not? Maybe we can grab a brew while we're at it. We sure earned it today."

They finished up, organized the shop, cleaned themselves, and were outside pulling on their helmets in thirty minutes.

The wind in his face felt wonderful as Troy retraced the path to Victoria's house. He almost missed one turn but made it without seeming to falter. He saw the house ahead on the left and pulled up in front of it across the street. There was no car in the drive.

They killed the engines and removed their helmets. Troy noticed Alphie's look of confusion.

"It belongs to Vickie. She wants me to move in with her," said Troy with a wave of his arm in the direction of the house. It wasn't how he planned to start the conversation. He had not formulated a plan, but he was sure that if he had his statement would have resided closer to the end of the conversation.

"Whoa, buddy!" exclaimed Alphie, a feeling of sudden relief washing over him. "You gonna do it?"

"That's what we need to talk about. You and I were going to get that place at Eden's Gate, and I hate to change up on you. You've helped me a lot since I've been in town, and I won't back out on you." Troy let the conversation drop but looked at the house. It seemed to be receding. His life had changed so much so fast. Some of his feelings confused him. He knew he loved Vickie and wanted to live with her whether in this house or somewhere else. But he had given his word to his friend and would stand by it.

Alphie saw a look of resolve on Troy's face and knew he had to move fast, or his escape hatch would close. He, too, had been wrestling between loyalty and desire. Now, it seemed everyone could have what they really wanted.

"That's some nice digs, Bro. To tell you the truth, I've been having some second thoughts about moving to Eden's Gate, but I didn't want to mess you up. Jill and I have been getting hot and heavy here lately, and who knows? When did Vickie get this?"

"I don't know. Her sister's been living here, but she's moving, so Vickie asked me to move in with her."

"If that's what you want, go for it. I'm happy for y'all. Just don't get all uppity and quit the shop. We've really got it happening there. I might even need a partner. Let's go get a beer and see what happens."

"You sure?"

"Hell yeah, I'm sure. A beer's just what I need."

"I mean…"

"I know what you mean. Yeah, I'm sure."

Alphie threw his leg over the Harley and kicked the engine into life. Troy did likewise. Neither of them noticed the movement of the curtains in the house.

Chapter Forty-two

Mary Alice let the curtain slip closed with her back pressed against the wall. Her heart pounded in her chest. Her breath was coming in gasps. "Shit!" was all she could think of to say. She reached her hand to her brow to wipe the perspiration, but it was like sponging the ocean with a river.

She had been packing the last of Craig's clothes for the move when she heard the roar of the motorcycles. She still loved the sound of a Harley-Davidson and hardly ever did one pass without her pausing to listen. Although that was part of another life, she couldn't help herself. The sound of the engine noise stopping instead of thundering past caught her attention. Since she and Craig had been living at Victoria's house, she had not heard a Harley in the neighborhood. She folded a few more shirts, but the seed of unease the sound had planted grew until she could no longer ignore it. She walked down the stairs and across the room to the front of the house. She almost opened the front door to go onto the front porch to check things out but thought better of it. Instead, she slipped to the window, parted the curtains slightly, and peeped through them. What she saw paralyzed her.

Across the street two Harleys had parked with the back wheels against the curb. Two men stood beside the bikes. She couldn't see clearly, but one was very likely Troy Jacobs, and he was waving his hand toward the house. She tried to rationalize him away. If it were

Troy, he had gotten a haircut and shaved his beard, something she could not visualize him doing. He was the right size, and the bike was the right color, but both men wore uniform shirts of the same design, which would mean they worked at the same place. Troy was a T-shirt man and never worked anywhere long enough to get a uniform. Still, in her heart of hearts, she knew.

She had known Troy would be pissed off when she left Cedar Creek. She even thought he might try to find her. Even so, she had always thought of Troy as a short attention span player who would quickly avert his notice to one of the many bimbos who could hardly wait to throw their legs over a Harley or the man who owned one.

She looked at her watch and saw it was 5:30. Craig would be home any minute. She had let him take the beetle to work this morning so she could spend the day packing. Now it was time for him, and he was going to drive into the middle of this. Would Troy cause a scene? Hell yes! Why else would he come all the way from Cedar Creek? Would Craig try to fight him? Hell yes, she thought, remembering the incident at his job site.

Two days, she thought. *Just two days, and we would be moved and maybe unfindable.* If Troy were to locate them, at least the ruckus would not be in Victoria's neighborhood. "She's gonna kill me!!"

As she watched, the two men talked. She geared up for confrontation, but they got back on their bikes instead of coming to the house and slowly rode away.

Maybe they didn't know for sure this was the house. Maybe she was wrong about it being Troy. Maybe he had ridden all that way and changed his mind or a cooler head had talked out of it. Maybe they could get the hell out of there before anything happened. Maybe, maybe, maybe.

The sound of the Volkswagen startled her. She looked through the curtains and saw Craig turn into the drive. Should she warn him or let it go? She would decide as the night went on. In any case, tonight would be a low-light, no-noise night. Troy might break the tranquility of the night, but he would not sneak up on her. One more day and the party on Saturday, and they would be free.

Chapter Forty-three

Craig Cotton faced Friday with a smile on his face. The alarm succeeded in waking him but failed to annoy him as it often did. He was sure nothing would aggravate him today. One more day of work, endure the party Victoria had planned, and then move on Sunday. In just two days, he and Mary Alice would really start their life together. Although the future intrigued him, it was the recent past, especially last night, that made him smile.

When he arrived home last night, he found Mary Alice in an agitated state, not angry, just excitable. Before he could ask her about it, she was in his arms, flooding him with questions about his day. She asked if they could go out for dinner and maybe ride by the new house. She had to know the answer was yes. When he finished his shower, she was dressed and waiting.

Mary Alice had never been a backseat driver, but Craig noticed she was paying a lot of attention to the traffic. He guessed she was just being superstitious. That was fine by him. He didn't want anything happening on the threshold of their new life either. Even in the restaurant, she kept looking around the room, although they had been there several times. Again, after dinner in the traffic, she remained tense and vigilant. He chose not to say anything for fear that she would take it as a reprimand, thus ruining the evening. His patience and silence were rewarded when they returned home.

When they drove into the driveway, she told him to pull way around back out of the illumination of the light mounted on the garage front. After they stopped, she exhaled a deep sigh, reached across the seat, and kissed him. After ten more minutes in the car, she squeezed his hand, opened the door, and whispered, "No lights."

They stumbled through the darkness into the living room, where she continued her sensual assault. Time is meaningless when you are in love and in the dark. By the time they felt their way from the living room, up the stairs, and into bed, they were both purring like kittens.

Craig smiled at himself in the bathroom mirror, remembering. He dressed and found Mary Alice downstairs, looking out through the closed curtains.

"Morning, baby," he said, squeezing her from behind.

She jumped, turned, and smiled. "Morning."

"You taking me to work, or do you want me to take the car?"

"I'll drive you. I've got a few things to do, and I'm going to take some things out to the house." In fact, she planned to stay gone all day and then repeat last night's events. That would leave only the party between her and safety. Even if Craig had known her plan, he would not have objected, especially if it meant another night like last night.

* * *

In Cedar Creek, Rodney Wilson was preparing to leave for work. When he was dressed, he stepped back into the bedroom to kiss Amanda goodbye. He lightly touched her cheek. She stirred, mumbled, and turned over.

"Rodney, if you don't mind, I think I'll go by Edna's this afternoon. I want to fix a pumpkin cake to take to your friend's party tomorrow, and she'll have all the fixings."

"That sounds great, hon. I'll swing by here and if you're not here, I'll meet you over there. See you then. Love you."

"Okay, love you too," she said, although it sounded like "Okay, l-m-m-m-m-m-m-m-m" as she turned back into the pillow.

* * *

When the final bell rang on a Friday afternoon at Cedar Creek High, there was usually a mad dash for the doors. This Friday was no exception except for a handful of young male students, the would-be wrestling team awaiting their first dress-out day. I had looked forward to it with both anticipation and apprehension.

I found Diane waiting for me in the hall outside my civics class, and we walked hand in hand toward the gym. As we turned the corner, she gave me a light kiss on the cheek and turned right to go out the door. I continued down the hall to the locker room. A notice hung on the door.

> **Please change and bring everything into the gym with you. The locker rooms will be closed for repairs at 4 p.m. No showers or changing facilities will be available after practice. Thank you.**
> **—Coach Alt**

When I changed into my uniform and looked at myself in the mirror, I again had mixed feelings. Everything was comfortable, fitting like a second skin. The combination of the tights and the three-quarter body suit made me look sleek and athletic, but the snugness and cling of the material revealed a bulge below my stomach, which I found quite disconcerting.

The fact that we would not be able to change back into street clothes failed to hit me until practice was almost over. I glanced at the clock above the gym door and saw it was almost five o'clock. At least everyone would be gone but us. I knew I would have to get over my discomfort to compete, but I wanted some time to taper out of it.

Practice ended with a series of stretches that left me feeling tired but relaxed. When Coach Alt dismissed us, I grabbed my stuff and headed for the door with the rest of the guys. I sensed I was not the only one who felt self-conscious because we all seemed to pause as a group at the door. I guess we were making sure that some sick soul had not notified the whole student body that we would be exiting in tights so they could form en masse outside the gym. The only thing out there was a line of cars, each manned by awaiting parents. Among them, I saw Daddy's old Ford. I breathed a sigh of relief. We burst through the doors and ran to our respective vehicles, sure that the parent inside was so intent on their own child they would not be inclined to look at the rest of us.

Once inside the truck's cab, I relaxed and told Daddy all about practice. He listened attentively and asked a few questions, but he mostly just drove and smiled while I talked.

I had given him all the facts by the time we got home and was probably on the verge of a little embellishment when we turned into the driveway. What I saw created a panic in me and almost certainly reduced the bulge that may have been apparent south of my equator. There in my yard was Ms. Amanda Cotton's car. I had to think. Then it came to me.

Ms. Amanda and Mama would almost certainly be in the living room talking. I would sneak around back, go in through the kitchen, rush up the stairs, and into my room to change before they even knew I was home.

When Daddy stopped the truck, he said he was going to the shop for a few minutes and would see me inside. That really worked into my plan. Daddy probably didn't want to become part of a hen party and believed that a sip of Jim Beam was a more preferable welcome home than a conversation with two ladies whose jaws were surely already loosened up.

I watched Daddy walk toward the shop as I got close to the house and slipped around back, sliding along the wall like a cat burglar, all in black. If I had faced the house, I would have realized my error before it was too late. I reached behind me for the doorknob and twisted it, slipping inside. Instead of a path to freedom, I was brought face to face with Ms. Amanda Cotton and Mama, both working over the freshly baked layers of a cake. How had I failed to smell that cake? I'll never know because, thinking back, it sure smelled good.

"Hey, Scooter," said Ms. Amanda looking up from the cakes.

The creek would have been mostly mud, the woods would have been full of mosquitoes, there were massive fires burning out west, and people were starving in Africa, but I would have rather been anywhere besides in front of Ms. Amanda Cotton with a pair of tights on. "Hey" was all I could say. I was slowly edging my way to the door, trying to maintain some semblance of dignity, when Mama spoke up.

"Scooter, look at you," she said, turning to Ms. Amanda. "Doesn't he look just like one of those man ballerinas? A regular Nu-re-yev?"

Looking back on that moment, it doesn't seem all that bad, but that Friday it seemed disastrous.

"Aw, Mama," I cried and broke for the door.

Chapter Forty-four

A certain genre of movie popular in the late 1940s and early 1950s always featured scenes in which masterful detectives like Charlie Chan and Nick Charles would work their way through a cast of characters in search of a vile criminal. The detective seemed harmless enough and the other characters even more so. In the end, the detective, with the full cooperation of the local police, gathered all the characters together and, through a clever reenactment of the crime, solved the mystery. In the end, everyone was always together, a room filled with people, one guilty of a felonious crime and everyone else with the weight of countless misdemeanors resting on their shoulders. They invariably squabbled about being made to endure each other's company, but in the final scene the mystery was solved, and everyone could get on with their lives.

While none of our cast of characters had committed a felony, the accumulated misdeeds of our group would take a volume to expose. In any case, they found themselves together once again on a Saturday afternoon in Asheville, reunited not by a master detective but by what some would say was pure circumstance and others would claim to be the act of a God with an ironic sense of humor.

* * *

Mary Alice got up early. Normally she and Craig slept in, but she arose early for two reasons. She wanted to be sure Troy had not set up surveillance during the night and lay in wait, planning to attack at the first sight of activity. The other reason was the promised arrival of Victoria to make all preparations for the party. Mary Alice knew she had embarked on what would be the longest day of her life. She only hoped to get through it without some scene that would ruin the party and probably her new relationship with Victoria. Tomorrow, she and Craig planned to move to their new home. While they couldn't disappear, they could handle any trouble without having to get anyone else involved.

She found the coast clear and breathed a sigh of relief. Maybe luck was with her. She showered and dressed, allowing herself to relax just a little.

Once Victoria arrived, there was little time for thinking. Victoria put Craig to work in the yard, and the two sisters started making their way through the to-do list Victoria had compiled. Side by side as sisters, they worked together in a way they had not done since childhood. Somehow, Mary Alice felt safe in Victoria's presence. By late afternoon everything was set.

"That's it except for the ice, and we can let Craig get that in a while," said Victoria as she looked around, hands on hips, seeming satisfied. "Let's have a beer."

Mary Alice smiled at her sister and said, "I'll get them."

"No, you don't," said Victoria. "You're the guest of honor, and you won't do another thing." With that, Victoria walked to her Saab, opened the trunk, and retrieved a cooler.

Mary Alice could not contain herself. She laughed aloud.

"What are you laughing at, Little Bit?"

"My prim and proper big sister riding around with a cooler of beer in the trunk. You're so full of surprises."

"Just wait, little sister."

Mary Alice thought about her preconceived notion of Victoria and Jillian's relationship. *What the hell,* she thought. *If it makes her this happy, I'm all for it.*

They drank two beers apiece. Craig had one too, even though he never drank.

When the time came, they went inside to get ready for the party. Victoria's last orders were for Craig to go get the ice as soon as he was dressed and for Mary Alice to relax and prepare for guests.

* * *

Jillian was the first to arrive. Craig had just left the driveway when she pulled in. Mary Alice watched from the upstairs window as Victoria ran out to meet her. They embraced and walked hand in hand back inside. "I'll just have to get used to it," Mary Alice said to herself, trying for conviction in her inner voice. She was just about to go downstairs when a Chevy pickup pulled up and parked on the other side of the street. She could plainly see the two men inside. They wore regular shirts instead of uniforms. They arrived on four wheels instead of two, but there was no mistaking Troy and the other thug who had cased the place a few days ago as they got out of the truck, crossed the street, and headed for the house.

Mary Alice panicked. What luck! What timing? Everything she had hoped for went down the drain. "Shit!"

Her hands came up involuntarily. She clutched her head between them. As quickly as the panic had come, it was gone. Replacing her anxiety was a calm as deep as the ocean. *You will not ruin this for me,* she thought. *If it's a confrontation that you want, it's a confrontation that you will get.* With that, she flung open the door and stomped down the hall. She was at the head of the stairs when she stopped, turned around, and opened the door to the hall closet. In the back corner was Lawrence's old golf bag. She reached in, selected the driver, and gave it a practice swing. It was too awkward, so she exchanged it for the nine iron. Much better. She inhaled, checked herself, and found the calm at her center. It was almost as if she were a spectator watching her body prepare for battle.

"Let's do this," she said aloud. Like many warriors before her, she struck a path toward the enemy. Unlike many warriors before her, she wore heels, swung a golf club, and negotiated a flight of stairs. The combination undid her on the fourth step from the bottom. Somehow, the golf club arced downward, struck her across the shins, and slipped neatly between two posts of the stair rail. If she had released the club, she might have saved herself, but it happened too fast. She lost her balance. She started to turn. She again faced the top of the staircase. She reached out with her left hand to find something to grab, but there was only a bare wall. Her hand slipped along the wallpaper as she continued to spin. Once again, her left hand grasped the stair rail, and the club was torn from her right hand by the weight of her body. She found the rail, but it was too late to stop her forward momentum. Her heel twisted, and she found herself falling. Her grip on the rail slowed her fall. Her butt hit solidly on the landing. The motion turned her ninety degrees on the landing, and her body flipped down the last two steps. When she stopped, she was sitting upright with her legs straight out in front of her, looking at Jillian embracing Troy's backup thug. A movement caught her eye, and she looked up just in time to see the golf club take one last pendulum-like swing and fall toward her. She rolled to her left to avoid being hit and came up, staring at her sister in the arms of her ex-boyfriend. The golf club fell across her lap as if it were an exclamation point.

* * *

Craig had every intention of going to the store, getting the ice, and returning home straight away. He had pulled the Beetle into the lot of the Sav-Qwik and parked along the side of the building. He liked this location because of the grassy area with shade trees and picnic tables behind the store provided a traveler's rest of sorts.

Sometimes, cars would stop, and their occupants would stretch their legs with a little stroll around the grounds, take a minute to sit at one of the tables and leisurely consume their purchases, or give the family pet some relief. Today, the place was empty. *What the hell,* he thought. *Mary Alice and Victoria are probably having another beer, so what's a few minutes?* He tapped his rear pocket and found his trusty pouch. *This'll be my last chance today and probably my last chance for a while.* He closed the door of the Volkswagen, pulled his pouch from his pocket, and walked across the grass to a table. An oak tree that must have been a hundred years old shaded the table. Craig put in his chew and sat down to contemplate the wonder of trees such as this one left in such an unlikely place.

* * *

On his way to Slugger's place, Rodney Wilson saw the same tree described in his instructions as the proper exit to take to get to the party. The day was warm but not hot, and not a cloud appeared in the sky. If he had been alone, he would have driven the Willys without the top and perhaps with the windshield down. When he did that, he had to wear goggles much like the old-time aviators. It looked weird, but it felt great. The feel of the wind flowing across his face and tossing his hair was worth the stares he got as he drove about. The people of Cedar Creek hardly looked; they were used to Rodney's ways. Outside of town, people would stare at him as if he were an escapee from some mental institution or some Howard Hughes-like recluse coming down from the mountain in his ancient conveyance. Yes, if it were he alone, that's how he would have gone to the party, but he was not.

Amanda sat beside him. She had consented to go to a party where she would not know a soul just because he said Slugger asked him to come. She even baked a cake for a party of strangers. She, whose hair was perfect and whose clothes were sparkling and crisp.

He could never ask her to arrive at said party in a 1948 Willys Jeep with tangled locks and bugs in her teeth.

As Rodney took the exit, he glanced at the gas gauge and saw it was down to almost a quarter of a tank. He spotted the pumps in front of the store and decided to gas up on the way to the party rather than after.

Amanda went inside to the restroom while Rodney pumped the gas. She wanted to check her appearance one last time and take care of nature's business so she would not have to seek a bathroom soon after arriving at the party. She said she would pay for the gas on the way back out.

After he replaced the nozzle and was screwing the cap back onto the gas tank, Rodney saw the Beetle parked around the side of the building. It looked a lot like the car Slugger drove, so he decided to investigate. He rounded the building and looked across the back lot just as Craig was adding another bit of tobacco nectar to the surrounding lawn.

"Hey, Slugger," said Rodney. "What are you doing here? I thought you were having a party?" He couldn't help but laugh.

"Rodney!" Craig said in surprise and wiped the back of his hand across his lips. "Yeah, I should be getting back. I just came for some ice but decided to take a little break while I was here."

"That's my boy. Grab a little R&R whenever the situation presents itself. You'll never be sorry."

"I heard that," said Craig falling into the job site slang. "But if I don't get back pretty soon, my R&R won't be rest and relaxation. It will be reprimanded and restricted if you know what I mean."

They both laughed. Rodney said, "I do know what you mean! Come on, partner, we'll follow so we can be sure to get to the right place." With that, Rodney threw his arm around Slugger's shoulder, and they both started around the building.

As they came to the corner, Craig saw the blonde walking toward Rodney's pickup. A feeling came over him that was both pleasant and confusing. Her back was toward him, but it was a back he would forever remember. He didn't know what to do. Just a short while ago, he had wanted to talk with her, but now panic filled his heart. If Rodney were not there with him, he would have turned tail and run, but he couldn't do that with his friend and mentor watching. He thought maybe she wouldn't see him until Rodney called out "Amanda, look, I found Slugger trying to escape his own party."

She turned at the sound of his voice, and her eyes fell on the two men walking together.

"Craig?" she said before she could think.

It was Rodney's turn to be confused but not for long. In a period that would shame some older computers, Rodney sorted the facts as he knew them and added a little conjecture to come up with the complete picture. When the picture came into focus, he could not contain himself. He burst into laughter.

Amanda, doing some sorting of her own, also came to the truth. She didn't know what to say or if she should speak at all. She looked at Craig and felt neutrality and a hint of sympathy for his situation at the moment. But when she looked at Rodney, laughing his fool head off in a predicament that would have discomfited a lesser man, she felt only love. Nothing else mattered. She, too, broke into laughter.

Craig looked from his best friend to his ex-wife and back again. They were both laughing uncontrollably. "Holy Jesus," Craig said as though it were a testament and a question. At that, the laughing renewed. He shook his head in disbelief and, without conscious thought, started laughing with them.

Rodney held his arm out to Amanda, and she willingly slipped into it. She reached her other arm around Craig as a sign of absolution, and his arm found her shoulder. To the untrained observer, they would have looked like a band of traveling idiots who had stopped along the interstate to perform some crazy ritual that only they could understand, but to Rodney, Amanda, and Craig, a little piece of the universe had just been set right. The party had begun.

* * *

Mary Alice quickly checked herself to make certain her modesty was intact. The top of her outfit had stayed up, and somehow she had landed with the hem of her skirt primly across her knees. She thought of a painting she had once seen of a little girl all dressed up for a party, sitting flat-bottomed with legs outstretched in her sandbox. She must have been trying to get in a few more minutes of playtime while her mother was taking care of some last-minute details inside the house. Mary Alice thought she must look ridiculous. No matter how funny she appeared, Troy obviously found nothing amusing about her presence.

His mouth was frozen open, and he looked like a mannequin, standing with his arm still around Victoria. His face started to melt as astonishment gave way to panic. It became apparent to Mary Alice that Troy did not come to Victoria's house in search of her, had no idea she was there, and, in fact, would give just about anything if she were not.

"Well, that's quite an entrance, Ms. Guest of Honor," said Victoria. "Before you go outside to practice your chipping, I'd like you to meet some friends of mine."

Troy's face changed expressions as quickly as a fourth grader flipping flash cards. Mary Alice saw surprise, recognition, and confusion, but mostly she saw panic. His eyes found hers, and in them she could see a pleading.

In contrast, Victoria was glowing and blushing like a schoolgirl. Although trying to act otherwise, she seemed to be a little embarrassed at being caught with her beau. Mary Alice had some sorting out of her own to do. The two major sources of discomfort in her life were her sister's sexuality and the fear of Troy hunting her down. While she had worried, one had seemingly taken care of the other.

"Little Bit, er... I mean, Mary Alice, I want you to meet someone who is very, very special to me. This is Troy Jacobs. He's originally from Cedar Creek but lives in Asheville now. You know Jillian, of course, and this is her friend Alphie McCann. He and Troy work together. Ya'll, this is my sister, Mary Alice Darnell."

Mary Alice could tell that Troy had no idea she and Victoria were related. His eyes were now filled with a look of fear that made him seem vulnerable. He didn't know what to expect. Mary Alice got up, brushed herself off, and walked directly to Troy and Victoria. She smiled at her sister and then looked into Troy's eyes. He was frozen.

"Hi," she said, holding out her hand. "Nice to meet you."

Epilogue

It would be easy to pass the whole thing off with a cliché: "small world." Instead, after close consideration of the circumstances and a few years of being able to observe life through the eyes of a journalist, I have come to see such occurrences as a "Cosmic Justice System" of sorts. No matter how far we run, how deeply we burrow, or to what lengths we go to avoid it, eventually we come face to face with our every fear. We are forced to acknowledge and somehow reconcile our mistakes and to repeatedly strive against our weaknesses. For the most part, the human spirit adapts, improvises, and overcomes. The only difference between a diamond and a chunk of coal is the pressure the precious gems were forced to endure.

The party was a resounding success. Victoria had invited many people from her previous life, and they all came bearing gifts. In the end, there were lots of gadgets for the new home, but the best present was one shared by Victoria, Troy, Mary Alice, Craig, Amanda, and Rodney: the gift of freedom. The freedom to forgive and forget the past and move on to a future they alone could influence. What better?

About the Author

Robert Wilkins, the author of The Reluctant Wizard, lives in Durham, N.C., with his wife, Debra, the world's smartest dog, Kady, and the universe's hungriest cat Bootsie. He also penned two Kindle Vella series, *Jukebox Time Machine* and *Dirt Poor*. Both take place in North Carolina.

Contact Information

Like the book?

Recommend it to a friend

Let the author know. You can contact Robert at

superchef1028@gmail.com

www.ingramcontent.com/pod-product-compliance
Lightning Source LLC
Chambersburg PA
CBHW061241210726
48293CB00003B/864